He'd been a mystery since she'd **...** **understand just who and what he** **...** **...**

"Hermit! Why are you leaving me?" she cried, but he did not pause. Saying a few choice words under her breath—decidedly not respectable ones—she scrambled up the slope behind him.

"Hermit!" she cried again, as she came to the top and a large hand reached over the crest to grasp hers. As he pulled her up, they were face-to-face, and she wasted no time in challenging him.

"What can you be thinking?" she asked, and then as a dreadful thought occurred to her, "Is it too late, then?"

"Too late?" he asked in a voice not like his own. "I say it is indeed too late."

"Penelope is dead?" Laurel gasped.

"Miss Croyden is sitting like a princess on a low stone, surrounded by roses and humming insects. She will live."

"Then explain your actions, sir. To run from a lady in need is despicable."

"It is not the worst charge that can be leveled against me, my dear Miss Gardiner. But I cannot help her."

"And why not?" Laurel asked, ready to push him over the edge herself, if need be.

"That is my business. And hers. Your interference is officious and will accomplish no good."

Laurel's hands dropped to her side, and she felt the bitter taste of a defeat she could not yet fathom.

"My . . . my friend is injured," she faltered. "I cannot move her myself."

The hermit seemed to consider the wisdom of this, and nodded. "I will borrow a horse from the stable, with your permission, and go for the doctor. You must go to the house and have your brothers arrange to have her brought there."

Laurel nodded, too numb to answerShe watched him run off, and some minutes later heard the whinny of the horses who witnessed his approach. She had not yet moved when she felt the shuddering vibration of hooves beneath her feet, and she looked up to see him ride away. Even at a distance, she recognized him as an experienced horseman, comfortable both with speed and the rocky terrain.

Only then did Laurel fully understand how he came to have such skills.

And how he happened on Penelope Croyden's family name, when she knew she never mentioned it.

For my Sister and Brother

Carole Kolodny Popa
And
Steven Kolodny

As a family, we grew up knowing
every curiosity,
every bit of information,
and every character we met,
were worthy of becoming stories
to share for a lifetime.

The Hermitage

***

Sharon Sobel

Forever Regency
a division of ImaJinn Books, Inc.

The Hermitage
Published by Forever Regency,
a division of ImaJinn Books, Inc

ISBN: 978-1-933417-53-0

10 9 8 7 6 5 4 3 2 1

PUBLISHER'S NOTE:
This book is a work of fiction. Names, characters, places and incidents are products of the author's imagination or are used fictitiously. Any resemblance to actual events or locales or persons, living or dead, is entirely coincidental.

Books are available at quantity discounts when used to promote products or services. For information please write to: Marketing Division, ImaJinn Books, Inc., P.O. Box 74274, Phoenix, AZ 85087, or call toll free 1-877-625-3592.

Cover design by Patricia Lazarus

Photo credits:
Kissing photo by forgiss@dreamstime.com
Leaves by Ilona, Bez and Lucie@Renderosity

Forever Regency,
a division of ImaJinn Books, Inc.
P.O. Box 74274, Phoenix, AZ 85087
Toll Free: 1-877-625-3592
http://www.imajinnbooks.com

Prologue

"I take little pleasure in the company of people, sir." The tall man shifted one shoulder, as if unburdening himself of a great weight, and his hood slipped away from his face. Mr. George Gardiner did not consider himself a worthy judge of such things, but he did pause to note the youth and comeliness of his petitioner's face, and the several days' growth of beard which, if unchecked, would undoubtedly obscure very fine features.

"You seem particularly bitter for one so young, my good man," Mr. Gardiner said, and glanced down at the papers on his desk. "Mr., ah, Robbie Darkwood. Might I ask what in your history brought you to such a state of malcontentment?"

Mr. Darkwood raised one hand and pushed the hood back over his eyes. "I do not know that it is your business to know mine, sir. I am here in answer to your solicitation. You desire a hermit to live in your hermitage. I am a hermit. I desire only a place to live in peace and solitude, far from the intercourse of society. I will ask nothing more of you, but you must tell me, straightaway, if there is more you expect of me." The young man pulled himself up and seemed almost defiant in his stance.

"I believe my solicitation is fairly direct in its wording, Mr. Darkwood. And of course it is my responsibility to know what I am about when I hire someone to do a job for me. I am a man of business, you see, though I have earned the privilege of some rare pleasures. I bought Greenbriars many years ago and have devoted a great deal of energy—and capital—to its improvement. Now my three sons manage most of the family business affairs in London, and I am entirely committed to my estate management. 'Tis a fine place, with much to recommend it. Several things, however, have gone lacking, and it my intention to make up for those things in which I have been remiss."

"Such as installing a hermitage, sir?"

"The hermitage was built into the stone wall on the northern edge of my park by the gentleman from whom I bought the estate," said Mr.

Gardiner, emphasizing the word "gentleman" ever so slightly. "The cottage was never intended to be anything else, and was inhabited by a succession of colorful individuals. Yours is a picturesque profession, Mr. Darkwood, though I am not sure there is much profit in it."

"Must there be? Is it not enough to live off the land and spend one's days in contemplation?" asked Darkwood, a bit arrogantly. He hesitated and then came closer to Mr. Gardiner's large desk. "But it is also my understanding there is a small stipend attached to the position."

George Gardiner smiled as he looked down at the papers Darkwood had thrust upon him fifteen minutes before.

"There is. If I desired nothing more than a tenant for the hermitage, I would be charging you rent to live there. But, as it is, I desire a hermit. I expect only that he live alone, and go about his business—whatever it might be—in complete solitude. He must dress the part, as indeed you have, and show himself whenever there are guests about. I will not have it said my hermit is a hoax. And I expect to get what I pay for."

"Must I speak to those guests?"

"Indeed, not! Such a thing would be entirely out of character!"

"Might I walk about the property?"

"I expect you must, in order to be seen. I daresay no one has been near the hermitage in years, other than the gardeners. So you may wander about, keeping yourself in the shelter of the trees and behind the statuary. That will do rather nicely, I think." Mr. Gardiner tapped his fingers on the desk, contemplating the prospect of Greenbriars, complete with a hooded man skirting the edge of the oak wood and artistically disappearing into the evening mist near the lake. He looked up suddenly. "You may wish to swim or fish in our water. It is well stocked with trout and turtles."

"It is my hope I might manage to live off the land—and water," Darkwood agreed.

"Entirely right. But I must insist you do so in the early hours of the day or at dusk."

"Would it not be entertaining for your guests to see your hermit so engaged?"

"I suppose it might. But I have other concerns." Mr. Gardiner lifted his restless fingers and rubbed his shiny forehead.

"Sir?"

"I have a daughter and she is somewhat . . . headstrong. Of course, it is out of the question for her to see you swimming. But if she sees you otherwise busy, and quite within her range of endeavor on the estate, she will almost certainly destroy your peace and solitude. That will not do. It is something neither of us desire."

"Perhaps you could simply explain our situation, sir, and warn her away. A child would surely obey."

Mr. Gardiner sighed heavily and continued to ply his forehead. "It is, of course, just the problem."

"Sir?" Darkwood repeated patiently.

"Miss Gardiner is not a child. She is a young woman, and even those who do not see her with fatherly eyes tell me she is a beauty. She will be in town for the season, of course, but that will not last forever. And she is fond of Greenbriars, so is likely to return often enough. If I prohibit her from speaking to you she will almost certainly see it as an invitation to visit you every day and follow you about. Perhaps I ought not say anything at all."

"I will avoid her as assiduously as the Prince does Caroline."

Mr. Gardiner dropped his hand and studied the hooded figure in front of him more closely.

"You do not speak like a man who has lived out of society," he said softly.

Darkwood stepped back, brushing against the finely polished bookcase. "One does not have to live in society to understand it. Or to decide to live within it, or without."

"I see your point, Mr. Darkwood. Do I then correctly assume that the attractions of beautiful young ladies hold no currency for you?"

The enigmatic Darkwood seemed to be weighing his answer, and Mr. Gardiner did not deny him the luxury of time.

"You have my word as a gen . . . as a hermit, sir," said Mr. Darkwood solemnly. "I have had enough of young ladies in my time and have every desire to avoid their company, as I do all company."

"Well spoken, my good man," Mr. Gardiner said as he rose from his large leather chair. He extended his right hand, and waited expectantly while Darkwood fished about for an opening in his robe to reveal his own hand. Mr. Gardiner was not surprised to see neatly trimmed nails and then, on the handshake to seal the bargain, feel an uncalloused palm. Indeed, he could scarcely resist the sense of satisfaction that he, a man of business, was about to hire possibly the only gentleman hermit in all of England. But then, he always endeavored to buy the finest furnishings for Greenbriars. Why should his hermit be any different?

"And welcome to Greenbriars," he added. "I hope your tenure with us is as lonely, desolate, and tedious as you can only imagine in your fondest dreams."

"Thank you very much, sir," said Mr. Robbie Darkwood.

Chapter One

June 1818

Miss Laurel Gardiner took great care to enter the Duke of Armadale's ballroom with all the advantages of her grooming, if not her birthright, on display. She knew to smile with the merest crescent of her white teeth showing, and to speak in short sentences, as her tight corset would likely cut off her supply of air if she rambled on too long. She had been taught to curtsy with her back rigidly straight, so as to deny any curious gentleman too generous a look at her curves as he stood above her. She had learned how to remove her elbow length gloves one dainty finger at a time, teasingly, suggestively, as if she might discard even more of her elegant clothes.

Indeed, on this evening, the notion was quite tempting.

The great crush of people, pressing through the arched doorway like a swollen river over a small cataract, filled the room and heated it almost beyond endurance. The odors of perfume, pomades, and too many unwashed bodies assailed her, and what passed for conversation nearly drowned out the melody of the musicians in the gallery above their heads.

Laurel looked up, studying the way a silver flute glinted in the candlelight, and gasped several breaths of fresher air. Her gloved hand fingered the neckline of her silk gown and felt moisture seep through the thin fabric. Truly, the evening was already unbearable.

How she longed to return to Greenbriars, to its beauty and blissful serenity. After years of living in London, she only recently discovered the blessings of the country, and now felt she could barely endure its deprivation. But this journey to town was full of great purpose, and if she met with any success, she might be rewarded with a long respite at home before abandoning it forever.

A bright ornamental fan slapped her wrist, and she swatted it as she would an irritating insect.

"You won't find much to amuse you in that direction, my dear," admonished her mother. "Your father did not arrange for this fine season so you could fall in love with a poor musician. You'll find riper fruit nearer our level."

Laurel dropped her chin. "Some of it a little too ripe, I fear," she said, wiggling her nose. Looking at her mother with the air of innocence that had always served her well in a household with three older brothers, she added, "But did Father not say I should set my sights high?"

The Japanese fan attacked her again.

"I am only teasing you, Mother," Laurel sighed. "But I so envy the musicians. It seems much more pleasant up in the galley."

"How can you say such a thing?" Mrs. Gardiner asked, apparently not in the humor for irony or teasing. "What could be more pleasant than the company here? I see Mr. Tidway and Lord Harings. And Lady Knollwood is here with her youngest son. And we know to expect Lord Ballister, for he can hardly resist you."

"He most certainly will find us before we find him," Laurel said, quietly confident.

"You do not sound like a woman in love, my dear," her mother pointed out.

Laurel once again glanced up at the flutist and his glistening instrument, and abandoned any hope of escape.

"In love?" she asked her mother. "Of course I am not in love with him. I hardly know him. Oh, he seems pleasant enough . . . "

" . . . and he is an earl . . . "

" . . . and he is an earl. That it is so, and I know that it is so, which may be the only thing we have in common."

Her mother's answer was drowned out by the fanfare of the horns in the gallery.

"The only thing," Laurel repeated.

"You will have Lindborough in common, and a houseful of children. And you will be a countess, which is more to the point."

It was, rather, to her mother's point, and not necessarily to hers.

"Penelope Croyden tells me Lindborough is in heavy disrepair, and sustained serious fire damage during the winter," Laurel reported, pinning some hopes on Penelope's information.

"And I suppose Miss Croyden knows about such things? Why, the poor dear does not even know where her intended is, and why he delays his entrance into town."

As her mother spoke, Laurel caught a glimpse of her friend through the crowd. Penelope's thick dark curls were laced with dark rose ribbon and swayed back and forth against her neck as she looked at the swell of people around her. Laurel did not doubt whom she sought.

"Westbridge is quite reliable, she assures me. After all, they have known each other all their lives, and live on neighboring estates. And he is an earl, Mother, so you can fault him nothing."

If the older woman felt Laurel's verbal jab, she gave no sign of it, for her attention was diverted.

"Lord Ballister!" her mother cried. "We did not see you in the crush!"

"But I saw you, Mrs. Gardiner," Lord Ballister said cheerfully. "And of course, Miss Gardiner's presence could not go unnoticed by anyone with eyes in his head."

Laurel looked knowingly at her mother.

"I am sure you are correct, Lord Ballister," Mrs. Gardiner murmured. "I have been aware of many appreciative glances in our direction, and I am not such a fool to imagine anyone looking particularly at me."

Lord Ballister smiled a little too broadly, and Laurel thought his response somewhat exaggerated for what was so blatantly an invitation to compliment. But if indeed the man's heart was not in it, his manners certainly were.

"Madam, there can be no doubt where Miss Gardiner inherited her beauty," said Lord Ballister, and brushed his hand through his pale hair, pushing it off his damp brow. He turned towards Laurel and looked at her intently, as if appraising her asset by asset.

Laurel stared back at him, silently daring him to come up with one original thought.

"But, my lord, you have never met my father. I am told I am quite like him," she said, giving up after a few long moments.

"It is true, we have not yet had the pleasure of meeting. But I have been told much about him."

"I am sure you have," Laurel said under her breath, and glanced at her mother.

But her mother, already satisfied with the turn of Lord Ballister's conversation, set her attention elsewhere.

"Ah, look who approaches! Miss Croyden is one of my daughter's favorite friends in town this season, Lord Ballister. And, as I am sure you know, she is engaged to marry the Earl of Westbridge, a very distinguished young man. It has been a love match since their childhood."

"Westbridge and I are acquainted from our school days, when we were not much more than children ourselves. Of course, he was known as plain old Robin Waltham then, but I heard that his father died some years ago."

"I cannot say, my lord," murmured Mrs. Gardiner, for once unable to demonstrate her vast social knowledge. "But what a pity his fond dream could not be realized—that of witnessing his son's marriage to the daughter of his neighbor and friend. Miss Croyden! Do join us!"

Laurel, quite silent during this preamble, and at a loss to explain how her mother managed to divine such information from the sparse facts Penelope had offered about her childhood and expectations, thought her friend did not look so much as happy to see them, as desperate. Penelope pushed through the teeming crush like a fish swimming upstream, and offered apologies in her wake. Her reticule caught on a gentleman's button and was nearly ripped out of her hand. An elderly lady walked headlong into her. Two gentlemen deep in conversation suddenly found dark curls bouncing between them.

Finally, to his credit, Lord Ballister stepped forward to clear Penelope's path. He reached out to take her by the elbow, and towed her into the Gardiners' safe haven.

"Thank you, my lord, I am very grateful for your assistance," Penelope said, a little breathlessly.

"I am sure if my old friend Robin Waltham were already here, he would have done nothing less. But I do not yet see him. Do you expect him?"

Penelope opened her mouth, and then seemed unsure how to answer this simple question.

"Lord Ballister has just explained how he and your intended were old friends at school," Laurel said helpfully.

"How delightful," Penelope said tersely. "Of course, that is one part of his life I was not privileged to share with him, and know little about his friendships there. For the rest, we are as well acquainted as brother and sister, and have been scarcely apart."

"As you have been these past weeks, poor dear," Laurel's mother reminded her. "Well, I am sure your young man will find his way here shortly. Indeed, he might already be in attendance, and we have only to see him in this crowd."

Penelope glanced around with the manner of one who already knows what she will find. Or not find. "Laurel. Miss Gardiner, I would like to speak to you in private, if I may."

Mrs. Gardiner opened her lips to protest, but changed her mind when Ballister said, "Ah, you have anticipated my own happy hope,

Miss Croyden, for I, too, would like a small portion of Miss Gardiner's undivided attention this evening. But perhaps I might yet exercise a privilege you are unable to share. Is it too much to hope that Miss Gardiner is still available for the first set?"

Laurel looked up into the gentleman's clear eyes, punctuated by his pale brows. For once she saw his looks in a more generous light than that to which she had grown accustomed; if not remarkable, he certainly was pleasant enough. He had little of great import to say, but when he spoke he was polite and solicitous. Did it really matter if he might be more interested in what she would inherit from her father, than the looks he imagined she had inherited from her mother? He could be a good friend to her, and a kind father to their children. And friendship, and kindness, and politeness ought to be quite enough; indeed, was it not all that Penelope seemed to require from her dear Robin?

"I am still available, my lord," Laurel said softly, wondering why it sounded so much like an elegy. Beside her, her mother sighed happily. "But will you kindly allow me to spend the next few minutes in conversation with Miss Croyden? I am sure we have time before the first set, for guests are yet arriving."

"As you wish, Miss Gardiner," he said, and bowed as low as he dared without risk of being jostled by the people around him. "Mrs. Gardiner, as you are otherwise unescorted, and quite as lovely as your daughter, will you do me the honor of entering the ballroom with me?"

Mrs. Gardiner blushed like a girl and tapped him playfully with her fan.

"I shall make all the young girls jealous, my lord, for you are surely the most handsome man here."

Lord Ballister straightened and looked directly at Laurel. She now thought his looks improved upon closer inspection and his fine jacket and well-fitted breeches gave him some advantage over many of the men in the company. She smiled at him encouragingly, and he seemed surprised. Goodness, had she been such a shrew?

"I do not wish to make all the girls jealous, Mrs. Gardiner. Only one," he said with a gallantry that belied his words, and nodded to Laurel. "But let us away, so our two companions might speak in private. I will know later this evening if I have succeeded in provoking my intended victim."

As they stepped into the crowd and were swept through the archway, Laurel and Penelope watched in silence.

"He intends to offer for you, Laurel," Penelope said softly.

"I believe you are right. And I believe it was only a minute ago that I realized I might be tempted to accept him."

"Laurel! Not truly!" Penelope gasped. "Was it not yesterday you told me you would only marry for love? Do not tell me you imagine yourself in love with Lord Ballister!"

Laurel frowned, wondering how many bridges she had burned in the past weeks by stating her opinions so candidly. Indeed, she could scarcely understand her great reversal of sentiments herself, let alone explain it sensibly to anyone else. She looked at Penelope, as loyal and true as her namesake, and realized how much she longed for what her friend already possessed.

"Come, let us away to the side of the room," she said, pulling on Penelope's arm. "I daresay we have sufficient privacy here, surrounded by a mob of hundreds, but I can scarcely breathe in this heat."

"We are both country girls at heart," Penelope said as she allowed herself to be led through the crush. "We need the air and the wide open spaces, and the grandeur of scenery. I can scarcely wait to return home."

"I was thinking very much the same thing myself. We are country girls at heart, if not in fact," Laurel corrected her as they arrived at a marble column, displacing one of the Armadale servants. "You recall I spent most of my life in the city, until my father decided it was time to impress our neighbors in Cambridgeshire. Unlike yours, our estate is redolent with the smells of fresh plaster and paint."

"It does not sound so very bad," Penelope sniffed. "Certainly it ought to be an improvement over stuffed drainpipes and smoky fireplaces. But come, you did not drag me to this corner to discuss architecture, nor have you yet answered me. Are you in love with Lord Ballister?"

Laurel hesitated, somehow believing that there was more of consequence in this answer than there might be if and when the man proposed.

"I am not," she said at last. "But perhaps I ask too much to demand it of myself. He is a good man, and a kind one, and I may very well come to love him some day."

"And if you do not?"

Laurel sighed. "Then I shall take comfort in other things. My children, perhaps. Our home. Friendships. It does not sound so very bad, does it?"

"It sounds dreadful! You are a little young to give up on the one grand thing, are you not?"

Laurel's wistful reflections turned to indignation. "You are a fine one to talk, Penelope Croyden! You scarcely looked beyond your parlor to find a man who suits you. What did you know of love when you were five or six years of age? Indeed, your own complacency about your dear Westbridge gave me reason to hope that a marriage of comfort could be a wonderful thing. I have never heard you speak of Westbridge but to add that you are as one in all your opinions, as like as brother and sister. If you can find happiness in such an arrangement, why might not I?"

Penelope's eyes seemed fixed on something or someone over Laurel's shoulder, but Laurel did not turn around. Instead, she studied her friend's face and for the first time realized there were lines of strain about her mouth and her brow was wrinkled in consternation.

"Perhaps it is because I may not realize happiness where once I took it for granted. I have received a letter from Robin, written days ago, but misdirected. In it, he says . . . " Penelope choked, and she swayed slightly towards Laurel.

Laurel caught her friend by the elbows, steadying her, looking her directly in the eyes.

"What? What does he say! If he has done anything to hurt you, I shall ask my brothers to challenge him! I will challenge him myself!"

Penelope coughed. "My dear! And you expect me to believe you will be Lord Ballister's acquiescent wife? It is quite impossible!"

Laurel bit down on her lip and gathered her wits about her. "Perhaps it is not in my nature to be acquiescent. But I will be a very loyal wife, as I am your loyal friend."

Penelope nodded. "I know you are. I would have thought to say the same of Robin. But in his letter he writes that he feels we must be apart for some time while he contemplates some grave matters. He has left the responsibility of his estate to his younger brother, and has otherwise abandoned everything behind him. It is so unlike him, I do not know what to do or say."

Laurel heard the hoarseness in her friend's voice, and the great effort it cost her to utter such words. Tactfully, she waited several minutes before she asked, "Has he abandoned you as well? And with nothing but this flimsy excuse for his actions? Then he is a villain! But is that all he writes?"

Penelope grew quite pale, though the room remained uncomfortably warm. Laurel, thinking she might faint, stepped closer.

"No," Penelope whispered. "He writes that he is not certain he can marry me."

Laurel felt the resurgence of anger and indignation, not only on poor Penelope's behalf, but for herself as well. Now that she had finally persuaded herself that an affection like the one her friend shared with her lover could be enough reason for a marriage, the cursed man dashed all her hopes. Who is a friend, but one to be absolutely trusted?

"Then he is an idiot," Laurel said with conviction.

"No, my dear, he is actually quite clever. He spends so much time in his library, for he is a great reader. And he understands everything about the estate and scarcely needs his steward. He writes poetry and has translated *The Iliad*. He plays several instruments, and is a patron of the Royal Academy."

"Yes, yes, he is a veritable paragon of excellence," Laurel said impatiently. "But what are such qualities if he will abandon the woman he loves? If he can cut you so deeply? I would rather have an honest man than a jack-of-all-trades, no matter how admirable his skills."

"He is an honest man."

"You defend him too warmly, Penelope, for surely he does not deserve it. In fact, when all this passes—as it surely will—I am not certain I can look at your Westbridge with any degree of composure. I am honest as well, and would surely like to tell him what I think of him!"

Penelope gave the barest hint of a smile. "I daresay you shall. And I do appreciate your defense of my poor reputation, but there is no hope. I doubt I will ever be truly happy again."

"Oh, but you shall! And you must not let anyone here even guess at what you hide. You must dance with other gentlemen, and put on a cheerful front. Then, if Westbridge hears of your behavior, he will be instantly jealous and return to you at once. It is an excellent strategy."

Penelope looked unconvinced. "I do not think it is so, Laurel, though I wish I could share your great optimism. For one, I have no evidence that Robin should ever hear of what goes on in London ballrooms, for I suspect he is quite remotely distant. And as for the rest," she began, and then blushed. "I have never danced with anyone but Robin. I do not even know what to say to a strange man."

Laurel sighed, wondering how her friend could prove to be such a shy simpleton. She knew her time was growing short, for the first set would soon begin, and she could scarcely leave Penelope standing alone among the Armadale columns. She looked at the late-arriving guests and found salvation, in the form of her older brother, removing his greatcoat in the foyer.

"You will find it very easy, and I have just the strange man for you to practice your skills upon. At least, he seems strange to me, because he is my brother. But, I assure you, he's quite harmless. Come, let us ambush him before Lady Pettrey sets her sights on him." Laurel caught Penelope's elbow and urged her forward.

"Good heavens, Laurel, you cannot mean . . . Is that gentleman your brother? You do not think that he . . . Why he is quite the handsomest man here!"

"We will not tell him that, will we? He will behave insufferably if he imagines it, and devise all sorts of torture for me. He is quite spoiled, you see. But come along, Penelope, I am sure he will do for an evening's diversion." Laurel marched determinedly back into the crowd. "Joseph! Mr. Joseph Gardiner!"

Joseph heard her through the din, as people attuned to the voices of their family members and friends often do. He turned and saw her, before settling his gaze on her companion. Laurel knew him well enough to catch the flicker of interest in his eyes.

"Miss Penelope Croyden, my brother, Mr. Joseph Gardiner. I did not think you would be here this night, Joseph," Laurel said.

"I had plans, but they changed at the last moment. So I thought I would humor Mother and come here, where I might prevent you from spending the evening consigned to the company of the elderly matrons. She believes no one else would have you."

"As it turns out, dear brother, both you and she are quite wrong about that. But, for once in your life, you can still make yourself useful. Miss Croyden's plans did not quite work out as she expected either."

Laurel knew she did not mistake the glint in his blue eyes. "Say no more, for to do so would be an insult to the lady," he said. "Miss Croyden, may I have the pleasure of the first dance?"

Laurel, still clutching Penelope's arm, felt her tremble. But when she spoke, she seemed calm enough.

"Certainly, sir. And thank you."

Laurel relinquished her friend to her brother's protection, and caught his wink as he looked at her over Penelope's dark curls. Perhaps some good could come of this evening, after all.

"Miss Gardiner? The first dance is soon to begin," Lord Ballister said, coming up quietly behind her, as he always did. For all she knew, he might have been standing there through her entire conversation with

Penelope. "I hope you have not forgotten it is to be with me."

"Of course not, my lord," Laurel said. "I have looked forward to it with pleasure throughout all my conversation with Miss Croyden."

But as he led her though the wide archway that was finally empty of the mob that had quite overwhelmed it only a half hour before, Laurel realized she had not looked forward to it at all. Even more disconcerting, she did not look forward to the lifetime of marriage for which he would surely try to secure her promise before the evening was over.

He was an excellent dancer. He moved with grace and confidence, and had pretty compliments for Laurel and all their female neighbors through each step of the quadrille. As she passed to his right, she heard him humming the melody of the piece, and she wondered if he was musically inclined. As Lady Winsted passed to his left, she whispered something in his ear, and Laurel wondered if he was Lady Winsted inclined. What did she know of him, after all?

She only knew that after they shared three dances, the very limit of propriety, he had every intention of making her a proposal of marriage. He caught her hand and suggested they take a turn in the garden to escape the oppressive heat and the even more oppressive gaze of other interested parties. As they made their way to the doors that opened onto the veranda, they passed Laurel's mother, who could barely disguise her expression of glee, and Joseph, who winked again over Penelope's head.

The veranda was not empty, but the air was cool, and a couple speaking in hushed tones could be guaranteed some privacy.

"This is quite a pretty garden," Laurel said. "It makes me think of Greenbriars, my family's home in the country."

"I have heard that your father did much to improve upon the estate after he purchased it from Lord Hanford."

"Yes, I am sure you have," Laurel remarked knowingly. "And did you also hear about his collection of Italian statuary, my lord?"

"It is the envy of all men who collect such treasures, Miss Gardiner. But I must confess that the treasure of your father's that interests me most is not made of marble."

"Very prettily said, my lord," murmured Laurel, conceding him the point. "Are you speaking of his Rembrandt? It is very small, I assure you. But very much like the man."

"Your father?"

"No, the artist. Rembrandt liked nothing so much as himself for a subject. But then, that makes him akin to most men, I suppose."

Lord Ballister looked disconcerted, and Laurel paused to wonder what little demon was compelling her to torment him. After all, she was nearly resolved to accept him, already decided that he would do as well for her as Westbridge would for Penelope. But now it seemed that Westbridge would not do for Penelope, that surely she deserved someone who would not abandon her for spurious reasons, and who would have a care for her feelings. If there was no hope for a love that was long-lived and true, what could a lady expect with a recent acquaintance who knew a good deal more about her father's estate than he knew about her?

"No, that is not the treasure of which I speak," Lord Ballister said, shaking his head. His flaxen hair fell down across his brow, and Laurel resisted the impulse to set it to rights. "Here is a poem I have penned, and you must guess its subject."

"It is a riddle, then," Laurel said wearily, wondering if she should trifle with his pride and guess at its answer before he even began. But instead she clasped her hands and attempted to look dotingly on the gentleman.

"I hope it is not so obscure," he said, and he fumbled in his breast pocket and pulled out a square of paper. He began to read words Laurel thought she had heard before, but in a voice uncommonly stiff and hesitant. But for the fact someone named "Laurel" was conspicuously named, she would have thought it a work of Andrew Marvel. After all, hers was not so common a name.

Nor was Lord Ballister's poem so compelling a riddle.

"How lovely, my lord," she said when he finished his recitation. "I did not realize you were a poet. And do you also produce translations of *The Iliad?*" she added, unable to stop herself.

He paused for a moment, as if trying to recall if he had ever done so, before answering. "I can only write for my muse, and you are she, Miss Gardiner. From the hour I met you, I was convinced that there could be no other woman suitable as the partner for my future life. You shall be my helpmate, my companion, the mother of my children, the mistress of Lindborough. Have I told you of Lindborough, my dear? It is a grand estate of a very rustic nature."

"You have not told me of it, my lord, but others have. By their descriptions, it sounds very rustic indeed. In fact, I heard that there is no roof over one wing of the house, and that a garden now grows in its rubble. I do not think my father intends for me to pluck weeds from flowerbeds in my own parlor."

Lord Ballister's eyes narrowed as he crumpled his poem into a ball and threw it over the balustrade.

"Then I shall ask your father for a generous settlement on his daughter, so you will never do anything of an odious nature. With his help, Lindborough will be restored, and my debts can be paid. I no longer will have to rent out my London townhouse, and I can bring my mother back from Scotland, where she has been exiled with my aunt." Then, having detailed his plans in the most odious fashion, he added with an uncharacteristic smirk: "Will that prove satisfactory?"

"I can scarcely say, my lord," Laurel said calmly but truthfully, as she knew nothing of the mother, the aunt or the townhouse. Of Lindborough and the debts, she had already been warned. "And what of your muse?"

"What muse?"

"Why, the muse who would inspire you to write poetry, be your helpmate, and the mother of your children. Might she not think it sadly unpoetic to realize she has been purchased to clear the ledgers—if not the weeds—of Lindborough? And might her father think he may not be getting a fair deal in auctioning her off?"

"Her father . . ." Lord Ballister could barely get the words out between his clenched teeth. ". . . *your* father will be getting an earl for a son-in-law, and a title for his daughter."

"I am not certain it is enough, my lord."

"Look here, Miss Gardiner. I am prepared to offer you everything I have in exchange for something your father has, and of which I am sadly deprived. I have approached you in all due courtesy, and have been solicitous of your mother. I have danced with you, and shared some thoughts with you, and have written you poetry. I have announced my intentions to other gentleman, so that they might stand off, and I am certain both you and your mother understood my intentions as well. I have told you honestly what I hoped to gain by our marriage, and pointed out the advantages to you and your family. Now I wish for your honesty in telling me if you will marry me."

Laurel looked at his plain face and sturdy shoulders. She considered how happy her parents would be to welcome such a man into their family. When the evening began, she had felt prepared to forego any foolish romantic thoughts she harbored and accept him for the decent and pleasant individual she thought him to be. With Penelope and her dear Westbridge as her model, Laurel came to believe marriage could be about many things, and passion need not be one of them. But as

Penelope's evening did not turn out as she expected, neither did Laurel's. With the defection of Westbridge came the collapse of not only Penelope's confidence, but also of any happy illusions about her marriage. Westbridge, on whom her friend had based all her hopes and dreams for her entire life, had proved a villain, the least worthy of all men. And if such a disappointment could happen to poor Penelope, who knew everything there was to know about the one she would marry, then what hope for happiness could there be for her by sealing her fate with a man she had known only for a few months?

"No, my lord," Laurel said, as her illusions melted and vanished like so many snowflakes on a warm palm. Lord Ballister closed his eyes and clenched his fists, allowing her to realize that this moment of great truth was even a greater disappointment to him. She sighed, reluctant to give pain to anyone. But he deserved to know precisely what she had decided, and that there was no possibility for a reversal. "No, my lord. I cannot marry you," Laurel said, and turned back to the ballroom.

* * * *

"I see no reason to remain in this tiresome city any longer," said Laurel, and hurled one of her new bonnets across her dressing room to land squarely in the open trunk. "It is a week since I refused Lord Ballister, and yet there seems to be nothing of interest for anyone to discuss but the great insult I delivered him by declining his proposal. Truly, Mother, the pleasures of the season are vastly overrated if one cannot be sustained by any sensible conversation. There is nothing here to amuse me."

Her mother walked across her daughter's dressing room, ducked once as a second bonnet sailed over her head, and gathered up the fashionable gowns that lay in a heap in front of the open armoire.

"I believe I warned you, my dear, that you would be very much on display here in London, and that your every move would be subject to gossip. Indeed, your disinclination to Lord Ballister does you no real harm, and opens the drawing room door to other men. I daresay much of the gossip is about that very real possibility." Her mother paused to pick up one of Laurel's discarded gowns and drape it against her own slim form. Frowning, she added it to the heap. "Just because Lord Ballister did not suit your fancy is not sufficient reason to condemn the society in which he and a hundred other eligible men mingle. He is not the only fish . . . "

" . . . in the sea. Yes, I know. But he is a particularly slippery one."

Laurel held up a lacy shawl to the light and realized she had not yet
worn it during her decisively short season in London. It would, however,
do very nicely on a cool summer evening while she walked the footpath
by the lake at Greenbriars.

"That is a disgusting metaphor, my love," said her mother. "But
surely it does you credit that you were able to catch him?"

"As to that, he very much desired to be caught. I, after all, was
only the bait, and he did all the pursuing." Laurel considered her words,
and thought herself at least as accomplished a wordsmith as Ballister.
But then she realized she had misstated the situation. "No, I was not
the bait. Father's fortune provided the bait. Lord Ballister did not even
trouble himself to disguise what truly attracted him to me. He might
have, at least, commented on my eyes or my sparkling wit."

"Which do you much credit, I am sure," her mother noted
approvingly. "It is now time to turn those assets in another direction
and find a gentleman who will truly appreciate them. The gossip is
nothing, for it will pass."

"But it is too late for that now, Mother. Matches have already
been made, and Lord Ballister effectively cut off the interests of any
other suitor. In fact, of everything he admitted on the night of the ball,
I believe I resent him the most for discouraging every other eligible
gentleman. I certainly did not give him cause to do so, and now, by his
precipitous actions, my season is quite ruined."

"It is not ruined, my dear. I can think of at least ten other men who
are in want of a wife. Lord Enfield has money enough of his own, and
is not so very old."

"Goodness, Mother! I would sooner marry a groom or a stableboy."

Her mother murmured something as she ducked down into the pile
of frills and netting.

"I am certain any man, even a groom, could be taught proper
manners and how to improve his speech. Then, I daresay he only
needs a proper suit of clothing, for underneath I imagine all men are
pretty much the same," Laurel mused.

"Laurel!"

"You need not be so shocked, Mother. I have three brothers, after
all." Laurel spoke confidently, but she had to admit to some curiosity.
It had been a good many years since she was dumped into the bath
with Joseph or Lewis; indeed, their nurse separated them just when
things began to get interesting. "But I imagine that grooms and
stableboys, and men who labor in the fields, might have additional, ah,

assets."

"This conversation is quite impossible. What if one of the maids should hear you?"

"If she does, I hope she goes out to find one of those stableboys. In that, she would have far more freedom than I do. I confess to some envy." Laurel sighed dramatically.

"A girl who marries a stableboy has the freedom to live above the stables or behind the carriage house. It might be very rustic and romantic. But on the other hand, Lord Enfield could give you several beautiful homes, a title, and children to carry it on. Your father did not build a shipping empire so his daughter would marry beneath her," her mother argued as she efficiently pressed Laurel's discarded gowns into the open traveling cabinet. "You do know we have maids for this purpose."

Laurel stopped suddenly, her arm poised to launch another projectile garment. "Yes, of course. To marry our stableboys." she agreed.

"To pack your garments, my dear," her mother answered tartly.

But Laurel knew she had won the battle. She might not be allowed to pursue a common laborer, but they were going home. She watched her mother examine a string of pearls before setting them into a small jewel case, and sigh over a tiara Laurel wore Wednesday last at Almack's. Lord Ballister had been present as well, and he had made a great show of avoiding her.

It was clear that her mother was in full despair. Her calm acceptance of Laurel's decision belied the real disappointment of returning to Greenbriars, to Laurel's father, with a daughter still unwed and the object of unflattering gossip. Instead, she might have been able to return triumphantly, like Titus to Rome, to present the rewards of her efforts: a daughter engaged to an earl, the young and thoroughly acceptable nephew of an unmarried duke. Perhaps more importantly, the marriage of Laurel to Lord Ballister would have thrust the Gardiner family through the doorway of society, at which they now stood yearningly at the threshold.

Laurel, understanding the nature of her mother's disappointment, decided to relent. "But these months have not been so very bad, Mother. We have enjoyed ourselves almost to distraction. We have shared the company of George, Joseph and Lewis, and it is not so often I find all three of my brothers in one place. And I have made some wonderful friends. Indeed, I have a notion of inviting Penelope Croyden to visit us at Greenbriars."

"Her Aunt Jessup assures me they will stay the season, even if you will not," her mother said pointedly.

"I cannot imagine why. Her dreadful disappointment surpasses all others', even poor, abused Lord Ballister's. It cannot be eased by going to a few balls and being thrust in front of the few other suitors who remain unattached. She will not so easily forget a man whom she has adored all her life."

"You talk as if you know, Missy."

"But I do know, Mother. If I do not have the interest to face other men after Lord Ballister's shallow behavior, what could poor Penelope be expected to endure? After all, the villain who abandoned her had been her childhood friend, a neighbor, a man known to all the family. They all had every expectation the wedding would take place, and why should it not?" Even as Laurel spoke, she realized there might be more to Penelope's story than they had been told. "They only lack the bridegroom."

"Miss Jessup fears something may have happened to the young man. He was a reliable sort, very comfortable and predictable."

Laurel raised her dark eyebrows. "He certainly does not sound very attractive to me, for all my friend adores him. Perhaps she can take heart in knowing that marriage to Westbridge might have bored her to death."

"And yet she loved him."

The words dropped between them, dissipating the argument.

"She loved him," Laurel repeated. "I suppose if I loved Lord Ballister, I might have forgiven him his self-interest."

"Sometimes there are things more compelling than love, my dear," her mother said.

Laurel looked into her mother's dark eyes. "If there are, you and Father have misled your children for so many years. We have always understood the deep feeling between the two of you, and how such affection can allow you to weather unsettling storms. I cannot speak for my brothers, but I will settle for nothing less in my own affairs."

"You did not love him," her mother said, and sighed.

"I did not." Laurel said solemnly, but then smiled brightly, as if everything turned out precisely as they hoped. "Therefore my story is happier than poor Penelope's, for I will leave London with my heart intact."

Her mother tossed another hat into the large cabinet, crushing the pheasant feathers adorning it. "And, isolated as we are in the country,

I daresay it shall remain so. There is nothing there."

"But you shall be reunited with Father. And I shall have . . ." Laurel hesitated, knowing her mother would not be very pleased with the prospect of her daughter reading at Greenbriars instead of flirting with young men in London. "I shall have the earth and sky and our lake and our gardens. There will be nothing to distract me from the beauty of nature!"

Chapter Two

Two days later Laurel opened her eyes onto a room that seemed part of her dream, and yet was achingly familiar to her. Blue and green vines imprinted upon white wallpaper grew in careful patterns towards the arched ceiling, stopping at a delicately carved border of molding. An artist's graceful hand continued the line of their sinewy paths against the plaster, so that the vines met at the summit, creating a canopy of painted leaf and sky. A warm breeze trifled with Laurel's spread hair, lifting it from the pillow on which she lay, and blowing it across her lips and eyelids. Unable to resist an impulse, she flung the linen bedcover off her body, allowing the same errant breeze to caress her bare arms and legs.

The faint scent of japonica mingled with the sharper odor of cut grass and filled the sunlit space. Laurel might well have awakened in a forest glade or a secret garden maze, or even in another world.

"If that girl does not get down to breakfast soon, I'll send in Mavis to pull her out of bed," growled a voice loud enough to startle Laurel from her enchantment.

It did. She sat up at once, pulling her cotton nightshift down below her knees, and looked around at her comfortable bedroom at Greenbriars. The walls, the furnishings, the Delftware pitcher on the water stand, were just as she left them only a few months before. It was a beautiful room, though it better suited her childish taste of only several years before than that of the woman she fancied she had lately become.

But it mattered not. She was home.

The door opened just a sliver.

"Miss Laurel?" asked a voice so softly Laurel barely discerned it from the rippling breeze.

"Why, it is Maggie, is it not?" Laurel guessed, knowing if it were not the young maid, it would be one of her multitude of cousins who all served at Greenbriars. "You seem to have grown a bit since I saw you last."

"You may be mistaking me for my sister, Miriam. Or mayhaps my cousin, Mavis."

Laurel felt a twinge of guilt for not being able to recognize a person who spent more time in this house than she. "But it is Maggie, am I right?"

"'Tis. But no matter. Mrs. Hills sent me to wake you and bring you breakfast, if you desire it."

"I suppose I do," Laurel said lazily, and stretched her body until her hands brushed against the delicate balled fringe on her headboard. "Is the day fair?"

It was a polite question, no more. Laurel had already guessed the June day to be as sunny and warm as they were ever likely to see at Greenbriars, and that the breeze would bring in rain by evening. Such was the pattern of days in the countryside; hours were marked by shifts in temperature and humidity. She had missed these natural barometers while she sojourned in London, where it could snow in May and hardly make a difference in one's daily schedule.

"It is, indeed, Miss Laurel. Shall I set out your riding clothes?"

"Yes, I would like to ride this morning. I may forego breakfast altogether, and bring a bit of lunch with me for a picnic."

"By yourself, Miss?" Maggie looked distressed.

"Indeed, by myself," Laurel said decisively, and started to pull her nightshift over her head. She felt the rise of goosebumps on her arms and breasts and wondered if it might be too cool to take her accustomed dip in the North Lake. "Why do you seem hesitant, Maggie? Do I have any reason to be fearful of riding unchaperoned?"

"I could not say, Miss. But Mavis said she saw a wood gnome when she went berry picking last week."

"A wood gnome? Would not such a creature avoid me?" Laurel buried her face in the warm fabric gathered at her shoulders, hoping Maggie would not see her smile.

"I could not say, Miss," Maggie repeated. "I suppose it depends on the lady. The creature dashed off into the woods when Mavis threw a stone at it."

"She attacked the poor fellow?"

"She meant no harm, Miss."

"Though I suppose the gnome could not know that." Laurel finally rose to her feet, throwing the nightshift into a basket near the bed. Her hair fell about her bare shoulders, caressing her skin. She had the sudden urge to ride as she was, as naked as Lady Godiva, across the park of Greenbriars. Perhaps the sight of her would tempt the gnome out of hiding, though she was not entirely sure a forest creature would find a lady more compelling than, perhaps, a plush bed of green moss.

"No, he would not," Maggie said firmly, and draped a sheet over Laurel's nakedness. "But if he thinks she did mean him harm, and then mistakes you for her, he might strike back at you. I would not ride alone, Miss."

"Oh, Maggie," Laurel protested, and turned so that the sheet twined about her. "I have ridden these hills and meadows for many years, and I have never found the slightest thing to give me a moment's hesitation. This is not London, you know. A lady can ride about unmolested: gnome, or fairy, or dragon take heed. Surely you do not think I might encounter worse than that!"

"Even so," the maid answered grimly, "I would be sure to hold the crop tightly in my hand wherever I go."

"I will take your caution to heart," Laurel promised solemnly, and stifled the image of herself accosting a small green figure of fantasy in a forest glen.

* * * *

Robbie Darkwood looked over his shoulder, making certain no one wandered through the meadow behind him. He had an obligation to his employer, to be sure, but it was almost impossible to chop logs with the vestments of his profession hanging about his limbs. He shrugged the unshaped linen robe off his back and let it drop onto the ground. Surely it could not get any more soiled than it already was.

The sun warmed his white peasant's shirt and the flesh beneath it. He gave a thought to removing his shirt as well, but after his recent encounter with a hysterical woman with predictably bad aim, he decided not to tempt fate any more than strictly necessary. He did not know her identity, but by her screaming, he did not doubt word was all over Cambridgeshire about the strange man in the wood.

Perhaps it was precisely what Mr. George Gardiner desired. After all, it could not be profitable to hire a hermit if no one knew he existed. And Rob did not doubt Mr. Gardiner always aimed to find profit in his investments.

Well, he, for one, could not fault that. Men of business had much to do to keep them occupied, intrigued, amused, concerned. Men of leisure—such as his own father, for example—owned far too much idle time and little enough to do in it. It then became too easy to turn idleness into mischief and waste, bringing despair and ruin to others.

Rob shattered a hefty log in one fierce blow. It did not pay to think of such things now. He could not take back the damage done twenty years ago; he could only seek to repair it. And that he did, though the medicine he applied would taint him and an innocent lady for a lifetime.

He lifted his axe again and took vengeance on the dead wood. There was merit in his choice of profession, odd though it may be. The sun and wind and leafy wood were his private kingdom to do with much as he pleased, and the pain of human intercourse was easily avoided. He no longer cared what was done in the gentlemen's clubs of London, or in the assembly rooms of Bath, or even in the drawing room of his own home. That life was gone to him now, but replaced by something infinitely purer, even redemptive.

He looked above him, the axe resting heavily on his shoulder. The blue green leaves of the surrounding elms created a verdant canopy over the glen, allowing only a solitary shaft of sunlight to touch the mossy ground. The breeze, bringing the scent of sea water upon it, ruffled his hair and his unaccustomed beard, which tickled his neck.

It was an absurd pretense, he admitted to himself. His beard was annoyingly scratchy and a damned nuisance when he ate the runny stews he managed to prepare in his meager kitchen. And he did not recall Mr. Gardiner including it in his very specific profession offering. But a beard somehow seemed to provide another barrier of defense against the world Rob had turned his back against, disarming any possibility he would be recognized. Indeed, he scarcely recognized himself.

The axe clattered to the ground as Rob spread out his arms to study his tanned forearms, muscled by only weeks of hard labor. The early blisters on his hands had calloused into hard knots of skin, and his nails were broken and rough edged. Before long, his disguise would no longer be artifice, but very much a part of his person. Transformation, it seemed, was not as hard wrought as he had first thought.

But what if he ever chose to return to the life he had abandoned? How long, he wondered, would it take to heal his cuts and bruises? Or soften his palms so that a lady might once again accept his hand for a reel? How long would it take to lose his gypsy's complexion? Or heal a broken heart?

Rob knelt down to retrieve the shards of wood and breathed deeply in the scent of the splintered cedar. He wrapped his robe about the logs to better carry them, and rose stiffly to his feet. His shirt clung damply to his back, and he thought the distant lake had never looked so inviting. And yet, the breeze brought up bumps on his skin, making him think the fine weather would not last.

He moved quickly down the path towards the stone cottage,

wondering if he dared expend some of his hard-won firewood on heating water for a bath. It would be a rare luxury, but one he might entirely justify.

If he had someone with whom to argue, that is.

He passed the small pen he had built for his goats and sheep and remembered the first few days at the hermitage when he thought he would go mad with loneliness. Mr. Gardiner's delivery of what he surely perceived to be a picturesque flock provided strange companions, but companions just the same. The addition of Prinny, a particularly exuberant mongrel, enlarged the circle of friends with more character than the hens and geese, and provided a swimming partner.

Rob looked ahead to the hermitage and saw Prinny racing up and down the pathway with all the enthusiasm of a puppy.

"Come Prinny! I have an excellent stick for you to fetch!"

Rob tossed a piece of his precious cedar down the slope of the hill, but Prinny would not have it. Instead he barked at the cottage door, and then, sensing Rob's attention, dashed around the back.

A dead squirrel, no doubt, Rob thought ruefully. Not tasty enough to tempt him, and not enough fur to serve any real purpose. Poor little creature, sport for a dog who would never be admitted into the echelons of real hunters.

Rob followed the sound of Prinny's riotous barking and caught the sudden movement of a larger animal at the edge of the clearing. A horse, perhaps? Did that madwoman with the stones return to torment him further?

"Stand!" said a decisive, feminine voice behind him. "Drop your parcel and whatever other weapons you carry."

Damn woman. Interfering harpy. Wretched crone. Did she think him defenseless?

He allowed the split logs to tumble to his feet, but held onto his hooded robe. He turned slowly, already framing a defense with which to disarm her.

And made the mistake of aiming his sight several inches too low.

"I beg your pardon," she said in righteous indignation.

Though the view of her full breasts proved tantalizing, he raised his eyes to gaze into a pair of deep brown eyes, framed by wisps of eyebrow that gave her a look—he guessed—of perpetual questioning. Masses of dark curls were gathered loosely at her neck, and she wore an absurd little hat that must be passing for fashion in London these days. He would not know. He only knew she was not that wretched crone.

Neither did she have a stone in hand.

She did, however, have a silver-tipped riding crop and looked quite ready to use it.

"I demand to know your purpose here, sir," she said, faltering over the last word. She frowned, which had the effect of heightening the red of her lips, and tapped her crop impatiently into the palm of her hand. "And once you state it, I will ask you to leave. This is private property."

Rob cleared his throat, wondering if he should don his rustic voice, so well practiced in rehearsal with Prinny.

"Have you no tongue? Or are you merely an idiot?" she asked.

That settled it. Hermits were members of a time-honored profession, and he had no intention of taking abuse. No matter how beautiful the abuser.

"I might ask the same of you, Madam. This is not only private property, it is my home."

She looked as if he had slapped her. "Such a thing is impossible. This cottage belongs to Mr. George Gardiner, of Greenbriars."

He took advantage of her dropped guard and flung his robe over his shoulders, slipping the hood down over his head.

She took a step back, undoubtedly repelled by the earthy scent of the fabric. But she held the riding crop with the same ominous stance.

"And I am in his employ. More specifically, I am his hermit." Rob drew himself up straight, and was absurdly pleased he had several inches on this unusually tall female. He wondered, just briefly, what it might be like to dance with her, or feel her body pressed against his, or . . .

But he was losing his mind to imagine such things with a woman about whom he knew nothing but that she surely wanted to murder him.

"His hermit?" She had the temerity to laugh out loud, and Rob heard music where he only had heard the sound of the wind blowing in the leaves before. "He has no hermit."

"Begging your pardon, Madam, but he not only has a hermit, but the hermitage to keep him in. I am told it is a very picturesque arrangement."

"The hermitage is mine," she said, and, ever so subtly, raised the crop.

Rob studied it a moment, before glancing to the right. The moment she followed his gaze, he snatched the crop from her tight grip.

"You have injured me!" she cried, and held out a palm with a sliver of blood across it. "You have not only taken my cottage, but have injured my person!"

Rob regretted his action immediately, for whatever else he pretended to be, he was still a gentleman.

"I acted in self defense, Madam, as well you know. I am not an animal you can take a crop to."

She looked at him speculatively.

"You are not. I am very sorry I responded so hastily," she conceded. "But neither do you seem defenseless against a woman."

Rob was grateful for the hood that almost completely obscured his face. The vixen looked appraisingly at his person and, undoubtedly, had seen a damn sight too much when she first accosted him and he had stood in his thin, damp shirt.

"I would not fight a woman," he said.

"And yet you would injure me."

He did cause her harm and it was regrettable. He did not know who she was, but she surely knew Mr. Gardiner. And direct confrontation with the guests was something his employer did not desire.

"I have salve within, and bandage to apply it with."

She looked at him suspiciously. "If your garments are any indication of the cleanliness of your bandages, I would rather chance the consequences of washing the blood away in the pig trough."

"There are clean cloths in the hermitage."

"I know, and they are undoubtedly mine. Unless you have destroyed them."

"I found many things in the hermitage, but thought them no one's property. I boxed them, and put them in the shed."

"In the shed?" she squeaked, and then quickly recovered. "You were sorely mistaken to remove them from the premises, for it is no different than stealing them. I repeat, they are mine."

"And will you make me free with your name? So you may properly claim them?" he asked.

She hesitated a moment, and took a deep breath. "I am Miss Gardiner," she said. "And as Mr. George Gardiner is my father, I believe my claim to this cottage is greater than your own."

Rob remembered his employer's cautious words about his interfering, but beautiful, daughter. Somehow, he had taken no heed of those words at the time, thinking a daughter who was to be in London posed no immediate threat to his recent vows. Then, he preferred to imagine himself quite done with women, and had not thought of being tempted by any feminine baggage.

Therefore, perhaps the most disconcerting thing about this first test of his resolve was the fact that he realized how easily he could be seduced by fair temptation.

"Well, Hermit? Will you add insolence to your many faults? Or are you once again deaf?"

Or temptation foul.

"I thought you in London, Miss Gardiner," he said quietly, and crossed his hands over his chest, lest he be further induced to drag her off somewhere. No wonder her father wished her in London; she could try a rational man's soul.

"And so you would usurp what is mine?" Miss Gardiner crossed her own arms, mimicking his bold stance. "Will you not agree my claim is greater than your own paltry one? A hermit, indeed. It is the stupidest thing I have ever heard."

"Your father does not think so. He advertised for a hermit, and I met his requirements."

"And pray, what are the requirements for a hermit? So far, you have demonstrated the abilities of the proverbial village idiot. What is it a hermit does?" She glanced around and sniffed contemptuously. "Surely you cannot boast of any knowledge of animal husbandry. And your gardening skills will not give sustenance for a month. Is wood cutting your expertise? Or are you skilled at fence mending? Do tell me, Hermit. I am at a loss to explain this life you profess to lead."

Rob gritted his teeth so tightly he thought he would pop a muscle in his neck.

"What I do is no business to anyone but myself. I live in complete solitude, with only the animals and the forest for company. It is what I have sworn to do, and what I most desire. Those who would violate my vows are as gravely guilty of trespassing as one who walks through the doorway of a home belonging to another."

"As you have done," Miss Gardiner said pointedly. Rob prayed that would be an end to it. But her questioning eyebrows warned him it was not yet to be. "Now I understand your mission, Hermit. I suspect, however, that one who chooses to live in such a way is hiding some great deficiency from the world. He must be either deformed, or ill featured, or guilty of some great crime."

"Perhaps I am all three."

Miss Gardiner looked up at him. "It is too late for that, as I have already glimpsed your face."

"For a moment, nothing more. You cannot have formed much of an opinion in so short a time.

"The beard is disgusting, to be sure," she said. "But it cannot hide your chin. And before you chose to cloak yourself like a mushroom, I saw eyes as blue as the summer sky. No, I would not think you ill featured, Hermit. Are you deformed? Unless you have a third arm invisible to me, I doubt it. You are taller than I, something many men of my acquaintance could not boast. So I know you are not a hunchback."

"You are, therefore, left with one option, Miss Gardiner."

Of course," she said and, absurdly, smiled. "But I already know you are guilty of a great crime."

Rob felt his body run cold, a strange reversal of the uncommon heat he had been feeling for at least ten minutes. Was it possible she knew his identity? Did rumors abound in London of the great injury he did to a faultless lady? Was he already labeled the most foul villain?

"You have found me out," he said, hoping to call her bluff and see what she really knew.

"I can hardly avoid it, since I shall bear the scar of that crime."

He said nothing, as he wondered if she called his bluff in her turn.

"I refer to my poor, injured hand, sir," she said, and held out her palm to reveal the sliver of blood across it.

Rob had nearly forgotten his recent transgression, but already suspected Miss Gardiner would remind him of it as long as they knew each other.

"Let us see to it," he said gently.

"'Tis a trifle," she answered too quickly, and waved her injured hand dismissively.

He reached out and caught her by the wrist, feeling the erratic beating of her pulse. "It is no trifle if you are hurt, and I am at fault. If you will not come into my hermitage, will you allow me to bring a bandage out to you?"

"Yes," she said, and then, "no."

"No?"

"I did not come all this way to be turned back from my own cottage. It is mine, for all you say, and I will have you out of it. You shall have to seek solitude elsewhere."

Rob dropped Miss Gardiner's hand and turned towards the door of the hermitage, knowing full well she would follow. He did not wish to seek solitude elsewhere, for the arrangement suited him very well. If he appealed to Mr. Gardiner, he would undoubtedly lose his employment, for having spoken to Miss Gardiner. And if Miss Gardiner appealed to her father, he would still lose, for having injured her.

They would settle this business between them; there was nothing else for it. He faced much greater trials than bargaining with a willful lady over possession of a hermitage, and the sooner he dismissed her suit, the better for them both. He would have his solitude, and peace.

"Good heavens! What have you done?" she cried out as she stepped into his sanctuary.

Chapter Three

Laurel felt a stranger in the place most dear to her. Her books, her rocks and shells, her beloved but poorly embroidered pillows had all been replaced by things of little interest and no delicacy. A wooden trencher replaced her china plate and an odorous horse rug was thrown over her lovely wooden chair. Lace curtains no longer provided respite from the bright sun, now streaming through the windows.

And the place seemed small to her now, through the hermit had removed much of the furniture and pushed whatever remained to the perimeters of the room. It was not until he turned to her, several moments after her outburst, when she fully understood the illusion.

It was not the place that was small, it was the hermit who was so large in its confines. She looked up at him, wondering how Mavis could even have dimly imagined she saw a gnome. Here was no otherworldly sprite, no strange creature of caves and woodlands, but as fine a figure of a man as any she had ever seen. In different garments, in a fine ballroom, this man could creditably mingle in society, drawing attention for his height and keen eyes, and not for oafish behavior.

And therein lay another curious piece to this puzzle of a man. His speech and words, not to mention his very demeanor, were not the trappings of a rustic. And yet, he was not a gentleman. No gentleman would ever have accosted her as he had, nor dare to invite her into his home. Of course, no lady would even imagine accepting such an invitation.

Laurel shrugged, casting off the last of her London lessons. She had never fancied herself a lady, in any case. And so she followed the hermit into his home.

It was his home now. She once used the stone cottage as a place of refuge, to escape from the grandeur of the great house, and to discover something of herself here. But he lived here, eating and sleeping, and spending all the hours of his day and night. She glanced at the bed, neatly made up in a dark corner of the room, and quickly looked away.

"Where are my books?" she asked. "You will not tell me you have also consigned them to a box in the shed?"

He had been rummaging in a drawer, and looked up in surprise.

"Your books? Books of history and art and of the Greek poets?"

Laurel stiffened in indignation. "Why do you seem so surprised, Hermit? Do you think a woman incapable of reading nothing but fashion magazines and frivolous romances?"

"It is my experience . . . "

"Your experience? Indeed! You are a hermit, so of what experience can you boast? Do you know the ways of women? What we admire and what we despise? What we desire and what gives us pleasure?"

He rose from where he knelt before the cabinet, and again, he seemed uncommonly large in the very small space. Though he did no more than meet her eyes, his speculative gaze suggested that he knew very well what would give her pleasure and that, with little additional provocation, he might be willing to demonstrate. Laurel's body swayed towards him, as if a gentle wind moved her, but then she suddenly caught herself before she revealed something she did not yet understand.

The hermit smiled, and finally glanced away. "I know a good deal more than that for which you would give me credit." He nodded towards the books which replaced hers on the shelves. "I read as you do. I daresay there is no subject I have left untouched."

Laurel rather wondered about the women he had touched, and doubted he was of a disposition to live his life through the pages of a book. What, then, made him wish to isolate himself from all society and connections with others? And what would happen if she asked that he be sent away, as she fully intended? He would find yet another hermitage, perhaps one deeper and darker, and estrange himself even further from his own humanity. What a dreadful pity it would be if society were to lose such a man

A notion, exciting and daring, started to tickle at the edges of her imagination, as it had on one of her last days in London.

"But will you let me touch you?" he suddenly asked.

Laurel looked up, startled out of her reverie. Dear God! Had she said something without realizing it?

"I beg your pardon?"

He slowly approached her, but her moment of trepidation had passed. Now she only saw a dark cloaked figure whose costume shadowed most of the features of his face, revealing the edges of an absurd black beard and hands that held some linens and a small bottle. How had she thought him threatening?

"Unless you want to wrestle with the bandage yourself," he said, softly, "I would have your hand in mine to wrap it up. Come to my water bowl."

"It is my bowl, Hermit," she insisted, as absurd as it was.

"Then all the more reason why it should not be offensive to you. Will you wash the blood from your hand?"

She studied him for a moment, wondering why the intimacy of the situation troubled her not at all. Slowly, she unbuttoned the sleeve of her sprigged muslin dress and pushed it above her wrist. Her actions were deliberate and intentionally teasing, knowing he watched her from under his voluminous hood. The injury truly was a trifle, no more than a scratch, but she would not lose the advantage she felt over him.

Without looking down, he poured water from her ancient pewter pitcher into the bowl, missing the center of the basin so that water splashed over the side and onto his robe. If he noticed, he did not seem to care.

"Did you throw out all my herbs, then?" Laurel asked, and moved towards the bowl, stepping in front of him so her back faced him. She found it easier to be indifferent, and even rude, if she did not have to speak to his tantalizingly obscured form.

"Green leaves hanging from the ceiling? Some dried stuff tied with ribbons?"

"A fine hermit you are, Hermit! I would think you an expert on herbal cures and potions, since you never avail yourself of physicians. If you did, you would know the value of certain plants in healing wounds. It would be very useful to me just now."

Laurel waited for her hermit to do the gentlemanly thing and offer to forage for what she desired in the woods. But of course he did no such thing.

He cleared his throat, and Laurel realized he stood only inches behind her. She closed her eyes and imagined falling backwards against him and having his arms close about her. What was it about this man that tempted her to forget herself so? Was it simply that he was so different from others of her acquaintance? Or was there something innately intriguing about one who so assiduously avoided the company of others, when most people craved it?

"What do you know of hermits?" he asked abruptly.

She opened her eyes. "I am sure I know as much about hermits as you do about ladies. I undoubtedly read more than you, as you surely know if you truly hauled all my precious volumes into the leaky shed."

"What is a man thinking when he decides to become a hermit, do you suppose?" he asked calmly.

Laurel decided to ignore the question. She deliberately tended to her hand, until the bloody scabs were altogether gone. She would have a thin white scar to show for it, nothing serious enough to explain away to others, but something that would remain her souvenir of her first encounter with this strange man. Perhaps this would be their only encounter, for she surely ought to demand he be removed from the premises immediately. But some nagging insistent notion not only made her want to stay and torture him, but to come back to do it again. And again. Therefore, she knew full well her answer to him mattered.

"I suppose a man who becomes a hermit is weary of worldly affairs, of society, and particularly of ladies."

"Why particularly?" he asked sharply.

Laurel was not sure why she said that, but suddenly saw a solution in an odd bit of Socratic reasoning. "Because he cannot escape the company of men altogether, since he is one. He can converse with himself, and have the full advantage of always sustaining an argument that is unanswerable. In any case, he could know precisely what he himself is thinking." Laurel thought her argument rather fine and circuitous. "And, for all you say, he cannot know the thoughts of a lady."

"I would disagree with you, but this extraordinary conversation precisely proves your point."

Even without turning around, even without seeing his face, Laurel knew he smiled again. She seized the advantage and said, "A man who becomes a hermit does so to meditate on that weariness, to find solace in nature and in books, and in the simple pleasures an animal companion provides."

"Very astute, Miss Gardiner. But do you not think a hermit may simply dislike people?"

Laurel turned around, but he was so close to her that she took a step backward, pressing up against the wash stand. "But you do not, Mr . . . .I do not know your name. I cannot continue to call you Hermit."

"I do not see why not," he said, sounding bored. "We will not likely meet again. Hermit will suffice."

"It will not." She looked up and saw his lips, thin and slightly parted, through the dark beard. His teeth were very fine and even. "To call you a thing and not your name, denies your very humanity."

"I believe that is the very point, Miss Gardiner. You seem to be something of a philosopher; you must see the logic in it." He glanced down and took her hand in his, turning her palm towards the light. For one so passionless, his hand was uncommonly warm and strong, his fingers lean and agile.

Laurel wondered if he could feel the erratic racing of her heart, as she struggled to calm herself."If you were a true hermit, you would divorce yourself entirely from society."

"I believe I have." He ran a finger over the thread-like wound, where the ridge was most sensitive.

"But I am here," she offered.

He said nothing, but continued to run his finger up and down the line. If he were anyone else, Laurel would expect him to kiss her, for such caresses were often preludes to the deed.

"So you are," he said, "but you will come no more."

She tried to pull her hand away, but he held fast. "I most certainly shall!"

"You most certainly shall not! I am under agreement to your father, and under no circumstances am I to have contact with his guests."

"I am not his guest. I am his daughter."

"I daresay the rules apply tenfold, then. He has hired me for a charade; there is no dialogue in the part I am scripted to play."

"You can break the rules."

"I will not," the hermit said, and then quietly added, "I need the position."

"It is hardly a living, I suspect."

"But it is mine. And as long as you see fit to interfere with my affairs, I might well ask you why you need to come to the hermitage."

Laurel felt surprise at his question, for she would have thought the answer obvious. "Why, I read and study here in my cottage."

"In this isolated place?" He laughed, a deep and hearty sound that warmed her heart. "I have been to Greenbriars, you know. Perhaps you can tell me why a young lady who can make herself free in a grand house need confine herself to a dusty stone cottage built into an ancient wall?"

"You have met my father. You cannot suppose he would allow me to read the works of poets and historians. He expects great things of me, that I should marry well. To his way of thinking, there are not many men who would tolerate the interests of a bluestocking. You, yourself, were surprised, and you are not a gentleman. So you must see my problem. I must find a place away from Greenbriars, and have time for myself."

"Why, Miss Gardiner, do you realize how very like a hermit you sound?"

"Yes. Therefore, I must have my hermitage back."

"But you cannot tell your father why you desire it. And I will give you no reason to complain to him of me."

"But, Hermit, you already have." She looked down at her hand, which he promptly dropped. Stepping away from her, he turned towards the window.

"I would ask you reconsider," he said.

"Perhaps I will."

"And I would ask you not tell anyone of this chance encounter."

"And risk my reputation? If anyone knew we spent time together here, my virtue would be compromised, and I would be ruined for the marriage mart." Laurel laughed, and her hermit looked back at her. "My hotheaded brothers, who can be perfect fools, would probably insist I marry you. And that would defeat everything."

"Indeed?' For a moment, he sounded not like himself, but somewhat arrogant and superior.

"Of course," she answered, disturbed by his unexpected tone. Surely he did not need to be reminded of the disparity in their classes and circumstances. "I am sure hermits cannot remain hermits if they marry. And my father wishes for his only daughter to be a countess, at the very least. He will be very disappointed to find her mistress of a stone cottage. And I will not disappoint him."

"Indeed," he said again, and it was not a question.

"But there is the problem of the books." Laurel added thoughtfully. "They cannot remain in the shed. They are volumes of some practical value, to be sure, but they are of infinite value to me."

"Let me suggest we retrieve them from ignominious storage and bring them back in here. I will make room for them somewhere about, and they will be safe. Perhaps, with your permission, I will read a few volumes myself. They will make for good company."

"But not as good company as am I," Laurel said impulsively. Too late, she also realized she spoke foolishly.

The hermit groaned and tapped his foot impatiently. "Did we not already decide we are not to meet again?"

"I recall no such thing. You told me your position would be compromised. And I told you my virtue would be compromised if it were known we were here together. Neither wishes to sacrifice the well being of the other," Laurel said, and tried to see his expression beneath his ridiculous hood. After all, she had just offered him her promise to allow him to stay. Now it was his turn to be accommodating. But he said nothing, so she added, "But neither do I wish to give up access to my books."

"What do you suggest? That we share the cottage?" He sounded impatient and frustrated. "Miss Gardiner, I believe the fastest route to earning a place of your own, where your privacy is assured, is to make a good marriage and be mistress of your husband's estate. And, as you yourself point out, you will not manage it if it is known you share a cottage with a lowly hermit."

"Lowly?" she said speculatively, and was pleased to see him frown through his dense beard. "But, in any case, I am not sure it is marriage I desire. I believe it greatly overrated. I have just come from London and saw no one to tempt me. If anything, I learned to be more cautious. My new friend in town is desolate because the gentleman she loved spurned her and has quite disappeared."

The hermit returned to stand before her and picked up the bowl in which she'd cleaned her injured hand. He carried it through the open door and poured its pinkish contents out onto the cinder path. Then he walked on, indifferent to the spill, dragging the edges of his brown robe through the glistening ash.

Laurel was determined not to let him escape so easily. "Wait! I have not yet given you leave!"

"I do as I please in my house and . . . "

" . . . and in mine? I will not be denied access to my books, and you have yet to give me an alternate proposal." She followed him out the door and into the bright sunlight.

He stopped at the goat pen, and the little beggars were immediately at his side, nudging his robe. From somewhere in its depths he pulled out a few apples and fed them to the greedy creatures. Laurel took one from his hand without asking, and delivered it to the smallest goat, who was being nudged out by her elders.

"You do not need them all at once?"

Laurel blinked, thinking he spoke of the apples. "What?"

"You do not need all your books at one time?" he said more specifically.

"I am sure I would not."

"Then perhaps we can develop a delivery system, of sorts. We establish a meeting point where you might leave a note telling me the volume you need, and I deliver it to you in a leather pouch, so it will not be harmed. Then you would have access to your books, and I my privacy, and your volumes will have a safe, dry place in which to be stored. I know it is a compromise of sorts, but it undoubtedly will not last for long."

His idea made some sense, though it would mean forfeiting the comfort of her little cottage. But what did he mean by it undoubtedly would not last for long? "Do you propose to leave, then, Hermit?"

"Indeed not, Madam. I intend to stay. I only meant when you marry, your books will go with you. I know you just told me you had no plans for marriage, but in my experience those ladies most opposed to the principal are most likely to agree to the practice. And when you do announce your betrothal to some gentleman hearty enough to endure your wit, I promise I will personally repack all your books to deliver to his home. Did you say your father intends for you to have an earl?"

"If there is one I would have," Laurel said primly. "I am not sure there is an earl good enough for me."

"Undoubtedly not. A prince, then." The hermit patted his goats affectionately, and showed them his damp, but empty, hands. "But what say you to my proposal?"

"There is some merit in it," Laurel admitted. "And I am willing to try. In fact, I can think of a suitable place. Near the lake there are the remains of an old farmhouse, a very small one."

"I have been there. It is in poor condition and not likely to provide protection for your books."

"But there is a small, stone smokehouse, its roof nearly intact. It has not been used for years and I doubt if anyone would notice our comings or goings there."

"I know the place."

"But will you come regularly?"

"I do not have much to fill my days, Madam."

"Though you would, Hermit, if you but learned to be a better farmer. Did no one ever teach you that human blood or hair or nail clippings would help to keep rabbits from your vegetables? The creatures do not wish to meet one of us when they are doing mischief, and our bodily leavings fool them into thinking we are about." Laurel felt absurdly smug for her trivial bit of knowledge. "Therefore, you wasted some excellent animal repellent when you drained the bloody water onto the cinder path. Better it had gone to the radishes."

"To make them all the brighter?"

Laurel laughed. She studied her hermit for a moment, thinking him clever for one who did not engage in conversation, and bold for one who professed to venture little into the world. He was a complete enigma, which, unfortunately, had precisely the opposite effect of what he surely intended. That is, rather than shy from his company, she wanted to decipher the riddle he was.

"To make them tastier," she said, and licked her lower lip as she contemplated a bite into the tart vegetable. She had his full attention now.

He cleared his throat. "Might I suggest we find a book for you right now, so you need not trouble to deliver a request for another for some time," he said.

"I am sure it suits you, Hermit, but I do not yet know what I will study this week. I will make a request within the next few days. There remains one problem, however."

He gave a small gesture of impatience. Laurel, who had grown up in a family of brothers, was not surprised. She knew that men, satisfied with a decision, had no desire to revisit it.

"I do not know the name of the recipient of my request," she went on. "To whom do I address the note?"

"Madam," he said wearily. "Do you suppose there is such traffic in an abandoned smokehouse that there might be multitudes of correspondents?"

"You have not answered my question, Hermit."

He stood firm, as if he had no intention of ever answering.

"Ah, well. Hermit it is. But even goats and mongrels have real names." Laurel patted the little goat on the head and picked up her crop from where he had dropped it some time before. She started on her way.

"It is Robbie," he called out suddenly. "Robbie Darkwood."

Laurel turned slowly, deliberately. "Robbie Darkwood?" she asked incredulously. "Did I not ask for your real name?"

Not waiting for him to respond, she turned back to the path, hoping he was enough of a gentleman to not fling something at her retreating back. She counted her steps as she walked, expecting some response, some reaction. Finally, at the goodly distance of forty footsteps, she took advantage of a curve in the path and glanced behind her.

The man who called himself Robbie Darkwood stood where she had left him, still watching her.

And she thought that response enough, for the moment.

* * * *

"Did I send you to London with the express purpose of getting yourself a husband?" demanded Laurel's father, in the very same moment he gestured for additional biscuits at his place setting. Hills, the head butler, moved swiftly in response. Laurel was not as energetic.

"Well, girl? You went with your mother, and with enough clothes to dress all the wives of the Admiralty, and yet you came home empty fisted."

"We were not in London very long, my dear," murmured Laurel's mother.

"Time does not matter to a Gardiner. We make our decision and act upon it immediately. Was it not so with us, my love?" Laurel watcher her father smile winningly at his wife of thirty years, who blushed like a girl.

"But I did make a decision," Laurel pointed out, interrupting her parents before the scene became embarrassing. "And if I had acted immediately upon it, I would now be a very unhappy bride."

"Lord Ballister is exactly the sort of match your mother and I encourage. He is an earl, his bachelor uncle a duke. Dare we aspire to higher reward?"

"I only dared to imagine he might care for me more than he cared for your money, Father. But he made his priorities clear only moments after he declared his undying love for me. Perhaps he heard about the legendary Gardiner decisiveness and thought he should waste no time on the matter."

"Your sarcasm holds no place at the table, Laurel," her father said sternly.

"I apologize, but I fear I use it somewhat indiscriminately, sir. It surely had a place at the Duke of Armadale's ball, where Lord Ballister addressed me. I let him know precisely what I thought of him."

Her father stuffed another biscuit into his mouth and rolled his eyes. "And yet you imagine another proposal might be made to you in the future? Where will we find such a fool?"

"Fear not, my love. Joseph will be arriving at Greenbriars within the week, and he brings with him several friends," Her mother reminded him, unaware of the implication of her words.

"But our son, for all his connections, prefers to befriend merchants and bankers. I will have more for Laurel."

"Might more be less, Father?"

"Explain yourself, girl," he answered gruffly.

"Do not begin your nonsense about marrying a groom," her mother cautioned.

"Marrying a groom!" Her father was on his feet, waving another biscuit in Laurel's face. "I will kill the beggar!"

"Calm down, Father, or you will suffer indigestion," Laurel said calmly. "I do not know of any grooms who wish to marry me . . . "

"Then they are all idiots!"

Laurel smiled, delighting in the whims of her father's inconsistencies, and knowing he could never stay angry with her for very long. "Just because they do not wish to marry me does not make them idiots. Indeed, one could think of few people stupider than Lord Ballister, and he probably is related to nothing less than an upper maid."

"Laurel . . . " her mother warned softly.

"I only meant . . . that is, I told Mother, I would sooner marry a groom who loved me than an earl who loved your money. Would you have me accept less than you wished for yourselves? You married for love when you were both still so young your parents could have dictated your preferences. But they respected the strength of your affections above all other things."

"We are not talking about your mother and me now. We are discussing your future," her father said. "I would like to know what you and a groom would share in common,"

Laurel looked down at her plate, imagining stolen kisses, intimate caresses, and the warmth of a man's arms embracing her body; but to even mention such things would be even less welcome at the dinner table than her sarcasm. She knew nothing of physical relations by experience of course, but she read a good deal, and her mother had not sent her out into the social world a complete innocent. Her father, unknowingly, nurtured her interest by installing an impressive collection of Italian sculpture in the garden. And, even worse, her father hired the hermit, a man who made her uncommonly curious about what was hidden beneath his dark robes.

"Well? If you have no answer, I will provide several for you. Your man would not be educated or share any of your sensibilities. He would not be able to offer you the things to which you are accustomed or provide your children with anything worth having. For all you ladies read romances, you surely recognize one could not survive merely on love."

"But what if there were such a man, one who worked hard and had great generosity of intellect, if not of pocket? What if he were tutored in some of the gentlemanly arts? Could you not believe him a man worthy of some consideration?"

Laurel knew her questions stabbed at her father's Achilles' heel. He had attained all he had, including his aristocratic wife, on his own merit. He allowed his sons to carry on his work, but he wanted no taint of industry to color his daughter's future.

"Of consideration, yes. But not for you, my dear child," her father admitted. "In any case, I do not believe your experiment would be successful."

Laurel had not thought her rambling notions sufficient to be termed "experiment," but she had already met the man who might prove very suitable to prove her point. And if she had her father's permission to spend time with Robbie Darkwood, her sojourn at Greenbriars might prove very diverting indeed. "If I should find him, an unpolished stone, might I endeavor to improve him? If not for me, then for a friend?"

Her father sat down heavily in his chair, rubbing his forehead as he often did when he tried to make sense of an irreconcilable business ledger. "Men are not to be trifled with, Laurel. Eloise, did you not tell our daughter anything about the ways of the world? This man will surely misconstrue your motives."

"Then I have permission to pursue such a project?" Laurel prodded.

"Yes. No! Of whom can you be speaking? What are you planning to do?"

Laurel avoided her father's eyes. "I met a young man in the village the other day. He appeared intelligent, though very untutored, and somewhat homely. He is just a farmer, scarred by some great sadness in his life. But there seemed something sincere in him, so sincere I doubt he could be persuaded to marry a lady for her father's money alone."

"And who will be his lucky bride? The man may be married with ten children, for all you know. This is a harebrained scheme, if ever I heard one."

"Rabbits are very clever little creatures, Father."

"Clever enough to mind their own business."

Laurel cleared her throat. "Clever enough to reap the rewards of another person's work. They do not grow their own food, but harvest the work of others."

"And get shot for their thieving ways."

Her mother gasped, and Laurel gently patted her hand. "I will not get shot, Father," she said, though more for her mother's benefit. "And certainly not by the man's nonexistent wife and ten children," she added, for his. "He appears entirely unencumbered."

"A situation you wish to remedy, not content to leave the poor fool alone," her father accurately pointed out.

"If he were a poor fool, I would not bother," Laurel reminded him.

"Ah, yes. Your unpolished stone. A man capable of being reinvented by a young busybody with little to do but interfere with the affairs of others." Her father now had both hands pressed against his forehead, and sounded pained.

Laurel's retort died on her lips. She would have liked to point out there was little enough for her to do on the estate, so concerned were her parents with giving her every advantage of a genteel upbringing. She would have liked to reveal she had a cottage full of books she enjoyed and studied, but that would have brought the discussion to the hermitage, and she did not wish for either of her parents to guess the object of her proposed experiment. And in both cases, the conversation would have turned on her, for her parents would be sure to remind her that she would not be so very bored if she had a husband and children. And that was an argument she couldn't possibly win.

"But why bother at all, my dear?" her mother asked.

Laurel ran a finger along the rim of her crystal wine glass, hearing the slight hum of the sherry's vibration. Her mother was a very literal sort, and would not be put off by vague references to rabbits and unpolished stones.

"I just feel I might do some good," she said at last. "I am blessed with a very cheerful life, and I am surrounded by people who care for me. Is it wrong for me to wish the same for others?"

"And so you wish to take a man from the path he has chosen and lead him down another? Perhaps he is happy being a farmer and cares not a whit for old Romans and Latin and mathematical computations. Perhaps he is happy just left as he is."

Indeed, had not Mr. Darkwood said just that?

"And yet I sense a great unhappiness in him," Laurel said.

"Perhaps it is because he is already married."

"Father!"

"George!"

Laurel and her mother protested in one voice, and her father had the grace to look chagrined.

"I am sorry, my dears. If he is a married man, then he must be, by definition, a happy one," he amended, and then, before they could respond to his sarcasm, "But who is to be the sacrificial lamb?"

Her mother looked up in confusion, but Laurel had lost none of the threads of the conversation.

"I made a new friend in London, Father, a very dear girl. She is much of an age with me, but seems sadder than her twenty or so years."

"Has she suffered many loses, then?"

"Her mother and father have been dead many years. She lives with her two younger sisters and a maiden aunt."

"That explains it, then." Her father removed his right hand from his forehead so he could slam it on the table in mock anger. The plates rattled by the impact and her mother cried out in alarm.

Laurel knew her father well enough to know when he poked fun at her. She ignored him, and continued, "And yet she seems contented with the arrangement. She has, however, been hurt in another way, and only recently." Laurel paused to strengthen herself with a sip of the neglected sherry. "She has been jilted."

"Poor, poor Miss Croyden," her mother murmured, and fortified herself in a similar manner. "She was to marry an earl."

"Is the man ripe for picking, then?"

Laurel stared at him, aghast. "Father! You cannot imagine I would be at all interested in such a man!"

"Aside from which, he has quite disappeared," added her mother. 'Vanished."

"Suggesting, of course, he eloped with another. No, my dears, you are quite right. He is far too ripe for our Laurel. But what is wrong with Miss Croyden? Is she cross-eyed or heavily mustached? Does she wear trousers or speak with an American accent? Is she a chattering idiot?"

Laurel recalled the list of defects she had offered to her father's hermit by way of explaining his separation from society, and she knew the business was never as simple as she—and now her father— imagined. Who ever knew what was in another's heart? Who ever understood what drove another to acts of desperation?

"No, Father. That is precisely the wonder of it. She is quite lovely and very personable. She is of good family and well connected. The Earl of Westridge was intended for her from the time they were children, and he gave no indication of any discontent with her or their arrangement."

"Perhaps they grew apart and entertained other interests."

"Do you not think she would have realized such a schism forming?

They lived on adjoining properties."

"Then I cannot say," her father said in a rare concession. "But why is it any business of yours?"

"It is not," Laurel finally admitted. "But I cannot bear to see such a lovely person so unhappy. And if she were to be introduced to another such person, perhaps they will find joy with each other."

"Harebrained, indeed," her father grumbled under his breath. "And somehow you imagine a girl once betrothed to an earl would be happy with a farmer?"

"A certain farmer, perhaps. There is something in him I see, something that might be nurtured and encouraged. At least, let me try. Please, Father."

Her father settled one elbow on the table and settled his cheek into his palm. He gaze went above their heads as he seemed to be appealing to a higher authority for advice. Laurel smiled and sat back in her seat when she saw this familiar gesture and knew what it would mean. He was concerned, to be sure, but she knew she would get what she wanted.

"Very well. But what do you want of me?" asked the voice of a defeated man.

"Why, nothing," Laurel said in surprise, wondering if she might have hatched this scheme without the knowledge of either of her parents. She was accustomed to such subterfuge, after all. "I only ask that you allow me to invite Miss Penelope Croyden to Greenbriars and introduce her to the neighborhood."

"Any friend of my daughter is welcome in our home," her father reminded her. "After all, your brothers have never thought anything of bringing rogues and hoodlums to our door."

"George! I am sure Joseph knew nothing of Lord Ledward's sticky fingers!" her mother protested.

Laurel quickly interceded. "I am sure you will find nothing objectionable about Miss Croyden, Father. She is so far above reproach you will be as taken as I by her sad story."

"I will dutifully shed tears with her when the name of the Earl of Westbourne . . . "

" . . . Westridge . . . "

" . . . is mentioned. But what will I find to commiserate with your melancholy farmer? Will you bring him to the house? Will you introduce us?"

Laurel frowned, having neglected to think through this difficulty.

"I am not sure he will come. He is very shy. I am not even sure the name he gave me was his own."

"And this is the man you propose to polish so brightly he will replace an earl in a lady's affections?" her father said disbelievingly. "I am not sure I want you anywhere near him, my dear."

"I am not fearful for my own safety," Laurel said quickly, though she recalled with uncomfortable clarity the strange attraction she felt for the hermit. "He has come to the neighborhood with references and has secured a position locally."

"As a farmer?"

"As a . . . farmer."

Her father said nothing, but Laurel was fully aware he did not entirely trust her words or her motives. Perhaps it was because he knew her too well. And with his quiet doubt, Laurel began to wonder if she knew herself too little.

"Well if the man has some talent at his work, perhaps we can introduce him to our hermit, a fellow who seems to have not the slightest knowledge of husbandry," her father said at last, his face still upturned. Laurel followed the direction of his gaze. "But then, the poor man is not inclined to conversation and will admit no visitors. I am much relieved you have not made him the object of your attention, Laurel."

"A hermit!" Laurel said brightly. "I had quite forgotten his existence."

She dropped her eyes and glanced towards her father, whose gaze held hers for a moment.

"A hermit?" her mother asked. "Do we have one, George?"

Chapter Four

Rob studied himself in the cloudy mirror and moved his head from side to side, allowing the flow of his black beard to caress the tanned skin on his chest. Unbidden, the remembrance came to him of a lady's dark curls spread across his neck and shoulders, tickling his nose as they lay together in the shade of a protecting beech tree—accompanied by the great shame that such memories now ignited. At the time, there seemed nothing reprehensible about their growing intimacy and the certain freedoms they enjoyed with each other; now he thanked heaven every day that it never went further than it had.

But for all their eventual difficulties, the lady's hair had been splendid, long and curling, and smelling suggestively of the lemon verbena in which he knew she bathed. His recent beard, by contrast, looked like a dead badger hanging from his chin. It was as odious as any hermit could desire.

But then, he was not quite a hermit. Or, at least, although he proclaimed himself as such, he had not yet sufficiently developed the sensibility of such a character, nor was he entirely convinced such a life would suit him for the duration of his years.

The doubting of his own commitment frankly surprised him, for he had once managed to convince himself—and the all-seeing Mr. Gardiner—of the righteousness of his choice. So he would have remained, and so he would have been content. Or, at least, this he told himself.

But since the unwelcome intrusion into his rustic paradise by Mr. Gardiner's bold and interfering daughter, he found himself thinking of certain things that would drive his fellow hermits to despair. Of course, that very bothersome lady would readily point out that a brotherhood of hermits would quite defeat the point, and that despair was the very password for men in his curious profession. But it seemed hardly the issue.

What was the issue was that he suddenly imagined Miss Gardiner's own dark curls nestling against him, warming his body and his soul, and that he would very much like to stifle her witty and sarcastic words with his lips. Since their meeting, he found himself wondering if she had ever slept in the small bed he himself now used in the hermitage, and if she once used the utensils with which he now made himself free.

Both his curse and his salvation would be received if she could possibly manage to stay away from the place.

He tugged at the beard, mentally picturing it several inches longer and curling towards his naval. It was impossible and absurd. It would drive him to distraction, and the lady would relentlessly bother him about it.

If she ever came to his door again.

Rob moved towards the window, in front of which stood a small, weather-beaten work table, and ran his fingers over the various implements he had set down upon it. He had not a scissors, but there was a fairly sharp candle snuffer. And, even better, his carving knife. As he raised this more effective tool towards his face with his right hand, he pulled out his beard with the left.

And realized if he misjudged his stroke he would damn near cut his own throat.

It would be bad enough for Miss Gardiner to find him half dressed, but even worse should she find him dead. She would undoubtedly be joyous to be rid of him, and start returning her own property to his shelves as soon as she could drag his lifeless corpse out into the yard, where it might fertilize the soil. But then she would be equally joyous to imagine her hypothesis correct, that he killed himself because of some deep sadness, and she would let all the world know how very clever she was. Consequently there would be questions about his identity, and too many questions asked, and others would be injured.

All this would quite defeat his purpose in coming to Greenbriars. Of course, if Miss Gardiner threw his body into the pig trough, as she was more likely to do, no one would be at all harmed.

But Rob could not take that chance. He returned to his mirror and took measured lengths along the beard before hacking away half its growth. Ready to discard what he now held in his hand, he remembered the knowing words of his lady tormentor and decided to mix it in the soil near his tomatoes, and see if the rabbits were as perturbed by his scent as he guessed was Miss Gardiner. He turned back to his own reflection, and decided he did not look half bad. More like a Renaissance gentleman, actually, which seemed to coincide with Miss Gardiner's taste in literature. He chopped away at the sides and upper lip, nicking himself just once, and restored himself to some semblance of humanity.

Not bad at all.

Then there was his hair, most of which tumbled about his face and neck, unless he remembered to gather it in a queue with a piece of gut. But it did not solve the problem of what to do with the stringy mop that fell into his eyes, occasionally blinding him as he read or cooked his food. He lifted a handful of hair just above his forehead, and with his newfound barber's skill, trimmed it with one clean stroke. If it seemed to be an inch higher on the left then on the right, it could scarcely matter. If he ever decided to abandon the hermit's life to pursue the profession of valet, he would work to refine his skills even further.

Musing on the infinite possibilities available to a talented working man, he thoughtfully scratched his chest. And decided that when he next operated on himself, he should remember to drape some rag over his shoulders and avoid decorating himself with his own prickly cuttings.

He briefly considered a swim in the lake, until he remembered Miss Gardiner's urgent message about a book she desired, and knew to procrastinate would bring the harpy back to his garden.

Rob picked up his white linen shirt from where he had dropped it the night before, and pushed his fisted hands through the armholes. The garment, a remnant from his former life, had lost its starched veneer and a few buttons, and now felt as comfortable as an old nightshirt. He thought it his best shirt, but in the past week or so noticed a certain tightness in the shoulders and arms. He knew when you washed garments, they sometimes shriveled. But he had not washed this shirt for a fortnight. He flexed his arm, and nearly ripped the fabric.

The fabric had not shriveled; he had muscles he scarcely knew existed. They first made themselves known to him in the first weeks of his new profession and now, old friends though they had become, they sometimes managed to surprise him. Undoubtedly they would surprise a few people of his acquaintance, as well.

A pity he felt obliged to bury himself in his voluminous robes, but truly, as there would be no one but a few field mice to greet him in the old smokehouse, he had no one to impress but himself. He flung the rough robe over his shoulders, fastening it at his neck. The hood would stay off for now; it would be hard enough to find Miss Gardiner's book in the dim shed without peering through the ragged edge of his garment.

* * * *

Laurel reveled in the warmth of the earth as it seeped through the thin leather of her fashionable boots and warmed her feet. The mud of the early spring, which she had abandoned to seek the dubious delights of London, had hardened into packed dirt, the ruts and footprints of

March still intact. Her experienced eyes saw the tracks of rabbits and deer, a large sized dog, and her own boots. Here and there another larger set of prints mixed with hers, and she knew them for the hermit's. A man as tall as he would have a suitably sized foot to match. And she doubted if anyone else ever ventured along these isolated paths.

Today she did not care to see him, for she had other objectives on her way. Though she intended his path to eventually cross with that of her friend Penelope, her present thoughts were all for the invitation she composed in her head as she walked. She desired Penelope's presence, and would make that patently plain in her missive. But should she hint at some future joy? Would Penelope be intrigued or offended that Laurel thought an earthy, untutored man worthy of redemption, not to mention as a possible suitor for her? Would Penelope feel the sting of pity, or the excitement of intrigue?

To be sure, Penelope had once confided her belief that the notion of marrying a man of position and title to be vastly overrated. She, herself, once intended to marry for love. The fact that the man she was to marry was, indeed, the Earl of Westridge, was mere coincidence.

And it ended badly.

Certain men were not to be trusted, they had agreed, although Laurel sensed some hesitation on her friend's part. Though Penelope had been jilted, virtually on the very eve of her marriage, she still wrote in her letters that she trusted her damnable earl, and imagined him hurt and wounded in a ditch, or set upon by brigands in his very drawing room. She did not doubt he would return to her one day.

Laurel, who heard nothing of the man to particularly recommend him, rather imagined him living with a lightskirt in Paris, or eloping to Gretna with another lady. She doubted very much he would return.

Which was why she believed she could ignite an attraction elsewhere, and do so with impunity. She knew other men who would do for Penelope, not the least of whom were her own three brothers, but there certainly was a challenge in imagining she might refine a rough man into a suitor worthy of her friend. She had read a good deal of and about Rousseau, after all. And, for all his superiority of intellect and association with other great men, did not the man find happiness with an illiterate housemaid?

A hermit, by contrast, seemed infinitely preferable than a housemaid for, unlike most members of the lower classes, he was not tainted by society. In some ways, Robbie Darkwood was closer to Rousseau's natural child than someone much younger might be.

Of course, he did not seem so very old, and Laurel imagined him of an age to her brothers. And she had seen enough of him through his damp white shirt to know he was not a child; Laurel's face grew warm just thinking of it. Additionally, he did confess himself a reader. Mrs. Rousseau—if indeed she ever married her tutor—necessarily learned all her lessons from her husband.

But a hermit usually did not have worldly experience, and therein remained a problem. Robbie Darkwood did indeed seem somewhat familiar with the ways of the world, and did not appear so very much at home with the earth. Why, the man did not even know how to nurture his garden!

Laurel smiled to think of it, and then, rather unhappily, guessed that most men she met in London would be similarly ignorant.

She stumbled on a stone and looked down at the path to see another very large footprint. Mr. Darkwood owned a fashionable pair of boots, she saw, one in which the left foot could be differentiated from the right. But that meant nothing, of course. He could be wearing a pair of her brothers' boots, or ones discarded by former employers. Even Mrs. Rousseau would have owned clothes better than expected for one in her poor station in life.

In any case, Laurel convinced herself, Mr. Darkwood only waited for redemption at her hands and she would mold him and model him until he proved himself worthy of a lady. And Penelope Croyden, poor abused and lonely Penelope, was almost certainly that lady.

Light of step, Laurel continued to compose her letter of invitation as she started up the slope towards the smokehouse. She saw a flash of dark brown disappear into the woods and realized she may have only missed Mr. Darkwood by minutes. It was not regrettable, for though she felt quite ready to embark on her little experiment, she did have an appointment with John Lyly this day. And she guessed Mr. Darkwood had just delivered her first request: Lyly's *Anatomy of Wit*.

She quickened her step and felt in her embroidered pocket for the small offering she intended for the hermit. He did not expect a reward. Indeed, the bargain was only for her to allow him to remain in her cottage. But she wished to give him something that would do much towards encouraging him to return to human society.

At first she thought he had left the smokehouse door ajar, and then realized it was off its hinges. Robbie Darkwood had propped it against the stonework, little realizing how difficult it might be for a lady to lift. She would be sure to remind him of it in her next letter, though it did not

solve her immediate problem. Laurel grasped the edge of the oaken
door and tried to pivot the boards to the left. Instead, in order to avoid
being crushed by it as it fell, she had to jump to the right. The errant
hinge caught her skirt and tore the fabric, but the injury to her dress
was nothing to what pain she would have suffered if the door had
fallen on her.

In but two meetings with the hermit, she had twice suffered harm.
By all rights, she should take warning and avoid him or demand his
removal from her father's property. But then, she admitted, the pleasure
of her own project would be gone.

She stepped into the smokehouse, breathing in the smoke-scented
air that somehow yet lingered after many years of disuse, and looked
towards the stove where she had left her message the day before.
There, upon the dusty iron, in a leather pouch, was something resembling
a book.

The moment Laurel lifted it she realized it not weighty enough to
be her *Wit* and wondered what mischief was afoot. In the sudden light
of understanding, she realized her hermit might well have been bluffing,
and did not know how to read at all. Perhaps his was the illusion of wit,
with nothing of substance to back it

Frustrated and annoyed, and knowing full well her task was now
likely to be a good deal more complicated, she stepped out into the light
and pulled the volume from its protective cover.

Lyly it was, but not his *Wit*. Instead, she looked down at a volume
hitherto unknown to her, though not apparently to that famous author.
When had he written *Euphues and his England*? It was not a volume
from her library.

A scrap of paper, of some rough fiber of the sort that booksellers
used, fell to the ground. Laurel, already seeing the blue ink of a bold
hand, bent over and retrieved it. The letter began:

My dear Miss Gardiner,

*As I suspect you already know the contents of the book you
requested, and may not be as familiar with Lyly's later work, I
thought it best to forward this companion volume to you. You may
be intrigued to find it a continuation of his well-known ruminations
and hence, appreciate it all the more.*

I am, sincerely, R.D.

Appreciate it, indeed? Was her father's hermit now her mentor
and she not his? Laurel threw his odious note on the ground, and

trampled it as she started to follow the path she knew he had taken to return to his—*her*—cottage. If she had desired another book, she would have told him so. But she had not. Nor was he expected to make his own judgements about what she ought be reading; if she sought such officious guidance, she would have remained in a corner of her father's library and read books of his recommendation. Not that she ever saw her father read, but he did have a rather impressive library.

As she looked up the path, willing her heart and lungs to slow their breathless rhythm, she saw Prinny wagging his spiral tail in cheerful greeting.

"Where is your master, you little interloper? A fine pair you make, of dubious parentage, and masquerading with authority on an estate not yours!" Even though she spoke harshly, Laurel could scarcely resist fondling the large dog's ears. A mongrel he might be, but he had lived at Greenbriars for many years, and he never failed to greet her with exuberance. "Well, where is he?"

Prinny barked loud enough to dislodge the ancient Vikings from their peaty bogs, and dashed ahead on the path.

Laurel lifted her skirts and would have run after him but that she saw her prey not many yards ahead.

Mr. Darkwood was aptly named, it seemed, for in the bright sunlight his hair was the color of the deepest mahogany. His odious hood was down about his shoulders, revealing a curling mane caught in a careless knot at his nape. Laurel's memory flickered, but did not catch fire, and something began to bother her as she approached him.

Something must have bothered him as well, for he paused in his tracks and seemed to be adjusting his robe about his body. And it was an excellent body, looking larger and larger with each step she took.

"Mr. Darkwood!" she called out. When he didn't slow, she called out again.

She saw him stiffen and, without turning, slip the hood back over his head. Laurel cursed herself silently, wishing she had caught him unawares.

"Miss Gardiner?" he questioned as he turned around, in a tone of apparent amazement. Who else did he imagine would be traipsing along this old path? "Did you not find your book?"

"Indeed not, Mr. Darkwood. I did not find my book. I found another, not quite fulfilling my needs." She caught up to him and faced him on the narrow path. Prinny danced around them, barking with delight. "Do you have, perhaps, another lady for whom you leave volumes of early Renaissance writings?"

He amazed her by laughing. "Would I knew another! No, I am sorry to say you are my only scholar, Miss Gardiner."

She stared at him for several moments, wondering what fantasies brewed under his brown lid.

"I am your scholar, sir? You are sadly mistaken, and presume far too much. I am not your anything, but the daughter of your employer. You are to obey my wishes, and do as I say. And I did not give you permission to undertake the business of my education."

Mr. Darkwood said nothing but dropped to his knees. Laurel, for one brief moment, imagined the most dramatic form of apology, and would have bid him rise, when she realized he did no more than fish about for a stick. Rising with it, he lifted it in the air and tossed it unceremoniously for a thankful Prinny.

"No, Miss Gardiner. It is once again you who are mistaken. I was willing to submit to your little plan for access to your books, though it went against my nature. I am a hermit, after all, and do not desire contact with anyone." He took a step back, as if emphasizing his point. "You may be the daughter of my employer, but you are not my employer. I obey the wishes of your father, that is all. And I will not be blackmailed into forfeiting my agreement with him."

"You would have had to forfeit nothing, nor would you have had to speak to me at all if you only did as I asked. You gave me the wrong book, sir, and what is more, not even one from my collection. Have you an explanation for it?"

Darkwood took a deep breath and glanced away from her. When he did so, she caught the briefest glimpse of his jaw, and realized his beard and mustache looked somewhat neater than they had when last they met. As she continued to study him, she saw his fingers creep out from under the robe, and reach out to scratch his neck. Fleas? Whatever advantage the hermit gained by his improved appearance was instantly lost.

"I could not find your *Wit*, though I looked through each of the trunks packed in the shed. Since most men have read the earlier work, I thought you might be intrigued by the continuation. Lyly published it a few years later, and it is not as well known."

Laurel was very much intrigued, though not by his explanation. "I am not most men, sir," she reminded him. "And most women are not encouraged to read such things at all. We are given novels, and light volumes of verse. And the occasional religious treatise. Our education is a poor one."

"But at least girls are taught to read in our language. Young men must endure years of training in Latin and sometimes Hebrew, and while away at school are expected to read texts only in those languages."

More and more intriguing.

"I might ask, sir, how you know that?"

Mr. Darkwood had the grace to look flustered. He seemed to glance about for another stick to throw for Prinny, who had not yet returned with the last one.

"Well?" Laurel broke a twig from a nearby bush, and handed it to him.

"I lived on an estate where there were several young men. We . . . ah . . . were of an age. When they went off to university, I heard many things about their lives there." He scratched his chest through his robe.

"I see. And I suppose they allowed you access to their books?" Laurel was not sure why she suddenly preferred to be so helpful, but somehow she very much desired for him to have a reasonable explanation.

"Indeed."

"And the book you gave me belonged to them?"

"You hardly can expect a poor man like me to own such volumes, Miss Gardiner."

"Of course not," she said, smiling. But she looked down at the book in her hands, and opened it to the flyleaf. As she turned the pages, she watched him closely, expecting him to grab the book at any moment.

But instead, he stood calmly, still scratching away at his chest. She looked down, and saw the ragged edge in the binding from whence the flyleaf had been ripped asunder.

"I may be poor, but I am not stupid," Robbie Darkwood said softly.

"No, you are not," Laurel said thoughtfully. "If I believed you were, I would know this meeting to be pure chance, and entirely undesirable on your part."

"As it is."

"Of course it is not, sir. You have intentionally provoked me, knowing full well I would follow you, seeking an explanation for the substitution you willfully made." Laurel stepped forward, daring him to withdraw yet again.

"I did nothing of the sort, nor would I. Ladies of my acquaintance do not pursue strange men though the woods, nor do they follow them into their homes."

"Ladies of your acquaintance?" Laurel was willing to overlook the insult if she could but catch him in a falsehood. "I understood you knew little of ladies in the flesh."

Mr. Darkwood stared at her; she knew it though she could not see his eyes. She regretted her unfortunate choice of words, not only for her own modesty but for his. Here stood a man who entirely renounced the company of others, and attempted to do it with some level of dignity. Tempting him with reminders of what he lacked was really very poor sport.

"Miss Gardiner, you may imagine you know much about any topic to come your way, but I assure you, you remain in painful ignorance of many things."

"As you are ignorant of social life and things that pass between men and women?" she asked tartly. "You are a hermit, my good sir."

"And you are a beautiful and intelligent young woman of good family who has just returned from a season in London with nothing to do but read dusty old tomes and harass a man who desires the company of no one. The evidence suggests you may be ignorant of certain things, as well."

Laurel felt as if the hermit slapped her hard across the face, though his hands remained hidden in his robes. She breathed in deeply, determined not to let him see her cry.

"Of what can you be speaking, Mr. Darkwood?"

He gave a slight gesture of impatience. "There must have been a dozen eligible men following you through the corridors of Almack's. If you accepted one of them, you would not be bothering a poor hermit in his wood. You would be planning a wedding. Therefore, my good Miss Gardiner, I suspect some ignorance on your part, for not getting yourself a husband."

Laurel closed her eyes, wondering if she had walked too far and if the sun were too hot, for she felt faint.

"Miss Gardiner?" The hermit took a step closer and held out his arm. Laurel grasped this anchor through his robe, and felt the firm muscle and bone beneath.

"Perhaps it is not due to ignorance I have come home empty-fisted, but to intelligence. I saw no man to tempt me, Mr. Darkwood. Is it possible for you, as a man, to accept such a fact?"

"Of course it is, Miss Gardiner." He turned and pulled her along with him on the path, her arm now tucked under his elbow. Though his garments were voluminous, the fabric itself was thin, and Laurel was keenly aware of the body beneath. "Inasmuch as I find no woman—or man—to tempt me either, I am in perfect harmony with your sentiments. However, since you went to London with a rather singular purpose, I will not believe you felt that way at the beginning of the season."

"What if I were to tell you I went to examine Mr. Elgin's marbles?"

"And, having studied the Greek notion of masculine beauty, you found real men lacking?"

"I believe this is not a topic for discussion between us, Mr. Darkwood."

"And yet we have thus far been honest with each other. Have we just established that we are in perfect harmony?"

"So we are. Well, Mr. Darkwood, I do not know if the Athenian men would have cared so very much for my father's income as did the real men in London. And as for the other thing—their physical attributes—I simply have no basis for comparison."

"Tis a pity," Laurel thought he said, and then, "I daresay the ancient heroes would have been bought just as easily."

"But I would not be in the market for one. Nor was I in London. Money might buy a new gown, or theatre tickets, or even a hermit, but I will not use it to buy a man."

They walked along for some moments in silence, Prinny nipping excitedly at their heels. Laurel fell into Mr. Darkwood's shadow, though she felt as warm as if she stood in the fierce sunshine.

"Do you not think a hermit a man?"

"A man, yes, but not one I might ever marry. If I felt otherwise, you realize I could not possibly walk with you thus, or confide in you things I have not even told my dearest friend."

"I am honored. I think."

"You will meet her, of course."

"Of whom can you be speaking?"

"Why, my friend, of course. She is wonderfully dear, though I met her just months ago. She suffered a terrible loss and is in a deep melancholy. I thought to have her here would improve her spirits, and mine. And now, yours."

"Miss Gardiner, you are quite forgetting yourself. And me. I will have none of this, nor should I. I desire contact with no one, and certainly with no woman."

Laurel smiled, happy to turn his words back on him. "Do you not think me a woman, then?"

"I think you too much a woman, Miss Gardiner," he said, and finally removed her arm from his. "And I believe our current relations not at all appropriate. In fact, I am sure we should put an end to it immediately. Shall we agree, we two in perfect harmony, that this should be our last meeting?"

"I will not promise anything, Hermit," Laurel said, "but I will say that unless you do something about the fleas, you will not see me at any close distance."

"Fleas?" he asked, and patted Prinny on the head.

"I did not see the dog scratch himself, but you are practically tearing the flesh from your body, Mr. Darkwood. It is disgusting."

As if on cue, he rubbed the area around his neck. "I think it not fleas, but my own hair. I . . . ah . . . gave myself a haircut this morning."

"Did you use a scythe on yourself?"

"Something like," he admitted.

"It appears so." Laurel noticed his beard was trimmer and his hair fell not so much in his eyes. He really would not be so very bad, once he cleaned up. "I left something for you in the smokehouse. See that you use it."

"I do not take orders from anyone but my employer, Miss Gardiner."

"Then I shall have to phrase my words in a prettier fashion."

"I doubt it possible, Miss Gardiner." He bowed very slightly, and his robe completely enveloped his face. He turned, nearly tripped on a fallen log, and set off alone down the path. Prinny remained with Laurel.

She looked down at the happy mongrel and rubbed his ears. "Did you not hear him call me beautiful and intelligent, Prinny?" she asked. "He cannot be so much an idiot after all."

* * * *

From whence came such a great longing for home? Did a firm mattress and polished cabinetry amount to so very much in the measure of a man's happiness? Would not his horses and pointers be cared for by a dozen servants? Did dinners taste any better served on fine china than on treenware?

Well, perhaps they did taste somewhat better. And one was less likely to have splinters in the gums. But did not the pleasure of growing and hunting for one's meal somewhat compensate for rich crème sauces and candied vegetables?

Rob looked down at the slab of undercooked venison on his plate and thought it surely would do him no harm. And a man had to eat.

He thought of his mother, who had taught him how to eat like a gentleman. And of his brother, who was always more resistant to such lessons, but who now would be expected to rise to the place at the head of the table vacated by his absent brother. Rob missed them, and he would have done anything to spare them the pain and uncertainty his absence must have brought. As he would have spared the woman he once loved.

But there was nothing to be done. Explanations would have cut far deeper than their current pain, and the damage would be irreparable.

And yet he missed them all.

His fork clattered to the floor, and in a moment of forgetfulness, he waited for a servant to retrieve it for him. Instead, Prinny jumped up from the rug near the hearth and gobbled up the morsel of red meat stuck on the tines.

"Let us go for a walk, boy," Rob said as he stood, knocking his chair to the floor. "I have supped full of such delicacies."

Prinny looked as if he would have preferred to remain with the venison, so Rob left the cottage door ajar, little caring if the wretched dinner was all gone by the time he returned.

Miss Gardiner was the cause of his current discontent; that much was certain.

Somehow, during the first months at the hermitage, he had managed to convince himself that the life of the hermit was grace itself, capable of redeeming him from the sins of his other life. He devoted his energies to forging a new existence, an identity through which he could be true to himself and be immune to the frailties of others. He found strengths he little knew existed and peace of mind unparalleled by anything he had yet experienced.

And then came a woman who thought nothing of following him about, asking him impertinent questions and arguing with him about matters about which she could know little, and pressing her long, thin fingers against the skin of his forearm. For all he imagined his damned robe to protect him against the world, he had felt her warmth as if the fabric did not even exist.

He patted his chest pocket and gently tapped the smooth oval of the sandalwood scented soap she had left for him in the smokehouse. He had not waited so very long after their meeting before he went to retrieve it, curious to see what gift she thought suitable. It was wrapped in tea paper, tied with a scrap of lace that undoubtedly was a discard from her sewing box. But he saved it, along with the paper. After all, in his profession, one never knew when such things could be useful.

The lake glistened in the late afternoon sunshine, and a swarm of bees hummed over the still surface. The trees, still lush with greenery, dipped their boughs into the water, joining their reflections in perfect union. There was a time, not too long ago, when such a scene mirrored the very harmony in his life, and lowered branches created a perfect place for an afternoon tryst.

Now, with his hermit's eyes, Rob could think only of firewood for a long, cold winter ahead, and if he might fashion a raft for himself from some sturdy limbs.

He reached for his penknife, but only felt the bar of soap.

Miss Gardiner again. Was it possible to pass five minutes without thinking of her?

She surely intended the soap as an insult, much as she did almost everything she said to him. Not that it could matter to her whether he was clean or no. Indeed, he knew gentlemen of power and position who probably bathed less frequently than Robbie Darkwood did, even as a hermit. But she did put a point on the general messiness—nay, he had to call it slovenliness—of the hermitage, and accused him of having fleas. Perhaps he did.

He descended the gentle slope of the riverbank and pulled the robe over his head. Punching it into a ball, he tossed it into the shallows, thinking he would not miss it very much if it happened to float over the dam. But it did not; it spread out on the water like a great brown stain, and rippled in the slight breeze. His once-white shirt followed. He hopped on one foot, and then the other as he removed his boots and wondered if his stockings were even worth the soap and water.

Deciding he might later regret their loss, he added them to his laundry. Finally, taking one last look around to vouchsafe his privacy, he removed his trousers and undergarments, and entered the water.

The chill of the early spring, when first he ventured into its depths months ago, was gone, to be replaced by a heady verdant smell enhanced by the sun's heat. Rob dove directly into an underground field of weed and heard Prinny splash in at his heels. Aside from his noisy companion, he heard nothing else but the sound of his own pulse in his ears.

Savoring sensation, Rob stayed down as long as he could, and finally came up gasping for air. His shirt was no more than an arm's length away, and he reached out to retrieve the soap from its pocket. Thoroughly moistened, the sandalwood was even stronger than before and would surely overpower the slight fishy scent that would otherwise prevail.

Rob set to work on his garments, on his hair, on his body. If Prinny came any closer, he too would have been a sudsy sight. But Prinny had no one to please but himself, and Rob had . . . well, Rob had no one either. He reminded himself of that as he rubbed the soap over his arms and chest, and rinsed it out of his hair. Hanging wet and straight, his hair reached his shoulder on one side, and his cheek on the other.

He wondered if Miss Gardiner owned a scissors she might spare.

Finally, as the shadows deepened and the air cooled his bare skin, Rob pulled his clothing and himself from the lake. Why had he not thought to bring a blanket in which to wrap and dry himself? He could not risk even the short walk back to the hermitage in such a state, and cursed himself his foolhardiness.

Deciding he would retreat under cover of darkness, he settled himself back down into the water, which was warmer than the air, and lay partially submerged on the bank.

Perhaps he slept; he did not think so, but when he opened his eyes it was dark, and the first stars glittered in the inky sky. Far in the distance, the lights of Greenbriars shone like some great beacon, and Rob wondered if the family entertained guests this evening. If those guests lingered, he might have to put in a vague, elusive appearance near the woods the next day; it was his job.

But as he studied the house, wondered if music played in the drawing room, and if Miss Gardiner danced with a gentleman, he became aware of other lights moving on the other side of the lake. The water, acting like an echo chamber, carried the sound of hooves and the creaking of carriage wheels. And then, over it all, the deep thrum of men's voices, as they approached the house.

It was no business of his, Rob reminded himself, feeling a jolt of jealousy.

And yet he wondered if Miss Gardiner did not yet dance in the drawing room of Greenbriars, if she waited for her partner soon to arrive, and if that unfortunate gentleman used sandalwood soap.

It was no business of his. Unless the fellow was so bothered by the delectable Miss Gardiner, he would seek refuge in a hermitage for the sake of his own sanity. Such things happened before.

Chapter Five

Laurel knew the moment her brothers entered the house. Even if she had not seen the approaching carriage from the windows of the hall, she would have recognized the subtle change in the atmosphere of Greenbriars as soon as they crossed the threshold. What they carried with them was indefinable but no less recognizable than a banner waved before an approaching army. And they were no less boisterous or demanding.

She reached the stairway the same moment as her mother.

"They are here, are they not?" Mrs. Gardiner asked, as she ran quick fingers over her curls to ensure all her pins in place.

At that moment, something crashed onto the white marble floor below.

"Oh, bloody hell," cried a voice too loud and too rude to be anyone but Lewis, the youngest of the three Gardiner brothers.

"I told you to box the damned thing, Lew. Now it's good for nothing, and it cost you a week's earnings," said Joseph, his elder brother by five years. "Mother will have . . . "

"Mother will have none of that sort of language in the house," interrupted Mrs. Gardiner as she pulled Laurel willingly down the stairs. Once they alighted on the main floor, she dropped her daughter's hand, and opened her arms to embrace her two returning boys. "Not while your sister can hear you as plain as day."

"And I bet poor Laurel has heard nothing of such things before," said Lewis, winking at her over their mother's smothering shoulder.

Mrs. Gardiner released her sons, and they turned to Laurel, picking her up off her feet in their enthusiasm.

"What the hell . . . oh, sorry, my dear." Mr. Gardiner came through the library door. "I should have known those young ruffians have returned."

Lewis and Joseph dropped their sister unceremoniously, and greeted their father with the same degree of energy.

"And what priceless piece of ornamentation now adorns our hitherto plain floor?" Mr. Gardiner asked sarcastically as he pushed a broken piece of porcelain with his boot. He studied his sons with very much the same look he might have used when they were little boys, and not the grown men, taller than he, they now were.

"It was a vase for Mother," Lewis explained. "A gift from one of our agents in China."

"Mr. Brady?" Mrs. Gardiner asked. "I shall have to send him a pretty note with my gratitude. I will not, however, let him know it will decorate the garbage pit behind the stable. Or that it came all the way from China to London, and from London to Cambridgeshire, only to be reduced to rubble at our front door."

"The floor was too slippery," Lewis protested. "Do the servants have nothing to do but spend the day polishing the marble as smooth as ice?"

"As a matter of fact, they scarcely have a thing to do with the three of you gone," said Mrs. Gardiner. She peered around them to the front door. "Is George with you?"

"The old man could not get away," Joseph said, looking at their father.

"The old man would not get away," Lewis amended, smiling at their mother. "There is a certain lady who has engaged his interest of late. I believe you provided the introduction when you were in town."

"Miss Corbett?" Mrs. Gardiner asked excitedly, clearly very pleased with the prospect.

"Then tis just the two of you?" Laurel asked. There had seemed to be a lot of noise, even for her two brothers.

"Did we ever say so, sweet sister?" Joseph teased her. "We have a few introductions to provide as well."

As if on cue, two more young men came through the doorway, carrying bouquets of wilted flowers.

"Have a care," cautioned Lewis, "the marble is more slippery than the dance floor at The Sailors Three."

"Lewis!" cried his mother, and then to Joseph, "Where do you take him? I expect you to . . ."

"Now, dear, I am sure our boys do nothing untoward," Mr. Gardiner said as he walked forward to receive their guests. In a lower voice he added, "And nothing I did not do as a young man."

Mrs. Gardiner glared at him, but remembered her manners in time to turn her attention to the two newcomers.

Joseph, as the elder, did the honors of the introduction, and though he dutifully named his parents first, he seemed to particularly emphasize their names to his sister. "Sir John Linden. Mr. Henry Winthrop. My sister, Miss Laurel Gardiner."

"I believe we met briefly in London, Mr. Winthrop," Laurel said as she curtsied. "But our acquaintance did not extend to my appreciation of your skills as a botanist."

Mr. Winthrop looked at her blankly until she gestured towards the untidy burden he still held in his arms.

"Oh, these are neither ours nor our gardeners', Madam. When a friend of ours understood we were to visit Greenbriars, he insisted we bring them to you as a token of his affection. Lord Ballister it was," explained Mr. Winthrop, as Mrs. Gardiner sighed her appreciation.

"I thank you for your troubles, but they look as worse for the trip as Lord Ballister's affections rest in my esteem. If he is your friend, you surely understand there is nothing between us," said Laurel.

Mr. Winthrop looked a little doubtfully at the array of lilies and roses.

"But fear not, Mr. Winthrop. I will trouble our housekeeper to find some pots to put them in and see if they can be revived. That is more than I can say for my feelings, however. Nevertheless, I will accept them." Laurel reached out and gathered the blossoms to her breast. "We are civilized here, Mr. Winthrop. I will not kill the messenger."

The poor man had not a notion of what she meant, and Laurel could not help guessing that her poor hermit would know precisely the reference.

"You have traveled long," Mrs. Gardiner reminded them. "I am sure Cook has more than enough remaining from dinner to serve up. We did not know when to expect you."

"Do not apologize, Mother. We thought we would stay the night at an inn, but made exceptional time on our journey. All the other carriages seemed to be making their way into London."

"And why not," asked Mrs. Gardiner, "when the season remains in high activity?"

"We are grateful you could come for a visit," Laurel added quickly. "I am sure you are depriving yourself of some delights in town."

The four men looked at each other, and she guessed whatever those delights, she would be most unlikely to hear of them.

"Can I offer you a glass of sherry, while we await your dinner?" her father asked, turning to the drawing room.

His guests did not answer, but Sir John and Mr. Winthrop bowed before the two ladies, and allowed them to precede them into the room. Mrs. Gardiner waved them on at the threshold, so she could have a quick conference with her cook and, presumably, with the maid who would dispose of Lewis' gift to her. Laurel left Lord Ballister's flowers on the pianoforte as they all found comfortable seats on the several upholstered sofas in the seating area.

"We miss you in town, Laurel," Joseph said.

"I cannot imagine why," his sister answered. "You hardly saw Mother and me when we were there."

"He does not mean your actual presence, Laurel. Just your coterie of companions. The ladies who always seemed to be hovering around you," said Lewis.

"I do not think they hovered overly much after my brothers entered the party," Laurel pointed out. "I assume they still feel at ease to do so, whether I am there or not."

Her brothers' glances at their friends told her what she needed to know.

"And how are my friends? Do you see much of them? Is Miss Croyden happy and well? I wrote to her this very week, but have not yet received an answer."

"Lord Westbridge's leaving?" Sir John asked.

"You are most unkind, sir," Laurel said sternly, even as she recognized the plight of all women to be forever identified in relationship to the men in their lives. "She is an innocent lady who deserves no censure for having been jilted. Westbridge is surely the most hard hearted of individuals, a villain who merits severe punishment."

"Forgive me, Miss Gardiner. I meant no ill of the lady. I only speak with the prejudice of my sex; I cannot believe a man to be wholly at fault in this. In any case, the gentleman is not available to defend himself," explained Sir John.

"I am sure he is off with someone else," Laurel said censoriously.

"We do not know," Joseph reminded her. "But the lady is nearly recovered and quite alone, but for her demonic aunt."

"I hope to remedy that situation by inviting her to join us at Greenbriars, with or without Miss Jessup" said Laurel. "How long do you intend to remain?"

"At least a week, if Mother can stand our company," said Lewis.

"What did you say, dear boy?" Mrs. Gardiner entered the room.

"I said, if we but knew there would be additional company, we would have invited even more of our friends," grinned Lewis.

"No matter," said his mother, calmly, quite accustomed to her sons' teasing. "I believe there is enough food on store for all of Wellington's army. Cook is already serving a buffet in the dining room. Would you like to clean yourselves up a bit before joining us there?"

The four men were out of the room before Mrs. Gardiner had the time to assign the guests to their chambers.

"No matter," she repeated. "They will figure it out."

"You have more confidence in them than I do," Mr. Gardiner grumbled.

"And yet you have trusted the business to the boys," Mrs. Gardiner reminded him. "They cannot be so muddleheaded as all that."

She reached for her husband's arm, but he was already out of her grasp and into the hall, shouting up the stairs.

Instead, she caught Laurel. "What do you think of Sir John, my dear?"

"He seems pleasant enough, though I am not overly fond of mustached men," Laurel answered, though there was one she could scarcely rid from her thoughts. "I hope you are not thinking of a match, Mother. It is extremely awkward if he is a friend of the family. Look what happened to Penelope Croyden."

"And is Miss Croyden the very model for all we do? I feel for the child; I really do. But it is always awkward when neighbors are brought together. If it does not work out, then the hurt is bound to run deeper and have lasting effects. Miss Croyden's aunt assured me the couple was very much like brother and sister."

"So we are always told. But Miss Croyden assured me that she and the Earl of Westridge did things I would never do with my brothers."

"Laurel!"

"Well, it is true, Mother. How am I to learn about what goes on between men and women if I do not hear about it from ladies more experienced than I?"

"I have told you what to expect."

Laurel patted her mother's hand. "You have. And George and Joseph have . . . "

"Your brothers! What could they be thinking!"

"Nothing inappropriate, I assure you. They simply warned me about certain things, and taught me how to protect myself."

"Like some hoyden, I am sure. You are twenty-three years old, my dear, and have rejected a very eligible suitor who continues to pay you court. Is it possible you are protecting yourself too well?"

"Is such a thing possible, Mother?"

Her mother sighed, and hugged her. "No, it is not possible. But yet

I would see you happy. Do you suppose Sir John or Mr. Winthrop worthy of some interest on your part?"

"We have only just met. But I will not discount any gentleman out of hand."

"Of course, so long as he is a gentleman."

As they entered the dining room, its candles relit to illuminate the late and unexpected repast, Laurel thought of someone else, most certainly not a gentleman, who would already be asleep in his dark hermitage. He was rough hewn, and had little to recommend him to a well born wife. And yet there was something there in his speech, in his intelligence, and in the mystery of his past that was surely worth cultivating. If there was ever a man to bring Penelope Croyden out of her melancholy state, it was Mr. Darkwood. And if there was ever a friend who could bring such a pair together, it was she. Penelope would necessarily have to be coaxed out of her valley. And Mr. Darkwood would have to coaxed out of his hermitage. But she had accomplished that much already for him, had she not?

She wondered if he had found her soap. Or better, used it.

"I think we shall plan a picnic, while the weather is yet warm," murmured Mrs. Gardiner. "We can invite several of the people in the neighborhood and enjoy some boating on the lake."

"If we set our tent near the rose garden, we will have an excellent prospect of the North Wood," added Mr. Gardiner, returning to her side.

"Oh, no, my dear," said his ever-patient wife, and glanced at their daughter.

"What is wrong with the North Wood?" Laurel asked innocently.

"Your father has a little project there."

"At the hermitage? I have met your project, and he is not so little," Laurel announced smugly. "I would have thought either of you would have warned me about a strange man roaming the property."

"You have met him?" Mr. Gardiner asked. "I warned the man . .
. ''

"It was not his fault, Father. And, as I have just told Mother, I know how to protect myself. I was merely curious to see the woodland gnome Mavis attacked a few weeks past."

"Mavis attacked him?" Mr. Gardiner shouted. The crystals on the chandelier clinked against each other and danced in the candlelight.

"I believe she threw some rocks at him. But you hardly can expect a woman who misses the dust on my dressing table to have very good aim. He seems to have survived, in any case."

"You are not to talk to him, Laurel," Mrs. Gardiner said sternly. 'We know nothing about him."

"And yet you allow him to live here?"

"Our hermitage needed a hermit. The other estates all have them, and he seemed perfectly suited to the job," Mr. Gardiner said. "He also was the only applicant."

"And so you desire him to be nothing more than an ornament, like the crystal or china? Or as Lord Ballister desired me?" Laurel snapped a fingernail at one of the glasses on the table and heard the inevitable ring. "It sounds very cold-hearted."

"I did not invent the profession, nor do I even guess why a young man would take it up. He plays the part, and I pay him a decent wage."

"Is it enough to support a wife and family?"

"Why would that matter? Hermits do not take wives. They have nothing to do with anyone else. The moment my man invites a woman—or man—into his cottage, he forfeits his position. I want the genuine thing."

"I thought, perhaps, I would draw him out into society."

Mr. Gardiner stopped where he stood, and seemed to be gasping for air. "I do not want you near him. I do not want you following him. I do not want you talking to him. Is that perfectly understood?"

Before Laurel could answer, Joseph entered the room. His hair was damp, and his skin looked as if it had been scrubbed with a hairbrush.

"Laurel not talk to a man? Is such a thing possible?" he asked.

"I will experiment with you, dear brother, and not talk to you for all the time you are at Greenbriars. You will see how very easy it is."

"Now, children," began Mrs. Gardiner.

"Father is forbidding me to speak to a guest on the estate," Laurel pleaded her case to her older brother, someone she had been able to manipulate since she was three years old.

"He is not a guest! He is a servant!" insisted Mr. Gardiner.

Joseph looked at his parent, the surprise evident on his face. "But Father, have you not always taught us to treat our servants with respect? To inquire after their health? To engage them in conversation?"

"We are talking about a man who does not engage in conversation!!" Mr. Gardiner's face turned bright red, and he looked ready to do damage to one of the crystal wine glasses.

Joseph went to his accustomed place at the table, though he did not sit down. He clearly was more interested in the roasted quail set upon a silver platter than in his family's squabbles.

"Is the man deaf? Was he a spy and his tongue cut out by Napoleon's troops? I have heard of such things," Joseph said, almost absently.

"He is a hermit!" Mr. Gardiner roared.

"A hermit?" asked Lewis, entering the room with Mr. Winthrop and Sir John.

"Yes," Laurel nodded. "Father has hired a hermit to live in the abandoned cottage at the north edge of the lake."

"Ah, yes, I thought I saw someone near the shore when we approached a while back. He . . . ah . . . was not dressed to receive company."

"He was not?" Laurel said with some interest.

"Let us sit," Mrs. Gardiner said a little desperately. "The boys are starving for nourishment."

As they moved to their seats, and the gentlemen waited for Laurel and Mrs. Gardiner to sit first, Laurel guessed Mr. Darkwood used her soap when he went into the lake. It was just as she planned. She regretted she had not also planned to be walking along the shore while he did so.

The "boys" certainly behaved as if they were starving, for all their manners. The food was quickly passed around the table, and spooned onto plates with a heavy hand, while Laurel and her parents,who had eaten some hours before, nibbled a bit in an effort to be sociable.

"So what is the news about a hermit?" Lewis said at last. "Is he part of a religious order? Or is he merely a deformed miscreant embarrassed to show his face in society?"

"He is neither, from what I see," said Mr. Gardiner. "He simply prefers to keep to himself."

"Did you warn him about our sister?" Joseph asked.

"As a matter of fact, I did," Mr. Gardiner said, and hid behind his glass of wine.

"Father!"

"Now, Laurel, please remember that I had every expectation you would remain in London for the whole season. And I thought there was a very good chance you would never return to live at Greenbriars. If all went as your mother and I expected, you might never have seen Mr. Darkwood."

"Is that the man's name?" asked Lewis. "You cannot expect us to believe it is real."

"I did not think so either. It is why I call him Hermit." Laurel said.

"I do not expect you to call him anything!" her father said again. "You are forbidden to have any contact with him, or he loses his position. Would you be responsible for a man being turned out?"

The hermit had said very much the same thing to her, when he made the case for secrecy. She had not believed her father would be so unreasonable, but now he confirmed it himself. And, she realized, she did not want the hermit to go.

"Are we allowed to speak to him, or is it just Laurel who is forbidden?" asked Lewis between mouthfuls of buttered rolls. "He sounds like an interesting sort of fellow."

Mr. Gardiner reached for his own roll and ate it as if he heard nothing of what went on at the table. Mr. Winthrop and Sir John looked somewhat uneasy and watched their host with dismay. But Laurel and her brothers just knew their father was carefully considering the words he would say. It was a habit well-formed from discretion and fear of heart disease.

"The hermit, Mr. Robbie Darkwood," he began quietly, "is only interesting because no one speaks to him. If he conversed and sat at our table, I believe we would find him a very ordinary sort of man. And that is why he does not. He is employed at this estate to give character to our property, and make some use of the hermitage, a building that was falling into disrepair before he arrived. He is not a damned . . ."

"My dear . . ." Laurel's mother murmured.

"He is not a guest, nor is he quite a servant. Is that understood?" Mr. Gardiner looked around his table, waiting for his three children to nod their agreement. They might have been sitting in the nursery. "Well?"

Laurel and her brothers nodded. But during the final course, hastily put together by Cook, and even more hastily devoured by the young men, their dark eyes met over the table. Laurel knew Joseph and Lewis would seek out their hermit, as surely as they knew she would do the same.

* * * *

Rob pulled an apple off one of the three scrawny trees comprising his orchard, and wondered how very difficult it would be to make a pie. He supposed it required a fair number of the fruits and something doughy to stick them in. He took a bite of the apple, which was so bitter the experience proved painful. It required sugar. He needed something to sweeten the burden.

Not for the first time, he began to think about the long winter ahead, when the immediate fruits of his labor would not satisfy his appetite. Perhaps he might apply to his employer for a temporary respite, and retire to warmer climes. But then, he would be so far removed from his home and family, reports of their lives would never reach him. And though he felt he could survive with nearly nothing of what he knew before, total exile would destroy him. He may be a hermit by inclination, but certainly not by nature.

He had understood the hypocrisy of his ambition the moment Laurel Gardiner had stepped into his cottage. Her eager interference into the matters of his life, and her bold wit, were precisely the weapons to disarm his camp. She could not know how much she tempted him, how he could barely turn his eyes from her dark eyes and unruly hair, and how the touch of her skin set him afire. She could not know these things because she would not; she would not because a man in his position was certainly beneath her.

There was irony in that notion, and Laurel Gardiner would be the first to appreciate it. But it was impossible for her to ever know the truth.

Rob threw the bitter apple as far as he could and heard it splash in the lake. A moment later, another splash followed, and he knew Prinny had appeared from nowhere to fetch the prize. He turned back to his trio of trees and considered the possibility of leaving the whole lot to the worms.

"You there. Hermit!"

Rob tried to place the voice, hearing both the authority and the London accent in it. He thought of the carriage he had seen the night before, and now knew he had not dreamed it. Regretting the loss of his robe, which hung from a line next to the cottage, he turned only part way to acknowledge his visitors.

"Will you not speak?" The voice lost nothing of its authority in its evident curiosity.

"You will get nothing from him, Joe. The man is vowed to silence," said a second voice, similarly accented.

"I never heard it said. Besides, did he not speak to Laurel?"

"Our sister could get vowels out of a stone."

Their identities were now plain. Rob, losing no ground, turned a little more, curious to see the men who claimed relationship to Miss Gardiner.

They were as like to her as he was to his own siblings. Tall, though not as tall as he, they shared the dark features and pale skin that made her so distinctly a beauty. On her brothers, the lines of the face were worn thicker, for they had not her delicacy, and the hair, cropped short in both cases, was not allowed to curl. But they most certainly were Gardiners.

The younger one, barely more than a schoolboy, stepped forward and extended his hand.

"I am Lewis Gardiner, the son of your employer. This is my brother Joseph."

Rob accepted the hand, and shook it firmly. He nodded, but he did not speak.

"We understand the nature of your business here, and that you are the new inhabitant of the hermitage," Joseph explained.

Rob raised an eyebrow, finding humor in the fact they were speaking to him as if he only understood a foreign tongue, and if they spoke clearly and loudly enough, he would almost certainly understand them.

"Our father has employed you to satisfy his vanity, and our mother undoubtedly considers a hermit to be a romantic sort of notion."

Rob wished he knew to what purpose these brothers offered such explanations. Were they prepared to dismiss him? Did Laurel send them on a mission to get him out of her cottage?"

"Neither seems to know very much about you, Mr. Darkwood. Nor do we. But if our sister is going to be traipsing about the wood, we feel a need to be concerned for her safety."

Rob cleared his throat. "Your sister has assured me she will not approach me or the cottage. Nor have I any intention of seeking her out," he said, speaking the truth and a lie at the same time. "And, in any case, she seems more than capable of taking care of herself."

Joseph laughed. "Damned right. Before our parents decided to make a lady of her, she held her own with the three of us. We have yet another brother, who remains in London."

Rob only nodded, realizing too late how easy it would be to befriend yet another few Gardiners. The sister was seductive; these two were easy, cheerful companions.

"Will you leave her alone, then? Ignore her when she tries to engage you in conversation? She will, you know," Lewis informed him.

Rob nodded again.

"We have overstayed our welcome, if we ever had one," Joseph said, and patted his brother on the back. "A pleasure to meet you, Mr.

Darkwood. You are just the man to handle our sister."

The Gardiner brothers laughed as they walked away, down the slope. Lewis turned suddenly, letting Joseph go on without him.

"You poor fellow!" he called out, and the brothers laughed again.

* * * *

Several days later, several riders and a solitary carriage stirred up the gravel at Greenbriars in their haste to get to the house. Rob heard the approaching storm and paused in his berry picking to stand dutifully at the edge of the wood, his crop in fruit-stained hand and his hood completely obscuring the rest of his features. He did not think they took any note of him, which was unfortunate, but he noticed them, which was even more so. Not that he knew the visitors—as he had never even heard of the Gardiners in his other life, he doubted he would know their friends—but as the gentlemen all looked young and rakish, and the ladies equally grand, he knew he was about to lose the company of the woman who was forbidden to offer it to him.

On the other hand, he might very well have already lost it. Although he had dutifully delivered Sidney's *Defense of Poesy* to the smokehouse the day before, he had already returned six times to find it still waiting for her. Did she not take her reading seriously? Did she not think his time valuable? Or was there, already, a suitor to distract her from the wild man in the forest? Yes and yes and yes. Rob was prepared to believe the very worst.

Once the dust settled back on the road and on himself, he looked down into the bucket and estimated he had gathered enough berries to satisfy a very small sparrow. True, he had already eaten his way through satisfying himself for a few hours, but there would be none to spare or save for the winter. Did hermits beg? He was not very sure of the rules of deportment, but he imagined he might ask the cook at Greenbriars to save him some remainders, for she would probably do no less for a stranger who came their way. Or, if he ever saw Miss Gardiner again, perhaps he could ask—nay, beg—her to bring a basket of food with every volume she returned to his keeping. He only knew he could scarcely survive on the slim offerings the landscape provided. And, as his small herd of livestock proved to be his only friends at the hermitage, he already knew he could never bring himself to feast on them.

Why had he not considered any of this when he ran from one life and flung himself into another? He, who always proved so cautious, so wise, so thoughtful, the arbiter of disputes in the neighborhood and the benefactor of dozens. He, who looked no further than to marry the woman next door and stay always close to that which he loved best. He, who never imagined a thing to disturb his utter tranquility and contentment.

Given such expectations, and such satisfactions, perhaps it could not be surprising he ran headlong into disaster. He had brought with him a collection of books and some few garments, but very little of practical value. But he had had a need to act quickly, before great damage could be done, and he had seized upon an opportunity much as a drowning man grabs a buoy. And Mr. Gardiner's rather strange advertisement had provided such a rescue. Or so it had seemed at the time.

Rob walked down the slope of the forest's edge and across the graveled drive over which the guests had only just passed. He again heard the sound of carriage wheels, and turned to see if he yet had time to dodge back into the shelter of the trees. But the vehicle—it was a cart, actually—was almost upon him, and he could do no more than step back and out of its path. The driver tipped his hat as he passed, but seemed more interested in the young woman in the scanty chemise who sat in his lap.

Rob glanced at the cart's burden as it slowly trundled past, and he helped himself to a smoked ham and a basket of eggs from the back of the cart. The driver never looked back, even when Prinny barked his loud approval of the acquisition.

"We have dinner for a week here, boy," Rob proclaimed, inordinately cheerful for having just stolen goods from his employer. "And I will see you have your fair share."

He hoisted the meat onto his shoulder, wondering only vaguely if his food had ever been seasoned with road dust before, and started back to the hermitage before guilt could detain him and require him to return that to which he had just helped himself.

It did not take very long before he felt its effects. The Gardiners were planning a party; that much was certain. The arrival of guests, the cartload of food supplies, and Miss Gardiner's inexplicable absence from the smokehouse, all suggested some great doings at the big house. Great doings in which he played no part.

But surely they needed their ham and eggs, for there were many people to feed, when he was just one.

"Sorry, old boy, we will have to return this," Rob said to Prinny, who barked as happily as he might have if Rob offered him the whole ham. "We would not want our Miss Gardiner and her fancy guests to go hungry."

Prinny barked his approval and dashed off into the meadow after some poor creature.

Rob skirted the wall by the lush pasture, and admired the horses that grazed contentedly within it. Once, he would have spent some time here, examining the creatures and having some conversation with the grooms. But, like all servants, he learned quickly that his responsibilities were most specific, and any interference into another's concerns was considered officious. He walked quickly and shifted the ham's weight on his shoulder.

The orchards came next, and Rob was absurdly pleased to see their fruit not much more impressive than his. He turned towards his cottage, some distance off, and realized he still needed to pass the smokehouse. Perhaps he might unburden both his mind and his body there. And, for the seventh time this day, he might check to see if a lady, who surely remained too busy to think of her books or of him, might have passed through.

Within moments, his heart began to race when he saw the broken door stood off its hinges and not set back in the frame. He began to run, imagining she still stood within and he might surprise her. He did not pause to examine the logic of his thoughts, or why he should be so anxious to spend time with a woman who sought only to torment him.

But yet he did, and that is why, when he saw her note on the door, he felt an illogical, irrational, but no less painful, disappointment.

Dear Hermit,

Please see to the door. I will not injure myself in the pursuit of something already mine.

Yours Sincerely,

L. M. Gardiner

The elegant fluidity of the script belied the economy of the message. Rob ran his stained fingers over the crisp paper and held it up to the light until he was sure its translucent reflection shone upon his face. He thought some care had gone into the wording and certainly into the presentation. He wondered if Miss Gardiner wrote notes to the guests who now arrived, and if all her missives were similarly scented with her lavender water. If so, it might explain the great haste of the carriages arriving at her door.

Rob turned so his broad frame could fit through the blessed doorframe, and he nearly decapitated himself on the damned lintel.

Cursing profusely, he dropped the ham and eggs onto a table poised in front of the massive hearth and turned to the place where he usually left Miss Gardiner's book. Sidney's volume was gone, but it had been replaced by the Lyly. And something else, which glinted in the shaft of sunlight that came through the smoke-fogged window.

He walked over, thinking it a dropped piece of her jewelry. It was, rather, something more useful to her, and, by her not-so-subtle suggestion, something to prove useful to him.

Neatly fitting into the palm of his hand was a pair of lady's scissors, designed like an egret, with the beak cleverly forming the sharp blades. And like an unfortunate fish, caught within that beak, Rob knew he was soon to be cut down.

Chapter Six

Laurel stifled a yawn into her third glass of sherry and wondered if it would be considered impolite to excuse herself from her father's gaming room, and retire for the evening. Her parents had left the party hours before, deferring the responsibility of entertaining their guests to their three children as they bade all the young people a pleasant night. But inasmuch as Joseph seemed intent on the game at the billiards table, and Lewis equally enthralled with the games the newly-arrived Miss Anne Fellows played, Laurel assumed the solitary role of hostess by default.

She doubted she gave it any measure of justice. Her brothers, undoubtedly at her father's instigation when she seemed indifferent to Sir John and Mr. Winthrop, managed to fill their quiet sanctuary at Greenbriers with enough guests to noticeably deplete the ranks of eligible bachelors in town and supply enough diversion for even the most fastidious of ladies. Mr. Winthrop was joined by his sweet-tempered sister Leona, and Sir John by his cousin Mr. Holt. They brought with them Miss Fellows, Mr. Milton, and the very young Duke of Montrose, and expected another party on the morrow. It really was beyond enough; if Penelope Croyden did not arrive shortly, there would be no available bed for her.

"Do you hunt much, Miss Gardiner?" The Duke of Montrose asked.

Laurel swallowed another yawn and hiccoughed. "Not at all, your grace. Though I have lived in the country for some years, I believe I grew up with the sensibilities of a city person. We do not think much about killing little animals whilst walking in Berkeley Square."

The Duke of Montrose looked perplexed. "Are there indeed animals in Berkeley Square? I cannot say I ever noticed any."

Oh, the little puppy! What on earth did Joseph think to invite a boy to their circle? Surely he did not imagine an eighteen-year-old, for all the Duke's wealth, an appropriate escort for his twenty-three-year-old sister? They could hardly sustain a passing conversation; the thought of being partner to the Duke during a long walk, or a formal dinner, was numbing.

"Your grace, I do not think one likely to find anything fiercer than some rather large rats in Berkeley Squres," Laurel said gently, "although there is a woman who often brings kittens in a basket. Their dam is reputed to be the best mouse-catcher in all of London. But one does not, of course, hunt the hunter."

"I should say not, Miss Gardiner!"

Laurel paused for a moment and looked into his earnest face, wondering if he yet shaved in the morning. She took pity on him. "Fear not, your grace. You may hunt as much as you wish, without any fear of retribution," she said as she patted his hand.

The Duke of Montrose blushed a fierce red.

"But know I will not accompany you to the fray. I will remain comfortably at home, embroidering little doilies," she said, though she wondered what she would do for a scissors since she'd left her only pair for the hermit.

"It is a very acceptable activity for young ladies," he admitted.

"And for slightly older ones, your grace," she said, hoping she sounded very wise and worldly. "And, indeed, some of us may have reached an age whereby staying awake all night is not at all advisable for our good health."

"But you are not so very old, Miss Gardiner!"

"How kind of you to say so, your grace," Laurel said sweetly, and stood a bit awkwardly in order to avoid touching him when he followed her lead. "But I fear I must retire."

Montrose looked stricken and glanced towards Lewis. What mischief were these two up to?

"Your sister is bored with the company, Gardiner."

Lewis removed his hand from Miss Fellows' waist, and turned very slowly.

"Is such a thing possible, Laurel?" her scoundrel brother asked very pointedly.

"I fear it may be possible, dear brother. But it is not the reason I must leave you now. The hour grows late, and I long for my chamber."

"It sounds very lonely," Miss Winthrop chirped.

Laurel wondered at this conspiracy against her—and that with no more provocation than she wished to sleep.

"My dreams are rarely lonely," she said, and let them imagine what they will.

"Please stay, Miss Gardiner. It can not be so very late as all that," Sir John said, taking his turn.

"It can be—and is. The servants are already abed." Truly, Laurel grew even wearier sustaining this ridiculous argument.

Joseph finally put down the billiards cue and entered the fray. "But, sister, they rise early to do their day's work."

And so do I, thought Laurel. She intended to visit the smokehouse before anyone was awake and deliver some of the remains of this evening's dinner, so the hermit could find it before the forest creatures did. However, she suddenly realized, perhaps she could set Montrose to the task and ask him to hunt down any curious squirrels or hedgehogs. Alas no—he would probably hit Prinny.

"I have an excellent idea! Why not light a bonfire!" Mr. Milton cried. "But would your parents object?"

"Yes," said Laurel.

"No," said Lewis at precisely the same moment, and frowned at her.

"May Day is gone nearly two months, gentlemen," she reminded them. "And I shall be gone nearly an hour before you set the sky ablaze with this mischief."

"Nonsense!" cried Joseph. "Let us do it! Montrose, do not let my sister escape."

The duke grabbed Laurel's hand before she could put it behind her back, and his grip felt surprisingly strong and warm.

"I beg you, your grace," she began, but too late. Neither he, nor anyone else, stood upon the order of their leaving, as their high spirits propelled them from the sedate room to the darkened hall. The night was warm, and no one save Laurel thought jackets to be in order, but her words seemed to go unheeded in any case.

"There is wood in the stable," she said wearily, and watched as her brothers went to raid the shed behind the kitchen.

"A torch can be found behind the flower pots," she reminded them, but realized Henry Winthrop carried with him two lit candles from the hall.

"You do not need my company; I shall retire after all," she said to no one in particular, but Montrose did not relinquish her hand. She pulled gently and then more insistently, until he finally released her from the trap.

* * * *

Rob wore nothing on his body when he slept. The many things he once took for granted, like food and good society, and the ability to purchase anything he desired, felt like immense luxuries now. Clean laundry, which was not to be had unless he scrubbed and soaked his own garments, seemed both a priceless commodity and a damned nuisance. Why waste his energy on that which provided no immediate rewards?

He turned in his sleep and knocked Prinny off the mattress. He waited for the dog to settle back down, but Prinny seemed preoccupied at the door, scratching and whining.

Rob opened his eyes, and at first thought he saw the eerie light of a strange dawn, white and flickering. But the sounds of the night, with which he had become completely attuned over the past few months, were still around him. It took but a moment before he threw himself out of bed.

Fire. Greenbriars must be ablaze!

He ran the few steps to the window and saw the torches outside the great house twinkle, as they always did to him, like bright stars of a distant constellation. They reflected in the black lake and made the light limestone of the grand steps and portico glow with warmth. And they did so now, but seemed to have some competition that was, at once, far brighter but less illuminating.

Greenbriars was not ablaze.

Rob rubbed his eyes a little too brusquely, wondering what he gazed upon. A fire it most certainly was, and closer to the lake than to the house. He tried in vain to remember what stood on that site, what could burn with such fever, what stood in jeopardy of its path. He rather thought the area sandy, as he recalled a little beach there, decorously planted with dry and scratchy shrubby things. They could, perhaps, catch fire, as could the several wooden rowboats overturned nearby. Then it would not be too far to the modest boathouse, and from there to the beech trees on the rise. And then Greenbriars itself would be vulnerable, while its inhabitants slept in their beds.

The house, he knew, was full of people, but he only thought of one as he carelessly threw on his clothes and thrust bare feet into his boots. He should bring a bucket, for he could scarcely run back and forth to the lake with cupped hands, and he should find a blanket to contain the flames as they set anew other fires. Four months ago, he might have acted on sheer intuition, but now he responded like the seasoned warrior he had become.

Why, only last week he would have burned down Miss Gardiner's shed, but for some quick thinking. Of course, he remembered ruefully, it was his own business for rummaging among her books in the dark of night, with only a sputtering torch for comfort.

But he thought of these things only briefly, for he was soon out the door, running sure and steadily along a path he had come to know as well as he once knew his own home and the people who dwelled within it. Or thought he did.

Prinny ran alongside him, excited about the evening's adventure, and seemed to know their destination. Where the path veered off towards the smokehouse, they stayed their route and brushed against the Italian statuary with which Mr. Gardiner enhanced the prospect. The sweet smells of mint and thyme, aroused by their trampling footsteps, nearly overcame the scent of burning wood. But they were now close enough to see the cinders rising like small fireworks.

And dark shadows moving against the flames.

As Rob circled the last stand of trees before the open expanse of the beach, he saw that others—many others—had arrived before him. And they did not seem to be overly concerned with the conflagration; rather, they appeared to nurse it along. Two men, louder than the others, threw logs on the fire, while a woman squealed with delight from the safety of ten yards off. A couple stood with their backs to the bonfire, finding heat of another sort, and a rather small fellow seemed preoccupied with skimming rocks across the water.

Rob slowed his pace, cursing himself for a fool. The Gardiners and their bloody houseguests could burn the whole place down for all he cared. Overly heated, his heart racing with anxiety and exertion, he flung off his robe and pulled at the twine that held his shirt together. Turning away before he could be seen, he reached down to pull up a stem of the mint on which to bite down his angry words. And then he walked headlong into a statue he had somehow missed along the path when he first approached, and knocked it, and himself, to the ground.

* * * *

Laurel allowed herself to be dragged down to the strand of beach her father fondly imagined to resemble Eastbourne, and she watched silently as her brothers and their friends pulled driftwood and miscellaneous timbers together to create a funnel of kindling. Henry Winthrop, who did not seem overly willing to soil his garments with the rough wood, appeared proud to have thought of the candles, and he set the whole thing ablaze. The wood, slightly damp in the evening's fog, sputtered but caught, and soon the absurd objective of her companions was fully met.

Nevertheless, having achieved it, no one seemed to know what to do about it. They had neither witch to burn in effigy, nor a recent kill to roast for dinner. The bonfire simply was done for entertainment and, apparently, to keep Laurel awake.

For Laurel, it accomplished neither. As soon as Montrose abandoned her to pull together a little pile of stones on the sand, she looked about for the best route of escape. She doubted, after all, that anyone would miss her, and she guessed they would soon tire of feeding the flames to no avail. She sat down on a bench, just slightly apart from the rest, and looked towards the house.

If she walked straight up the slope, her departure would be too obvious and surely prevented. If she excused herself to go to the boathouse, she would necessarily tramp through a thicket to reach the lawn, and undoubtedly emerge with her evening gown in tatters.

However, if she went along the path towards the Via Italiano—her father's grand name for the gravel path on which he placed his valuable, and well-endowed Roman copies of Greek statues—she might be able to cut back past Venus and hide behind Mercury and Hercules to approach the house from the west side. It made perfect sense, unless she fell asleep on her way.

Laurel stood up, swaying slightly. She did not think the sherry completely disarmed her, but that it, combined with sheer weariness, slowed all her senses.

Yet she was alert enough to realize no one seemed to notice her rising. Nor did anyone protest when she took a tentative step backward and yet another. Miss Fellows shrieked, but not for Laurel's escape.

Seizing her opportunity, Laurel lifted her brocaded skirt and ran towards the trees, avoiding the gravel which would be both noisy and injurious to her slippered feet. Of course, the damp grass would do its own work on the pastel satin, but she would sooner sacrifice them than another minute of her life. Nevertheless, she was also grateful for the flames glowing behind her, which illumined her way and allowed her to escape in relative silence.

Up ahead, she saw the outlines of the great trees and the first of the alabaster Romans. Glancing once more behind her, she was reassured no one followed. And in doing so, she ran directly into something solid that knocked her off her feet.

The ground was damp beneath her, and she slipped as she tried to rise. Unexpectedly, firm hands gripped her shoulders and pulled her to her feet, as if she weighed no more than a poppet. They tightened as she wavered, but even as she steadied herself, they did not let go.

"Miss Gardiner!"

She dropped her head back, feeling the tumble of her hair pins as they dropped to the ground, and squinted up at her assailant.

"Oh, Mr. Darkwood. Thank heavens it is only you. I thought I met a gypsy, or knocked into one of Father's precious statues or . . . "

"Hush. There are no gypsies here. Your father employs a hermit and a dozen groundskeepers to keep his daughter safe and free to go about as she pleases. Though I will say it is not usually advisable to run about in the dark in the wee hours of the morning, when other things are hunting their prey."

Please do not lecture me about hunting or the late hour, or any of the other things that have bored me this evening, Laurel silently lamented. She looked up into his face, for once rid of its odious hood and highlighted by her brothers' fire, and thought his blue eyes as dark as the waters of the lake.

She knew not whether it was the sherry or her own honest curiosity that asked, "But who is it who will keep me safe from the hermit?"

Mr. Darkwood sucked in his breath, but he did not relinquish his hold on her.

"And why is the hermit trusted with my care?" she pushed on, daring to see where it might lead them. "I understood you were to scrupulously avoid me. Why should it matter to you whether or not there be gypsies about to harm me?"

The hermit shifted slightly and frowned as if the question pained him. "I need to protect my connection to civilization," he said, his voice deeper than usual.

"Your connection to civilization? I am much relieved to hear it, Robbie Darkwood, for I thought you eschewed society's ways. Perhaps there is hope for you yet."

"My only hope is that I be allowed to live as I please."

"But that is not my hope," Laurel said softly and studied his face through the darkness. For all his bold words, he looked like a man who did not know himself. "'No man is an island.'"

"'Entire of itself?'" he quickly responded.

Laurel studied the smooth, thin lips that had just so easily quoted of the poet John Donne. Oh yes, Robbie Darkwood would do very well for Penelope Croyden. Or for any other young lady who desired an intelligent man of rare sensibility.

"'Entire of itself." Laurel continued to study him, wondering what he thought of her, and if she could be the one to return him to Donne's richly imagined, metaphorical mainland. Suddenly, she realized she wished to do it not just for Penelope's benefit, but for his, as well. "I see you made some use of my embroidery scissors. It is a start, at least."

"A start for what, Miss Gardiner?"

Laurel knew what she would say to any other man of her acquaintance, and what she ought to say to this large and very real man she had discovered amongst the statuary. But somehow, no words would come, so instead she raised her hand to his butchered hair and fingered the smooth, dark strands.

The hermit, the man who preferred to be an island in and of himself, grasped her wrist and pulled, but she did not loosen her hold on him. He winced, but nor did he loosen his hold on her.

"Why are you here, so far from the hermitage?" Laurel asked a little desperately. In a startling heated moment, she suddenly knew how wrong she was about everything. She wanted him not for poor lonely Penelope, but for herself. She wanted to touch him, to taste him.

Whether intentionally or not, Robbie Darkwood brought her hand to his chest and held it against his beating heart. He looked down, as if wondering how it came to be there.

"I thought a fire had been set and threatened you in the house," he answered huskily. "I did not imagine, when I dashed around the lake like a madman, that some fools had set a blaze to amuse . . . "

"Why should it matter to you if I burned in my bed? You barely tolerate my presence." Laurel whispered, knowing she now wished for something she had not even realized she desired moments before.

The hermit caught her by the waist and pulled her hard against him. His mouth, warm and tasting of mint, effectively closed off any further questions, even as it answered them all, and savored hers as if he were a starving man. Laurel opened her lips and allowed his tongue to plunder, as he pulled her so close her damp slippers found warmth atop his sturdy boots. His hand finally freed hers, allowing her to caress his firm chest through the thin linen shirt until she found the gap in the fabric. Then, hungry for more, her lips explored a line from his mouth to his chin to his neck, until she reached the tantalizing hollow revealed by his open shirt, and kissed the salty, warm skin there.

"Laurel, my dear," he protested, and effectively stopped her as he shifted again, so that his hips met hers as he lifted her just slightly off the ground. One hand pressed her against him, leaving her in no doubt of his arousal, as the other moved up her back until his fingers combed through the tangled mess of her long, loosened hair. Her nose brushed against his scratchy beard and she sneezed.

Robbie laughed and finally pulled away, though he still held her in the circle of his arms. He drew in several deep breaths before he bent closer and licked her lower lip.

"I fear I have taken advantage of a woman who has had too much to drink his evening," he said solemnly. "And we may yet regret this in the light of day."

She ran a finger over his lips and he bit down gently as she said, "Undoubtedly I did have too much to drink, but you did not take advantage of me because of it." She thought about what she'd said, and quickly amended it. "That is, you did not take advantage of me at all."

"I doubt if your father and your three large brothers would agree."

"They are not so large as you, Hermit, for all that. And it sounds as if you do not know my father very well. I know he cares for me, but men in your profession surely are not so easy to find. He may just as well think I took advantage of you, of your loneliness." When he did not answer, she said softly. "And perhaps he would be correct."

"I do not think so," he said, and she could hear the sadness in his voice. "It is my choice to be lonely, not his. And, whether by drink or no, we made a mistake tonight, Miss Gardiner."

Laurel leaned back again to look into his face, and she studied the shadows made by his straight nose and long lashes.

He caught a fistful of her hair and sniffed it.

"Smoke, I daresay. And you may call me Laurel now," she invited.

"I think not. I think we ought to forget about what just passed between us, for it can come to nothing."

Whatever else Laurel wanted this night, it was not good sense. She wanted much more from him, and none of it could come from the books he dutifully left for her. She wanted him, and felt not the smallest bit of shame for it. But looking up at him in the darkness, seeing the light of the bonfire flickering in his eyes, she realized the truth of what he said. Perhaps it was already too late to reverse the effects of what had happened, and she may have lost a friend. Indeed, while neither of them could have anticipated they would find each other in the firelight, nor could they ever go back to what they were.

Laurel stepped back, but the hermit still held her hair, so she returned to find warmth in the shelter of his outstretched arm. It felt right that she should be there, and she realized it was where she wanted to remain all night

For all her bold speech to her mother, she knew very little of lovemaking, but she decided she wanted more of it. None of the gentlemen in London had kissed her like her hermit, nor could she imagine any of them—especially Lord Ballister—invoking such an uninhibited response in her. But Robbie Darkwood was absolutely correct—there was no future in this. Laurel lifted her arms, easing her hair from his loosening grip, and attempted to tuck her wild curls into some semblance of order. But it was as hopeless as their present situation.

Robbie reached for her again, and then must have changed his mind, for instead he bowed low and picked up something she could not distinguish in the darkness. But once he threw it over his shoulders and pulled up the hood, she knew he was once again her hermit. The cursed robe was his shield from the rest of the world, his protection, the mask behind which he hid. She had learned some important lessons tonight, not only about herself, but about him as well.

"Good night, Hermit," she said, and wondered if he heard the catch in her voice.

"I will not allow a lady to walk unescorted through the woods in the middle of the night," he said gallantly.

"There is no need, Hermit. I am quite capable of taking care of myself."

"I do not doubt that, but you now have ample evidence of how tempting you are, Miss Gardiner. I have no excuse for what I did. But the other gentlemen, your friends, seem to be having an altogether rowdy time. I would feel better if I could bring you safely to your door."

"They are not my friends, Hermit, but my brothers. And you forget, bringing me to my door is no guarantee of safety, for they will sleep under the same roof."

"So long as they sleep," he said beneath his breath, and caught her hand, tucking it in the voluminous folds of his robe.

They walked wordlessly past the alabaster statues, over the scenic ruins of a stone wall, and across a wooden footbridge that scanned nothing more than a drainage ditch. Laurel's father had designed his estate with every notion of the romantic, but his only daughter had been immune to its artificial charms until this evening. And how very suitable she should receive her first taste of passion with Greenbriar's most decorous bit of scenery of them all.

When they neared the house, she glanced up at her hermit, a tall shadow against the waning lights. Though he was completely shrouded, she doubted she would ever forget the warmth of his skin, the taste of his lips, or the hardness of his body against hers. To continue thus would have been grace itself, but Laurel accepted the impossibility of such bliss for herself. She could not be so selfish.

But in the spirit of her generosity, she confirmed her commitment to a friend who desperately needed her. And him. Robbie Darkwood would, indeed, be a worthy lover to heal Miss Croyden's broken heart, she nobly resolved.

"Miss Gardiner, I can guess what you are thinking," he said suddenly.

She gave a long, low whistle. "Oh, I rather think not."

He turned, though his face was now in complete darkness.

"I will apologize again. The evening has unexpectedly given us much to regret, and we must forget it."

She stopped on the path, no longer eager to seek her bed. "But Robbie Darkwood, I shall only have regrets if I do forget it."

"You are an outspoken lady, Miss Gardiner, but I wish you would have a care. Your future husband would not appreciate knowing what passed between us, would not like it a bit."

"Dear Robbie, your future wife might not like your hermitage, but will you always remain silent about it?"

He caught her arm and began walking again, a little too quickly. "I do not intend to have a wife."

"Poor man. I think it will be a great waste if you do not."

He said nothing for the rest of the way, but she was very much aware of him, and each time their bodies pressed near along the pathway. Under his robe, beneath his mask, he really was quite splendid, and would, in the proper clothes, in the proper place, be incomparable.

"Will I see you tomorrow?" she asked.

"It is already today. And you will not."

"Will you bring me my Homer?"

"Tis waiting in the smokehouse. And we are now at your door . . ."

Will you come in? Laurel thought, and looked quickly at him to be sure she had not said it aloud.

It did not matter. With a brusque turn of his shoulder, the hermit abandoned her on the doorstep and walked steadily back down the path, farther and farther away from her, until he disappeared into the wood.

* * * *

Laurel sat in her mother's elegant morning room and raised her hand to defend her eyes against the onslaught of the sunlight. But once it was aloft, she scarcely had the energy to keep it there, and it dropped heavily onto her lap. Bowing her head, under the pretext of studying the tiny rosettes embroidered onto her day dress, she closed her eyes and nearly drifted back to sleep.

"You will not dismiss yourself so easily, Missy," her mother said loudly. "Your father and I called you here for a reason, and I do not intend to let you escape before I have some answers."

Laurel shook her head slightly, though it hurt terribly to do so. "I do not have anything to explain, for I do not think . . . "

"What will you have us do, Father?" Lewis's voice, loud but throaty, entered the room with a veritable stampede of footsteps. "Clean the stables with our hairbrushes? Are we to be punished like schoolboys?"

Mr. Gardiner entered on Lewis's heels, followed by Joseph. The parade of her brothers and father did nothing to improve Laurel's spirits.

"If you do not wish to be punished like schoolboys, you should not behave like ones," her father answered gruffly, and sat down on his favorite chair. His sons remained standing, although Lewis looked as if he needed something on which to prop himself.

"What, precisely, is our offense, sir?" Joseph asked quietly, helping himself to some of the dry biscuits that had been brought for Laurel to stave off sickness. "If it is the fire, I can assure you we took every precaution."

"If it is the matter of the ladies' wet slippers, we offered to replace them. But truly, they did not look so very bad," added Lewis.

"And if it is the matter of the Italian vase . . ." Joseph looked earnestly at his mother.

"My vase!" the lady shrieked. "Not another!"

"I will have it repaired when I return to town," he promised.

"I care not for the fire nor the damned . . ."

"George!"

" . . . the regrettable slippers, nor for a vase not to my taste. Any damage caused is easily fixed. I am more concerned with what cannot be mended."

Laurel finally looked up at her father, suddenly knowing what would come next.

"I expect my sons to be respectful of the ladies in their company, and particularly when one of the ladies is their own unmarried sister."

Joseph and Lewis exchanged a look of some puzzlement.

"The ladies were untouched, sir," said Joseph slowly, as if he still thought about the events of the night before. "We were all together, each in plain view of the others."

But Lewis studied Laurel, even as she would not meet his eyes.

"And Miss Winthrop has the advantage of her own brother in attendance. You cannot imagine Henry would let Leona off her tether for an instant? Their mother is a bear of a woman and would do him violence if the poor girl got so much as a splinter while in his care," Joseph added.

"And what of poor Laurel Gardiner's mother? Must she also be a bear to command any respect?" their mother asked.

Laurel watched as, predictably, her brothers smiled at their mother, knowing her to be the gentlest of souls.

"Why 'poor Laurel Gardiner,' Mother?" Laurel asked.

Now, like Lewis, they all stared at Laurel, and she regretted her forthrightness. She was not so certain she could stand up to any level of scrutiny this morning.

"You have gone to London and come back unmarried, little sister," Lewis said pointedly. "Is there any greater remorse?"

"If you saw your sister last night, you would understand there is," their father said sternly.

Laurel turned in her chair and stared at her father, scarcely daring to imagine of what he might be speaking. "Did you see me last night, Father?"

He tapped impatient fingers on a table, looking for words Laurel was not so certain she wanted to hear.

"I did not," he admitted. "But a certain woman in my employ did. And reported to me that my only daughter, the one on whom my fondest wishes rest, entered the house at an ungodly hour with her dress in disarray, twigs in her hair and her cheeks flushed and soiled. In short, she who might have been a countess instead looked like a wild woman."

"Your fondest wishes, sir? My brothers and I thank you very much," said Joseph tartly, and then met his sister's eyes. "Montrose?" The name was a silent question on his lips.

Laurel made a face and shook her head. Montrose, indeed. The little pup did not have the beard to scratch her cheek, as another's had.

"I did not realize you had spies in the house, Father," she said, feeling a burst of anger.

"Perhaps not just in the house, but also in the woods," said Lewis, suddenly on her side. "I think the hermit may have reported your comings and goings."

"The hermit?" Laurel said a little too loudly. Surely Lewis was mistaken. But what if Robbie Darkwood was duplicitous and played both herself and her father at the same time? "Whatever makes you say so?"

Lewis shrugged. "Why else would a seemingly healthy man condemn himself to such a miserable existence? When Joe and I spoke with him . . ."

"You spoke with him?" his father demanded.

"Indeed, we did. He is a pleasant enough fellow."

"He is not to speak with anyone! It is his job not to speak with anyone. And I know it is his preference, as well."

"You must have spoken with him yourself, Father, or else you would not have hired him for the position. And I know he spoke to . . ." Lewis's voice dropped off as he met Laurel's eyes. "Other people."

"Is the man holding court in the damned hermitage?" Their father was out of his chair, and he started rummaging for something in a desk drawer.

"George! You forget yourself!" Mrs. Gardiner raised an admonishing finger.

"Sorry, my love. But I daresay our daughter has heard such words before, and often enough from me. Ah, here 'tis!" Mr. Gardiner pulled out his old telescope from beneath a sheath of papers and went to the window with it.

"Now you no longer require spies to do your business, Father, for you can accomplish it yourself," Joseph said dryly.

"Can't see a blasted thing with the trees in the way," his father muttered.

"Most people believe the trees enhance the beauty of the property, Father," Laurel said sweetly, as she tried to divert him from his mission. "And your hermit would scarcely be out in the open, would he? You told me yourself he avoids people like a mole avoids the light."

"I said that, did I?" Her father nodded approvingly. "Very clever of me. And indeed, the hermit is not reporting anything to me other than news of the occasional problem with drainage in the pasture. He retrieves his salary, and stays very much to himself. Or so he ought."

"Perhaps it is time to bring him out into the light. Would you mind very much if we did so, Father?" Laurel asked, telling herself she thought only of her friend Miss Croyden. She ran her tongue over her dry lips, still burning from last evening's heated indiscretion.

"Mind? What can you be thinking? I will mind very much if my hermit proves to be even the least bit social. Men with his qualifications are hard to find. However would I replace him?"

Laurel had been thinking pretty much the same thing herself. She realized how much she wished to be with him, how she awoke each morning hoping their paths might meet.

"What are his qualifications, sir?" Joseph asked.

Mr. Gardiner dropped his useless telescope onto a sheath of papers. "He dislikes people and stays to himself. And what are yours, young man?"

Joseph, usually so cool and businesslike, was clearly taken aback. "To be a hermit?" he asked.

"I did not raise my sons to be hermits. I know not what the elder Darkwood accomplished in his lifetime to deserve such a son, but I suspect he misstepped most severely."

"Perhaps it was a lady," said Mrs. Gardiner, sympathetically.

Laurel flushed, remembering the hermit's kisses and wondering what sort of woman might have rejected such divine favors. But then, she necessarily would herself, as she groomed his ardor for Miss Croyden. She realized how stupid she had been, for now she truly wished him all for herself.

Her father looked at her and frowned. "A lady could very well reduce a man to desperation." Turning back to Lewis and Joseph, he said, "I question your qualifications to keep your sister protected and safe."

This surely had to be the end of this business, Laurel thought angrily. She had not come home to Greenbriars to be shuttled around as she had been in London. She sought to escape the censorious eyes of elderly matrons and jealous rivals for gentlemen's attentions, and the fickle passions of suitors who needed to make an advantageous match. It was no business of her brothers to oversee the freedom she now attained.

And, of course, she could not continue to see the hermit if Lewis and Joseph were always hanging about.

"They are not so qualified, sir," Laurel said, as she rose. "The only one who needs judgement in the matter of my own protection is myself. I am not a shy little thing, untutored in the way of the world. I can take care of myself."

"Well said, Missy, but you did not seem so very successful in the business last night. Can you explain what happened?" her father asked.

No, indeed, she could not. She knew not why she fell so readily into the hermit's embrace, nor why she responded to his kisses like a starving woman. She could not explain why she could scarcely sleep for thinking of him. Or why she longed to seek him out this day and taste of him again.

"The gentlemen had nothing to do with it, Father. I left the beach earlier than the rest and wandered a bit through the statuary. A small creature, a fox, perhaps, startled me, and I fell on the path. The detriment was to my gown, but not to my person. And certainly not to my reputation." Laurel smoothed down the fabric of her skirt, hoping her father's temper could be assuaged as easily. "I know not which of the servants delivered such ridiculous gossip to you, but if all the people you hire were as reticent as your hermit, there would be much less trouble in our lives."

Lewis began to applaud her, until Joseph stayed his hand.

"However, we appreciate your words, Father," the older brother began, returning to his usual formal demeanor. "If we were more attentive to our sister, she would not have fallen on the path in the dark."

"I do not need to be led about by a tether," Laurel insisted.

"You do, if you persist in walking about by yourself," her father said with equal conviction, and a good deal louder.

"She will, Father. Be assured of it," Joseph continued, and clasped his fingers around Laurel's wrist. He pressed very slightly on her palm, which she took as a sign to let the matter drop. "Lewis or I will know where she is at all times. If we cannot do it, we will enlist George's help."

"Oh, not George!" Laurel cried as he started to pull her from the room. Their oldest brother, to whom Mr. Gardiner had entrusted the bulk of the business, was such a stick. He would be happy to marry her off to anyone on the street who offered a good investment prospect.

Joseph drew her out into the hall, with Lewis fast on their heels.

"This is not about the hermit, is it?" he said the moment they were out of their parents' earshot.

"The hermit?" Laurel asked, her voice a little shrill. "Of what can you be thinking? Can you imagine me happy for two minutes with a man who does not speak?"

"Men can do many things that do not involve speaking," Joseph said knowingly. "Or thinking, either, for that matter."

Laurel knew precisely what he meant.

"But I do not lack sense," she lied. "And you have delivered an impressive array of gentlemen to my door. Why would I be tempted by an unkempt and mysterious hermit when I can choose between the likes of Mr. Holt or Mr. Milton or Sir John? Or the Baby Duke, for that matter?"

"Montrose is of an age with Lewis," Joseph said slowly, emphasizing each word.

"Then I suggest they both look to the nursery for romance. If there are no girls available for them, perhaps they would enjoy the hobby horses and hoops there."

"Laurel!" Lewis's protest was justified, she supposed.

"Oh, leave me, both of you," she said wearily. "If I have even the vaguest sense the two of you are following me, I shall make your lives miserable. I truly will."

"She can do it, Joe," said Lewis, with the unmistakable knowledge of the youngest child in a family.

Joseph dropped her hand, and she started to rub her wrist as if she had been in shackles.

"Will you tell me, will you promise me, you have no interest in the hermit as a friend or anything else?"

"And what is 'anything else?'" she demanded.

"Must I spell it out? If you are as worldly as you claim, you know precisely my meaning."

"Oh, that. You wish to know if I plan to take the hermit as my lover?" she asked, meaning to provoke them.

Her brothers, one older, one younger, blushed for embarrassment, and Laurel felt no small degree of satisfaction.

"Let me think on this," she said slowly, playing out her hand. "I have no such plans, brothers. Now, may I ask about your expectations? Will it be Miss Winthrop, Joseph?"

He puffed up like an angry toad. "I do not think it any business of . . ."

Laurel raised a finger, stopping him mid-sentence. "Precisely. I fail to understand why my own desire for privacy has less coinage than yours."

"Because your reputation is worth more. Once tarnished, it is without value," Joseph said.

Laurel looked at her older brother, seeing something eloquent she never had noticed before. Some lady would be very lucky to have him, if she could only fan the flames of the fire he kept so carefully banked.

"Then it would be my loss, would it not?" she asked sincerely. "If I gamble and do not succeed, I have no one to blame but myself."

"If you gamble and lose, then you will be dependent upon your brothers for life," Joseph said, and Lewis nodded in agreement.

"Fear not, boys," she said glibly. I would not wish to corrupt little Gardiners in the nursery like some dotty old spinster. I could instead hire myself out as a hermit, and manage very well on my own."

"Laurel!" Lewis's frustration was all too clear.

She ignored it and said, "And then, other men could reflect, as our own father did just now, that the fault must lie with the family that could cause a person to take such desperate measures." Laurel realized her father's words, though spoken in haste, were not entirely without merit, for she resolved to soon uncover her hermit's history. "Therefore, the blame will not be upon me, after all. It will be upon all of you."

She smiled, knowing, as she had all her life, how easy it was to torment these two.

"Our father did have it wrong when he asked us to guard you, little sister," Joseph said solemnly.

Laurel continued to smile, feeling she had earned her little victory.

"The only solution is to lock you in the tower and send all the charming princes away in disappointment," Joseph said as he shrugged.

"Have a care, dear brothers, lest I lock the two of you in that tower and throw away any hope of escape." Laurel threw an imaginary key over her shoulder. "But do not expect any princesses to be in the least bit disappointed!"

Chapter Seven

Laurel's heated resolution to seek out her hermit and hear an explanation of his history and what had caused him to come for her as he had last night, cooled as the day ran through its course. The family interview in the drawing room did much to dampen the flames, of course, as did the new awareness of an insidious spy in the sanctuary of her own home, who seemingly would not hesitate to report if the young mistress of Greenbriars had lips too red or lost her lace among the statuary. Laurel would discover the traitoress—for she did not doubt it a woman—and make her regret every blasphemous word she had uttered.

Except, of course, her revenge would be tempered by the fact that what was reported was absolutely true.

Laurel Gardiner, the innocent rose of an illustrious family that desired nothing more than to succeed where their humble ancestors had failed, had acted most inappropriately. She did not need her father's stern lecture, or her mother's tearful face to tell her this. She did not need her brothers to play watchdog and allow her only enough freedom to flirt with the men—or boys—of whom they approved. She knew it herself, almost from the very moment Robbie Darkwood released her from his arms.

She grew warm just thinking of it, of him. Every moment of their illicit encounter seemed at the time to be something in a dream, and yet held up in the light of day with startling clarity. She thought of his body, warm and damp from his race through the woods, pressed against the length of hers, and how hard and unyielding it felt beneath her loving, exploring hands. She still tasted his lips, and the sweet freshness of mint on them, when she had allowed them to savor her own. But knowing the sherry she had last night had been the prelude to the unexpected dessert they shared, Robbie nobly refused to claim too much of her because of it. He proved far more sensible than she, and more gentlemanly than most men of her acquaintance.

For Laurel had been sufficiently sober to know the sherry provided no excuse for what she had done, nor for what she would have been fully prepared to do if the hermit had allowed it.

She sighed and dropped her chin onto the headrest made by her open hands as her elbows leaned on her dressing table. One glance into the angled mirror offered three times the punishment of her reflection, wherein she saw a woman who had been transformed by the events of the night before into someone she did not yet recognize. She was an original; goodness knows, she heard it pronounced often enough. The season in London, to which she had come months before as a nervously expectant innocent, proved not to her liking and so she had abandoned it. The young men her brothers provided as likely contenders for her affections offered nothing of interest to her, and so she ignored them. And yet, inexplicably, she had allowed the least eligible man in Cambridgeshire to seduce her, and she had done nothing to push him away.

And worse, she realized she wanted more.

It would not do.

Her dark eyes looked back at her in the center mirror, their color heightened by regrettable smudges on the thin skin beneath them. Her hair, no longer a smoky tangle of curls and twigs recklessly combed by a man's long fingers, had been groomed into compliance after her morning bath and was braided into a proper coronet. The look, she had been told, was regal, and she glanced at her profile in the two side mirrors to confirm that pronouncement. The woman who had been kissed so thoroughly the night before looked very regal indeed.

But a woman, a lady, of substance did not make love to a man who lived in a stone cottage and covered his body, no matter how splendid that body, in threadbare rags. No matter her self-proclaimed status as an original.

It would not do at all.

Laurel ran her fingers over her tightly plaited hair and closed her eyes, remembering the path they had traced the night before through the hermit's dark, thick curls. Most women would envy such a crown and regret the waste of it on a man's head. But thinking on it, Laurel realized she knew someone with just such a treasure, and it was the very woman who would provide Laurel with an avenue of escape from her current difficulties.

She opened her eyes, but she no longer saw herself gazing back in weary indecision. It was Miss Croyden she saw instead, a lady whose hair was as dark and unruly as the hermit's and whose eyes were of a deep blue to match his own. Why had she not seen this before, even as she resolved upon a scheme to bring them together? Robbie Darkwood and Penelope Croyden were more than perfect for each other; it seemed destiny to bring together two so similar.

Revived with a sense of purpose, with the determination to bring two damaged souls to a state of perfect happiness, Laurel abandoned her dressing table for her *escritoir,* and found her scented stationary. Her mother called it the paper of love letters, and indeed it would be. In her insistence that Miss Croyden join them at Greenbriars as soon as possible, the letter would be the Cupid's arrow bringing together two people for whom she cared very much.

* * * *

Rob tossed the last of the wood onto a pile taller than his own height and thought it would have to be a very cold winter indeed to justify the amount of energy he'd expended this day on chopping down half the forest. If Mr. Gardiner would but give him permission, he would clear the eastern woodlands as well, and build a few bridges over the river into the bargain. He would do anything, in fact, if it did not require thinking overmuch. And did not bring him into the society of women.

Well, of one woman, particularly.

If he owned one grain of sense he would pack his trustworthy books and his precious few other belongings and move on to Scotland. How easy it would be to reinvent himself and find refuge in the Highlands, free from interfering ladies and companionable gentlemen with far too much time on their hands. As he recalled, his mother had people in Glasgow; perhaps he could claim some passing acquaintance and find employment with them.

But the plan, like every other he'd considered since last night's complete loss of discretion, was hopelessly flawed. After all, he could not hope that his distant relatives, like his present employer, would be entirely indifferent to any references or evidence of a past life. And the last thing he needed in the complicated business of his present life was polite inquiries to his forsaken home.

Home. He found himself thinking of it more and more these days, even as he expected the initial longing that accompanied his escape to wane over time. It seemed not so much that he missed the comforts, for he preferred to believe both his mind and body were now accustomed to rougher, earthier pleasures, and might even be better because of them. And it was not that he missed any one other than his mother and brother, for the rest had been the cause of his precipitous departure. Indeed, he missed his horses and dogs more than most of the human company, though Prinny now proved a congenial mate.

No, it was none of that. Rather, it seemed to Rob in his darkest moments, that the lie he now lived was as dangerous as the ones that had cut him so deeply in recent months. Because of it, harm might come to one for whom he cared.

And he did care for Miss Gardiner. He had not intended to, and had avoided the possibility assiduously in the first days of his acquaintance. Indeed, he'd somehow imagined he'd succeeded altogether until last night, when he thought her in danger and ran like a madman through the woods to rescue her. That she was perfectly safe, and possibly a little drunk, provided no excuses for what he'd done, or any explanation for why she'd answered him with a passion equal to his own.

For she'd answered him quite clearly, and might very well have answered a good many other questions as well, if he had not managed to finally regain his equanimity and exert some measure of sense. He was not, after all, one of the fine gentlemen with whom her family had populated Greenbriars in recent days, presented to her so that one of them would do precisely what he, a soulless hermit, had accomplished last night.

Had Miss Gardiner believed he was one of the other men in the party? The thought suddenly occurred to him, as unwelcome as a squirrel in his chimney. Had he interrupted an assignation among the statuary?

Well, the more credit to him, then. What did her brothers mean to let her go off unescorted and bent on ruining himself? Indeed, it was a good thing he had come along, for who knew what trouble the little vixen would have found herself in!

Rob hoisted a log onto his shoulder and brushed off a splinter that pricked his ear. The pain, as trivial as it was, nevertheless managed to restore him to his present bitter reality. Truly, the lady was driving him to distraction.

Laurel Gardiner did not need him any more than she needed another glass of sherry. She had servants enough to anticipate her needs, and gentlemen of rank who would prostrate themselves at her feet before daring to take advantage of any weakness. She had three burly brothers, who surely knew they must preserve her reputation, and two parents who cherished her. There was nothing the lady lacked but for some entertainment to keep her mind lively. And he, Robbie Darkwood, was not the one to provide it.

With luck, one of her suitors might, and take her away from Greenbriars in the bargain. Then might he live his life here in some peace, and not have to remind himself that he was not a gentleman who could dare seduce her along a dark garden path.

Still holding the unwieldy log, he started up the hill towards the smokehouse, where he hoped to split the wood and repair the leaky roof. He knew little about the business, lacking any experience in this regard, but thought he might put together something to prove adequate. He also knew Miss Gardiner had retrieved her book earlier in the day, for he caught a glimpse of a pale yellow gown and heard something that might have been singing in the woods. Despite his resolve to avoid her, and his good sense that urged him to stay away, he barely managed it. Next time, he would have to follow Odysseus' example and lash himself to a tree in order to resist the Sirens' call. This morning, however, he merely worked off his impulses, by cutting down her father's trees.

Prinny awaited him on the slope, wagging his dust-mop of a tail and yelping his excitement. If Rob ever returned to his home, the scamp would accompany him, but the name would have to stay behind. Prinny might do for the pet of a hermit, but he would have to be elevated to Prince if ever . . .

"Miss Gardiner!" Rob's fingers slipped on the log and he nearly dropped it, when she came into view.

He had been right about that yellow dress, for she wore it still. There was some lacy thing at her neckline that attempted to conceal one of the most admirable parts of her anatomy but which would have better served them both if there were more of it. Her hair, coiled up around her ears, looked a little austere, but allowed her small ears to be better appreciated. He supposed the flowery thing in her hand to be her bonnet and wondered why she did not wear it. It was always his understanding that ladies did not wish to brown their skin in the sun.

But perhaps that was why Miss Gardiner always looked healthier and more vibrant than the pale ladies with whom he once was acquainted.

She sat down on a fallen log, spreading out her yellow skirt. "Do join me, Mr. Darkwood," she said, quite as if she were asking him to tea. If that were the case, he would wonder if the tea contained something unexpectedly potent, for her manner seemed studiously guileless.

Rob looked at her with uncertainty, feeling very much like a schoolboy again. To sit beside her would be a punishment. And the greatest delight.

"I am not going to hurt you, sir," she said in a coaxing voice he scarcely recognized as hers. This was some scheme afoot; he knew her well enough for that. But even as he considered turning his back, as his conscious dictated, he wondered if she recalled nothing of last night's kiss and knew not how she tempted him.

"It is not your behavior I fear, madam, but my own," he said cautiously, testing her response.

She raised one of her finely arched eyebrows, and looked beyond the waters of the lake to where more than one fire had burned so brightly the night before. The smell of smoke lingered still in the warm air, and Rob imagined he heard the crackling of the flames.

"You have done nothing to give either of us cause for reflection, sir. I recall none of the events of last night."

As reassurance, it proved, of course, entirely ineffective. For all his misgivings, Rob could not help smiling. The lady said she recalled nothing, and yet she somehow knew something had happened between them last night.

"I do recall something, Madam, but perhaps it is of no consequence."

He saw something that might have been dismay in her expression, but her congenial manner did not waver.

"In any case, it will not be spoken of again," he added, and finally dropped the weight off his shoulder. The log nearly hit his foot.

She visibly brightened, and he knew it was not simply the work of the sunshine on her delicate skin.

"Then do sit with me, for we have much to discuss."

"If neither of us sufficiently recalls last night, then I am not sure we have anything to discuss." Rob stepped back. Here was one web he would avoid. "Have I not been diligent in bringing you your books? And have I endeavored to remain out of sight and out of your business? Have I interfered with your entertainment of your guests?" He believed he'd managed to sound righteous, but he knew full well he could be faulted on all counts.

"You have noticed them, then?" she asked, ignoring his obvious infractions.

"How can I not? I even observe one gentleman who is particularly desirous of your attention. The short one, with the flaxen curls."

"Oh, the Duke of Montrose. He is of no consequence."

"My dear Miss Gardiner. If he is a duke, then by definition he is of consequence."

"To my parents, perhaps. And to Lewis, also. But I am not convinced a gentleman has more to offer a lady than a common man, even a laborer. After all, my father and brothers have managed on nothing more than intelligence and ambition. Who is to say a groom will not succeed where an earl has not? Or even a hermit?"

Rob cleared his throat, fully aware the divine Miss Gardiner was about to make him suffer for kissing her amongst the statuary. "A groom may dream all he likes, but hermits do not desire any advancement. It is the very point of being a hermit, to throw off the trappings of our civilization."

"But you do not."

Nor would he, if there remained the slightest chance his life and honor could be restored to him.

"Do look around you, Miss Gardiner," Rob said with a sweep of his arm. "Are these the comforts of a gentleman of refinement?"

"I might ask you the same question, Hermit."

Rob slipped his hand up under his robe and loosened the fastening at his collar. It was an uncommonly warm day.

"They are not," he said clearly. "A true gentleman would never condescend to live under such conditions, for they would be abhorrent to him."

She nodded thoughtfully, and Rob suddenly felt he played a rhetorical game of strategy with this exquisite creature, and an unthinking comment on his part might very well lead to a verbal checkmate on hers.

"Precisely," she said, effectively checking him. "Which is why I have come to realize I do not prefer the society of gentlemen."

Rob sat down on a wood chopping block, onto which the woodsmen who had once used the smokehouse for its intended purpose had undoubtedly slaughtered all manner of beasts and fowl. Worse and worse.

"But you cannot prefer the society of hermits," he said bluntly, trying to make her believe it.

She sat up straighter on her log, and her bonnet slipped to the ground. "That is just the point. I do not know that I do, for you are the only hermit of my acquaintance. I imagine you may not be entirely representative of your ilk."

"I assure you, Madam, I am as singular and unsocial as any man of my profession."

She laughed out loud, and Rob knew he had been bested at the game.

"You are an excellent group of men, then!" she pronounced, and then looked thoughtful, as if something had just occurred to her. "I am tempted to join you. But are there women in your ranks?"

Unbidden, an image came to Rob of Miss Laurel Gardiner living with him in his little stone cottage, nestled naked and warm against him in the narrow bed.

"I daresay there are, Miss Gardiner. A woman may wish to escape society as much as any man. Only, the two may not do so together if they wish to remain hermits."

Her dark eyes looked directly at him, and yet he had the uncanny feeling she did not see him at all. She pondered some plan, of that he was certain, and he, quite at a loss to imagine it, continued to think further on the image of the divine Miss Gardiner as a hermit's companion.

"I know a woman who wishes to escape society, Mr. Darkwood."

He shifted uncomfortably on the altar.

"Will gentlemen allow her to do so?" he asked, thinking about her and the Duke of Montrose.

Her dark eyes shifted downward, and the sunshine created a halo of her bound plaits. Was she thinking of last night's misadventure, and wondering how she might bring up something they had already decided did not happen?

"A gentleman has already pushed her out of society, Mr. Darkwood."

He jumped to his feet, ignited by some of the same impulses that drove him the night before. "Did one of your guests offend you in some way? Behave inappropriately?" he demanded, silencing the insistent voice in his head that reminded him of his own reckless behavior and that he was guilty of the very same thing.

The dark eyes were upon him again, their surprise not to be misread.

"You are not my champion, Mr. Darkwood, whatever you say," she said quietly. "And I am not talking about my own circumstances."

He remained standing, feeling entirely the fool.

"Who is the lady, then?" he asked.

"A London friend, a very sweet and innocent lady who has been much imposed upon by the man to whom she is betrothed. Was betrothed," she corrected herself.

"Has she begged off from the engagement, then?" he asked, feeling a quickening of his heart.

"She has asked for nothing. But the gentleman has jilted her in the most unexpected and damaging way and left her with a broken spirit. There was nothing to be had in town to amuse or delight her. Or, indeed, to distract her from her unhappiness."

"Save your company, I expect," he said, without irony.

Her dark eyes brightened. "Of course."

"Then I expect she lacks for nothing."

He may have forgotten many things in his tenure as a hermit, but it seemed he still remembered how to flatter a lady. And yet he did not say anything he did not mean.

"Perhaps you are my champion, after all," she said. "And I require your services, it seems."

Rob could scarcely believe what he heard, and he had no words to answer her. He took a step forward and held out his hand.

"I wish for you to make love, "she continued.

Dear God!

"To her."

"Miss Gardiner!" he said, in a voice only somewhat resembling his own.

She looked up at him, obviously indifferent to the fact that he had nearly had a heart attack.

She stood and stepped over her bonnet as she approached him.

"It is my plan, you see. I have been thinking on it since I was in London myself."

"I did not know you then."

"No, you did not," she said and touched his sleeve. He stepped back and would have tripped over a fallen branch but that she caught his coat sleeve and held him tight. "But I knew there would be someone like you to answer my need." Her voice was low and sultry, rippling with the cadences of seduction.

Rob removed her hand from his arm and steadied himself.

"Miss Gardiner, I fail to see how I can be implicated in a plan I know nothing about, with those who are unknown to me. She is a London lady, you say?"

"We met in London," she nodded. "I shall properly introduce you, of course. She has been hurt, but I will not believe the damage is irreparable. She requires someone who is thoughtful and kind. Someone who can remind her that there is a great deal to discover in the world aside from what society offers us."

The lady in such great need might have been one he knew, if not for her London identity. Perhaps he might absolve himself of his recent indiscretion and enduring guilt, if he managed to make another lady happy. But the possibility, slight as it was, could not make him a ready conspirator in Miss Gardiner's absurd scheme.

"There are many men who will fulfill your requirements, my dear," he said sensibly. "And many of them are gentlemen who are a good deal kinder than the lout who jilted her."

"I do not have a high opinion of gentlemen. I believe I already told you so."

"So you did," he answered warily.

"And I confess I made a wager, of sorts, with my mother."

"I hope it did not concern me."

"As a matter of fact, it did. I told her my opinion that the very best men are not to be found among the aristocracy at all, but in the lower classes. Any ruffian can be taught to speak well, and dance without trampling a lady's toes."

"And there are titled men who could do neither." Rob saw her look at him with a question in her eyes, and he quickly went on. "But that is hardly the point. A lady does not marry a gentleman for his dancing skills, but for his property and wealth. It is about class, Miss Gardiner; that is everything."

"The lady in question already possesses property and wealth. Why should she not marry where she chooses?"

"An excellent point. But we are not talking about her choice, but your own. For her, that is," he added, stumbling over his own words. "And to make matters more complicated, you seem to have made a choice for me as well. I fear I am not interested in your friend, Miss Gardiner. Nor in any woman."

She licked her lips, as if she already knew the truth of it. But if she understood how he adored her, would she continue to tempt him so?

"In addition to which, your father would remove me at once from the hermitage, for breach of promise." Indeed, Mr. George Gardiner could already toss him out on his ear with sufficient provocation.

"My father need not know."

"I may not be a gentleman, but I am a man of honor. I would not so deceive him," he said stiffly.

"And yet you agreed to deceive him about our association."

"That is different, of course."

"Why? Because I blackmailed you into silence?"

"Miss Gardiner!"

She grinned and leaned slightly forward so that the lace in her neckline slipped slightly. He looked away towards the water, where Prinny chased a hapless duck. Poor little feathered devil; Rob knew precisely how he felt.

"Perhaps I could blackmail you again," she said, and he knew in that instant she had forgotten nothing of the night before.

"But you will not, because while you profess to disdain gentlemen, you are still a lady."

"'Tis a pity, is it not? But then, I shall have to rely on my abilities to cajole you."

Rob held up a hand in surrender, and the lady seized her opportunity. And his hand.

As she clung to it, she fervently said, "I wish for you only to meet her. She is a sweet thing and very gentle. Her features are not unlike your own, or at least what I can see beneath that hood and your ridiculous beard."

"I beg your pardon!"

"Surely you could have made better use of my scissors? I have had to borrow my mother's for all my embroidery."

Rob brought her hand to his chin and ran her fingers over his scratchy beard. He watched her expression, waiting for a sign of her repugnance. Instead, she seemed intent on smoothing down the rough hairs, trifling with the finer growth at the corners of his mouth. Wondering how those gentle fingers might feel on his bare skin, he wished he could be rid of the mess altogether. Indeed, the reprehensible beard seemed a metaphor for his whole cursed life. If only it were possible for complete honesty between them. But when she paused and looked up at him, her parted lips only inches from his, all thoughts of rhetorical allusions vanished.

"Hermit?" she asked in that same seductive voice. Truly, where would a proper lady learn to speak like this?

"I only need to meet her?" he asked gruffly.

"And talk a bit, perhaps," she said, smiling. Her lips were still close, and he noticed, for the first time, a tiny birthmark on her upper lip. He wondered if there were any others on her body, and who would be the one to discover them.

"I am not happy about this at all," he said, meaning a great deal more than she could imagine.

"It is settled then," she said, and stood on her toes to plant a kiss on his chin, sealing the bargain. Rob would have pulled her into his arms and reminded her of what a kiss ought to be, but the minx backed away, looking around her until she saw her discarded bonnet and picked it up. "She will arrive within the week, I hope. And we will have much to do before then."

It took a moment before he truly heard her words, and by then she was already walking down the hill towards the lake.

"What will we have to do?" he called after her, his mind and body centered on one thing only.

She turned in the path, her yellow gown swirling about her. "I am not yet sure," she called back, and then, in what he suspected was a rehearsed afterthought, "Do you know how to dance?"

He wondered, for the second time that afternoon, how quickly he might pack his belongings for Scotland.

* * * *

Laurel's heart skipped a beat when she recognized the tiny script of Penelope's hand on the small envelope passed to her by one of the servants. She glanced around at their small party to see if anyone would notice or care if she excused herself to read what she prayed—and expected—to be a confirmation of her friend's visit to Greenbriars. But truly, her energetic brothers provided amusement enough on this warm day to keep even the most interfering partner engaged and away from her.

Most of their guests were out on the lake in the freshly painted rowboats, wherein Sir John, Mr. Winthrop, Mr. Milton and Lewis were able to demonstrate their prowess in navigation, and Miss Winthrop and Miss Fellows were able to suitably admire them. Montrose, sharing a launch with Sir John and Miss Fellows, freely shared the remains of their picnic luncheon with a family of ducks who appeared to be inordinately found of watercress and biscuits. Closer at hand, Mrs. Gardiner was attentive to Mr. Holt's narration of his recent travels through Cornwall and his exploration of the caves beneath the ruined castle at Tintagel. Laurel knew her mother, who counted King Arthur's reign as somewhere after the Plantagenets and before the unfortunate Charles, could be absorbed for hours.

Joseph sat alone, and would appear to any of the onlookers to be asleep. Laurel, who knew him better than anyone, recognized for a certainty he was not, but she did not give him away. Her gaze went from where his lean body sprawled in the narrow wooden garden chair out to the lake, where Miss Fellows brushed an insistent dragonfly from Sir John's hat, and immediately understood the reason for his deception. Things were not going quite as he'd planned.

Fanning herself with Penelope's letter, Laurel reflected on how her perspectives had been, perhaps, somewhat prejudiced. She, too, had been hurt in London, and therefore, she had sided herself with Penelope because of that hurt. The art of courtship and marriage was taught to young girls as the dance during which they gracefully moved to attract the right partner; if no men sought such a partner at the time, then the disappointed girls moved on to the next dance, by which time they were young ladies. And so the seasons went, as young ladies became more mature ladies, more practiced dancers, and possibly aged spinsters. But always, it was assumed that men did the choosing, and women remained constant, to be either gratified or disappointed.

And, while Laurel was hardly a green miss, and knew of a good many circumstances in which a suitor had been refused or a gentleman's attentions rebuffed, she scarcely ever thought about the plight of a man with dashed hopes. Certainly, society did not wish to think much of him. It was merely assumed he would dispute the matter like a man, and go on to the next dance with nary a backward look.

But looking at Joseph now, at his studied insouciance and casual mien, she understood that gentlemen could feel the hurt of disappointed hopes as strongly as ladies. She did not know what had already passed between her older brother and the sweetly flattering Anne Fellows, but her newly experienced sensibility allowed her to make a guess. And to know it had not gone well for Joseph.

Poor boy.

Laurel slipped Penelope's letter into her sleeve and stood. Mr. Holt politely did the same, though he did not miss a note in his recitation of the glories of Tintagel.

"Are you leaving us, Laurel?" Mrs. Gardiner asked, squinting up at her.

Mr. Holt continued to talk, and Laurel suspected that whatever she answered would not be heard.

"Only for a while, Mother. I would like to see if any rose hips need to be clipped."

As soon as the words were out, she regretted them, for it might seem an invitation for Mr. Holt to join her. But she need not have worried, for it appeared he would not lose so eager an audience as her mother for the chance of an indifferent flirtation among the bees and blossoms of the rose garden. When she stepped away, he promptly sat down, and Mrs. Gardiner turned to face him once more.

Laurel made good her escape and went off in the direction of the sweet garden, though she guessed she might never get that far.

Penelope's letter rubbed against her wrist and she pulled it from her fitted sleeve. Lacking a desk knife, she ripped the paper apart and glanced over the page for the words she hoped to read.

Indeed, she would get her fondest wish. Penelope was at present with her younger sisters at her aunt's cottage in Warwickshire, but she expected to be able to leave with her sister Aurore two days hence. The season in town had produced no happy diversion for her, for she could meet no man to make her forget her beloved Earl of Westbridge, and so she had retreated to the country even as Laurel's first letter passed her en route. Thus, both Laurel's letters reached her nearly at the same time, and while both were on nearly the same theme, the latter appeared somewhat more compelling. What was a friend, after all, but a communicant of one's dearest hopes, deepest fears, and happiest triumphs? Who better to share the loneliness of a disaffected heart than one whose own unfortunate experience brought her so close to the perils of despair?

Laurel sighed and spared a thought for her own unremorseful deceit. Had she so much thought of Lord Ballister for five full minutes in all the weeks since her return to Greenbriars? Indeed, she considered Penelope's disappointment a good deal more often than she did her own. And it would be the fullest measure of her success if the cursed name of Westbridge could be as effectively removed from her friend's heart, as Ballister was from hers.

There was more from Penelope, of course. One of the reasons Laurel wished for her companionship was because Penelope never lacked for conversation.

And she went on, in her letter, to report on rumored sightings of her errant lover, and what news had already reached them of his doings. Laurel rushed through this information, for what did she care for such a man? But she noticed he had been seen in so many places—from London to Wales, from the docks at Liverpool to the beach at Brighton— he must surely be a man of considerable energy. And yet, for all that, he somehow lacked the strength to pick up his pen and provide his betrothed with an explanation for his disappearance.

The man deserved a miserable death and all manner of torture.

Penelope feared such a thing had already occurred. Laurel guiltily dismissed her unladylike thoughts and read of her friend's fears that something dreadful had happened to her beloved and she would never hear of or from him again.

When she finally finished the letter, sealed with Penelope's promised time of arrival at Greenbriars, she refolded it to fit inside the envelope. Westbridge dead could solve one potential problem, of course, for what if he should reappear after Penelope fell in love with Robbie Darkwood? Surely it would break the hermit's already damaged heart. And what would she, Laurel, do then? She could not hope to find a succession of young ladies to entice him from his withdrawal from society. Nor would she ever be able to convince him that her little experiment was conducted with the purest of reasons and with every hope of success. She would no sooner trifle with him than with her dear friend Penelope.

Indeed, thinking of the body she had felt against her when he pulled her to him on the night of the bonfire, and the delicious plundering of his lips, she wondered if she was being a good deal kinder to her friend than she was to herself.

Chapter Eight

On the next afternoon, when Joseph and Lewis escorted their guests into town to show them off to the townspeople, Laurel begged off from the excursion. She supposed she ought to be as indignant as her poor mother when none of the gentlemen looked in the least bit disappointed, but she had work to do and precious enough time in which to accomplish it. So she stood in the grand hallway of Greenbriars, enthusiastically waving them on, and quite ready to forcibly push them all out the door if they took yet another moment to leave.

Her mother frowned at her, but did no more than suggest that they bake bread together with the cook. Although her mother endeavored to present her daughter as a lady in society, she was imbued with a keen practical sense that demanded all her children know how to get on in the world if their circumstances should ever be reduced. So it was that Laurel knew the best ingredients for a silver polish, and how long to knead the dough when making a perfect rye bread.

Laurel, wondering if it would be useful to teach some of these skills to Penelope when she arrived, felt sorely tempted to join her mother in the kitchen. It would be very neighborly to deliver a loaf or two of bread to the hermit when she visited him next, and thus warm him to the expectation of the imminent arrival of Miss Croyden. But, knowing her brothers, she reconsidered that men were as easily seduced by a sweet trifle as by a beautiful woman, and thus he might prefer the food to the lady. Or worse, by her offering, the hermit might think she hoped for a renewal of his kisses.

To tell the truth, she did, she thought longingly.

"Well, my dear? What are you thinking?"

Laurel blinked at her mother and vowed the good woman would never know what her innocent daughter was thinking—or with whom she thought to do it.

"I am thinking it is a glorious afternoon, Mother, and I would prefer to spend the afternoon outside."

"If you are so enamoured of nature, you should have joined the others on their walk to town."

"I am very fond of nature, but I fail to see how an afternoon spent in the shops will add to my appreciation of it."

"Perhaps it would add to your appreciation of Montrose. Or even Mr. Holt."

"Mr. Holt?" Laurel smiled. "But he has already found a rapt audience in another."

"Do not be ridiculous, Missy," her mother whispered. "Mr. Holt only turned to me when he could not ignite even a flicker of interest from the lady whose attention he sought."

"I do doubt it, Mother. The man has not said two sentences altogether to me since his arrival."

"But what of Montrose?" her mother, surely understanding she could not win on that front, quickly changed tactics.

"Montrose plays a very fine game of *vingt-un,* something he presumably learned in the nursery. I cannot credit his memory much for remembering it, for surely he has only recently departed his nanny's leading strings."

"Impatient girl! He is not so very much younger than you, and will surely grow into his position before too many years are gone. Then some other girl will get him, and all that is his, and you shall regret ever slighting him."

"I do not think I shall, for I would always think of him as I see him now—a little boy fond of his toys, and hardly aware of what to do with a lady." Laurel's voice faded off as she spoke the last words, recalling with perfect clarity the responses of someone who knew precisely what to do.

Mrs. Gardiner looked at her suspiciously. "And yet your good friend, Miss Croyden, entertained us with stories of her own beloved, a man she knew from the time he was a boy. They played together as children, and she did not disparage his youth or inexperience at all."

"But still he abandoned her, so perhaps she did not know him as well as all that."

"Who is to say?" Mrs. Gardiner sighed. "I only hope in your preoccupation with your friend you do not allow her to get what you, yourself, desire."

"What do you mean, Mother?"

"I mean Montrose, of course. She may see an opportunity once she senses your indifference."

"She is welcome to him, though I give her more credit than that."

"She may consider him a bargain when she discovers your ridiculous scheme to pair her to a groom or a chimney sweep, or whatever you have planned." Her mother managed to look very knowing, very superior, which was not altogether unjustified. "I have not forgotten your determined words in London, my dear. And I have never doubted your ability to do anything to which you set your mind."

Laurel felt oddly touched. "I only wish to see my friend happy."

"And I only wish to see my daughter happy," said Mrs. Gardiner, and opened her arms. It took Laurel but a second's time to find comfort in the protective, soft warmth she had known since babyhood. Perhaps she proved not so much more mature than Montrose, after all. Indeed, she would have liked to remain thus, until her mother reminded her they both had purpose for this afternoon without the guests. "I shall roll up my sleeves and retire to the kitchen now. But you will not join me?" she sighed, into Laurel's hair.

"Not today, Mother. I have other work to keep me busy, and all of it in the sunshine."

"Then do not forget your bonnet. When Montrose grows up, he may prefer a woman without freckles on her nose."

"I would not entertain such hopes, Mother. But I will find my bonnet, just the same."

Mrs. Gardiner nodded and started towards the stairway to the kitchen. Laurel went in the opposite direction, up the grand staircase that led to the family chambers above, and grateful for the easy excuse of finding her bonnet. There were other things she required, and she preferred not to answer any questions about them.

She moved along the hallway, waiting until one of the maids passed her with the day's collection of laundry, and then she ducked into her oldest brother's chamber. The room was dark and smelled faintly of the bay rum with which he liked to shave. She missed George, she realized, and knew they would soon lose him to Miss Corbett, a highly fashionable lady who fancied his wealth a good deal more than she fancied his business interests. But George was not one to decline a move that would be advantageous to him or to the family, and so Laurel preferred to believe that the couple genuinely cared for each other. They would not be considered unusual by anyone in society if they did not, but George deserved better than that.

He also, she briefly reflected, deserved better than having his younger sister ransack his armoire and shaving table, but the damage she did to him this day would in no way affect his future happiness. She was certain he owned many garments newer and more stylish than what she now appropriated from his wardrobe, and would never miss the soap and razor she discovered among his other personal possessions.

Feeling like a common thief—which she supposed she was—she stuffed her brother's things into a carpetbag and stood cautiously at the door to his room before she made good her escape. She moved quickly to the back hallway, leading to a veranda which added much to the symmetry of Greenbriars but nothing to its comforts, and passed beneath the portraits of austere looking men and women with whom Mr. Gardiner endeavored to legitimize his ownership of the estate. She knew not who they were, only they were in no way related to her. Nor might they wish to be, if they knew what she was about.

The stairway was deserted, as she fully expected, and she made her way down with impunity. The bag proved heavy and she considered borrowing a cart to transport it to the smokehouse. But then there would be questions, and someone would surely mention her request to her father, and the whole purpose of her errand would be defeated. So she hoisted the bag onto her shoulder, and went off in the direction of the path around the lake.

The smokehouse was deserted, though the odor of freshly sawed wood alerted her to a repair of the ceiling. She knew nothing about such things, but recognized amateurish effort when she saw it. She guessed Robbie Darkwood had been at work here to protect her precious volumes from the elements. The knowledge moved her as no gesture from a suitor ever had, and she felt a renewed sense of purpose in introducing that enigmatic man to her friend.

Leaving the unwieldy bag in the smokehouse, she went out to find him.

The hermitage was empty, something Laurel quickly determined when she glanced through the windows and entered through the door that was slightly ajar. Or became slightly ajar when she pushed against it. She paused in the doorway and studied the cottage that no longer bore her distinctive stamp but that of another, and thought he did it credit. The main room, comprising nearly all of the space, was neat and tidy, and filled with the comforts of a rugged life. She walked over to a bowl of apples on the table, and thought her use of the word "comfort" might be a little overstated, as the fruits were small, wormy, things.

But perhaps that did not matter too much to a hermit.

What did matter? Would he appreciate the crisply laundered shirts she brought, and the spicy soaps? Did he know how to tie a cravat in a style considered fashionable—or at all? Would he think George's fitted jacket constricting after his robe? Would it even fit?

Somehow, Laurel needed to know these things, and she could not continue to deceive herself into thinking it entirely on Penelope's behalf. From the moment she'd met the hermit, accosting him outside the cottage she believed to be entirely her own, she'd wanted to know more about him, and could scarcely keep away. She told herself it had to do with sudden boredom, as she readjusted to life away from society. But even as her brothers filled the house with lively and attractive guests, and particularly elegant, well-groomed men, she found herself thinking of little else but him.

It was absurd, to be sure. But then, many things were absurd.

She glanced around the room, remembering how her books once lined the wooden shelves along the walls. Some would say it absurd a young lady read books to gain knowledge for which she could never have use. But the hermit never said that. And perhaps that was one reason why she wanted to know more about him.

She walked out of his cottage, leaving the door just as she found it, or nearly so. He need never know she invaded his privacy, unless he just now came down the path.

Laurel looked up, half expecting to see him, but knew Prinny would have announced their entrance with his usual fuss and enthusiasm. Instead, the goats and sheep grazed placidly in the nearby pen, and a few plump chickens pecked about beneath an oversized sunflower. Surely there was something most significant about this place now, for what for her had been a simple refuge was for the hermit a real home.

The path she took towards the orchard was muddy and slightly overgrown, but he must have used it recently to harvest the meager crop she saw within. Neither he nor Prinny were there now, nor, she realized as she set off on a long walk, were they in the wood, in the meadow, or near the lake. She understood perfectly the hermit's mission to remain hidden from view, but thus far that had not included her own view, and she became increasingly frustrated with his absence.

The day was warm, and her exercise made it even warmer. Her bonnet, instead of protecting her from the sunshine made her damp hair cloying and uncomfortable, and so Laurel removed it. In doing so, several of her pins came loose, and her hair fell down upon her neck and shoulders. With impatient fingers, she pulled the recalcitrant tresses into some order, though probably not sufficiently to make her appear respectable. Indeed, she probably looked a fair partner to the hermit this afternoon.

Thinking of him yet again, and with no more provocation than she usually required, she decided to retrace her steps through the woodlands, his veritable kingdom. Wherever else he lived, whatever else he had known, remained a mystery to her, and one he did not care to explain. It seemed as if he had sprung up on this very spot, with no history or past, and a future that held little ambition but to remain. This did not seem to pose much of a problem for her father, who must have seen some credentials before hiring him, but it proved a problem for her.

Robbie Darkwood could be a murderer, for all she knew. Or a French spy. He could be hiding from ruthless creditors. Or from pirates.

Or from a wife.

Laurel stopped on the path. How strange the notion had never occurred to her until now; how disastrous it would be should it prove true. Of course the hermit could be married, for though he denied real knowledge of women, Laurel possessed sufficient evidence he was not a novice in certain pleasurable arts. He might very well have a wife and even children, poor wretches all to have been abandoned by him.

And yet she would have her good friend meet him?

The more she walked, the more bothered and warm she became, until she thought she would like nothing more than a swim in the lake. It was impossible, of course, for it was something she had not been permitted to do for several years. But she remembered how it felt to be enveloped by the cool water, to have it stream through her hair and over her heated body. And when she would finally emerge, sometimes blue-lipped from the chill, she seemed renewed and redeemed, and quite prepared to meet any challenge.

Laurel closed her eyes, wishing she dared to do such a thing again, and silently cursing the proprieties that made such a thing impossible. Even so, with the vividness of memory, she imagined herself still immersed in that other world. And in doing so, cooled her heated soul.

"Would you be a statue in your father's Roman landscape, Miss Gardiner?" a voice asked so quietly Laurel thought it only the wind.

"And have the sunshine beat down upon me so relentlessly that it would burn an admirer to touch me?" she nevertheless answered, and smiled.

He groaned. "You do not require the sun to have that effect on an admirer."

Laurel opened her eyes and saw the hermit directly in front of her, not five feet away. His hood was pulled off his face, though the fastener at his neck held it secure, and his black hair stood up in spiky damp peaks, as if he had run anxious fingers through it.

"Where have you been?" she asked abruptly.

He looked surprised. "In the lake, doing what most men do when they have worked hard in the hot sun." He seemed to reflect on this a moment, and added, "And when they cannot afford the luxury of a proper bath."

"Oh," Laurel said, and felt her face burn from more than the sunshine. "Even those who can afford such a luxury sometimes enjoy a swim in the lake."

The hermit shifted his arms under his dark robe. "And what, might I ask, does a lady of refined tastes know of bathing with the fish?"

"A good deal, as it turns out, which proves my point that you know nothing of ladies. And I certainly never made claims to refinement, in any case."

"One need not make claims, when the proof of it is self-evident."

"My parents would be very glad to hear it," Laurel said, trying to deflect what seemed to be his second compliment in only a few minutes. She was not quite sure his comment about people burning at the touch of her was entirely intended to flatter. "They are possessed of fears I did not turn out well, though I suspect it is the concern of every parent. I wonder, what do your parents think of your chosen profession?"

Robbie Darkwood did not answer, but his eyes never left her face. Laurel knew he was not avoiding her question, but answering it in his own way. Indeed, he seemed to say, what would any parents think of a son closeting himself away from society?

"Were you in need of me?" he asked suddenly.

Oh, yes, she thought, though he was not to know how much. She looked at him, not sure how to answer.

"You said you were looking for me?"

Good sense returned like a dowsing of cold lake water.

"I most certainly did not. I merely wanted to know where you were."

"And I have told you. Now, perhaps you could tell me why it matters?" His eyes finally left her face, and looked beyond her, up the hill. Catching the light of the sun, they appeared very light against his tanned skin.

"It matters little, but I wished to thank you for the repair to the roof of the smokehouse." Laurel paused, trying to remember the real reason why she had just hiked an hour through field and wood trying to find him. "Oh, yes. And I brought you a small present."

The light eyes returned to her and visibly brightened. And why not? One of the sacrifices one made by living a solitary life surely was the deprivation of small unexpected pleasures.

"It is not proper for a young lady to give a gentleman a present, you know."

Laurel looked at him knowingly, wondering if he yet realized his slip of phrase. "But you are not a gentleman, Hermit. And I have already told you I do not make claims to refinement, though it would please my parents very much if I did. In any case, when you see my small offering, you will agree that nothing about it is proper."

His look of surprise would have been wonderfully laughable if he did not take himself so very seriously.

"Then I do not want it," he said. "Please take it away."

"I will not, for I want for you to have it. In fact, you must have it before you can meet my friend."

"Your friend from London?" he asked carelessly, and shrugged. "It is not a thing I prefer to do, as I have already said. I have enough ladies in my life."

Surely he meant a wife or a lover. And yet, somehow Laurel believed that there was no lady in his life but herself, and that she engaged him completely. She took a deep breath, and prayed for sanity to return. "It is a great pity you do not wish to meet my friend, for it most certainly is going to happen. You shall have to endure the great hardship of acquaintance with a lady of elegance, refinement and beauty. But for now, I would ask you to accompany me to the smokehouse, for it is where I left your gifts some time ago."

Laurel saw his reluctance but dismissed it, feeling a growing confidence that beneath his robes, he was a man who would refuse her nothing. But still he did not move and stood in the way of her progress. She hesitated, not daring to think what might happen if she provoked him, and tried to understand what was going on in his mind and—God help her—his body. Lifting her chin, she stepped forward and brushed against him on the narrow path. And got precisely that for which she asked.

The hermit caught her around her waist and pulled her even closer to him, so close she could smell the fishy scent of the lake upon his skin. Laurel breathed it in, invoking the cool and redemptive waters that might calm her spirit.

"Why will you not leave me be?" Robbie Darkwood whispered into her ear, his lips pressed to her skin. She heard the plea of a drowning man, of his floundering desperation. But she also felt the sweet thrill of seduction and knew that if he drowned, she would willingly go down with him.

"I cannot leave you be," she confessed, and it was the truth. She did not know what made her continue to seek him out and wonder at his life, or made her think of him in her dreams, both day and night. It somehow had become a fact of her life, igniting her passions, and the very reason why she looked to each day with a new sense of purpose and excitement. Laurel moved her head back and forth, as his lips grazed against her ear, her cheek, her hair. As gentle as the pressure was, she felt as if he branded her with his mark. She sighed and turned so that she faced him, her eyes at a level with the twisted collar of his robe. "But I might ask why you do not simply run from me each time I approach and abandon me to the witless society of Misses Winthrop and Fellows."

"Because I cannot," he echoed. "And the more fool I."

"Then you must gratify my desire, Robbie Darkwood," Laurel said into his collar, and heard him suck in his breath. She thought of a hundred ways in which he might gratify every desire of every dream from which she awoke damp and trembling, but she reluctantly willed herself to restore some sense of reason to them both. "You will come with me and see what I have brought you."

"Why not come with me and see what I can give you, instead?"

Laurel opened her lips, but no words would come. Her head dropped back so she could look up at him and truly understand what he was offering, and what he would want of her.

The answer was there, as plainly as if he spoke the words aloud. It was in his eyes, the tense lines around his mouth, his overall questioning expression.

"Come with me," he repeated.

"To the shed?" Laurel asked.

"To your hermitage," he corrected, and pulled her along the path. He nearly had to carry her, for all her legs could hold her. It was not fear that incapacitated her, for she wanted him and trusted him. Rather, it seemed to have to do with the very strength of her desire, centered at the core of her being, and handicapping all else.

Whatever Robbie Darkwood was feeling, all his parts seemed to be in working order, for he finally lost patience with their slow progress up the slope and lifted her into his arms.

"Dear God," Laurel sighed, though loud enough for him to hear her.

He stopped short, and looked down at her, so close that their noses nearly touched.

"Tell me now if you wish to abandon this foolishness, my dear," he said. "For whatever reason, whatever discomfort, whatever fears."

"Is it foolishness, Hermit?" she asked.

"Almost certainly. But, so help me, I never wanted to do a thing so dearly, nor wanted anyone as much as I want you. It defies everything I have determined for myself."

Laurel leaned back against his shoulder, refusing to consider how very much they were about to complicate their lives. She studied the rough roof of the hermitage as they came close to it and felt the jolt to the Hermit's body as he kicked open the door. He turned slightly so they could pass through the narrow portal into the earthy, musty main room of the dwelling, and she breathed in deeply the scent of ripe fruit, dry hay, and rich sandalwood soap.

He brought her to the narrow mattress and bent at the waist to settle Laurel on its edge. For all the rustic charm of the place, the furnishings seemed clean enough, and certainly no worse than when she sought sanctuary here with her books and dreams. Indeed, looking up at him now, with doubt and desire alternating in the expressions of his face, Laurel knew that some of her dreams were about to be realized.

"I wish you would not hide yourself with this," she said, tugging on his cape. "I want nothing more than to see what you look like."

He loosened the cord at his neck and shrugged off the offending garment, revealing a form and features even more beautiful than she remembered from their first meeting. "It is the very reason for it, for I do not wish to be seen by anyone." His eyes never left her face as he amended, "I did not wish to be seen by anyone."

Laurel lifted her legs beneath her and rose onto her knees, so they would be once again face-to-face, or nearly so. She set upon his threadbare shirt with a determination that bordered on reverence, already knowing what she would find beneath, for she imagined it often enough. The shirt fell off his shoulders to join the wretched cape on the ground, and she wished her own stifling garments consigned to a similar fate. But first, she only wanted to look at him.

His skin, tanned and smooth, was warm to her touch, and the

sprinkling of freckles across his shoulders revealed a habit of working shirtless in the summer sunshine. Whorls of hair lighter than that on his head made a pattern on his chest, thinning to a fine line over his taut stomach and brushing his navel. Laurel caught her breath, barely able to breath, and allowed her hands to travel down the sinewy muscles of his arms to rest upon his wrists.

"A bit of a disappointment," he said hoarsely, "especially for a young lady accustomed to the ideal proportions of the Roman gods in the Via Italiano?"

What could he be thinking? Was her hermit so far removed from society he did not understand how he would look to someone who desired him as much as she did?

"I believe the last time I passed through my father's sculpture garden, I only saw you. I was not disappointed then, nor am I now. Now I believe your ridiculous cape is something more than a hindrance; it is a desecration. Tell me, Robbie Darkwood, are all hermits as beautiful as you?"

The hermit made a noise deep in his throat and sat heavily on the sagging mattress. The shifting balance of the pallet made her fall back against him, and he seized his advantage, for, from behind her, his hands caressed her neck and shoulders.

"I care not about other hermits, bless their wretched souls. I only know that I am here with you, well beyond anything I can deserve, and that there is nothing that can make claim to beauty while you are here. All else falls into your shadow. I hope you have been told how very exquisite you are and have believed every knave who said so in the past," he said against her ear.

His warm lips tickled her, and she laughed in complete defiance of the solemnity of the moment. "If they were knaves, why should I believe them? And how do I know your words are any different?"

He hesitated, and she knew the moment was as difficult for him as it was for her, fraught with complications that would belie desires if their passions did not run so strong.

"Because we are about to risk everything, my dearest love. There could be no going back, no matter what happens this afternoon," he said gently, and as if to punctuate his point, started unfastening the row of tiny mother-of-pearl buttons that followed the line of her spine. Laurel sat quietly, patiently, trying to will her heart to calm its tumultuous pace. It did not get any easier when her yellow gown slipped off her shoulders and Robbie Darkwood brought his large hands under her arms to cup her breasts, still restrained by the stiff fabric of her corset.

Her gown pooled around her waist like some brilliant flower. But the Hermit impatiently pushed the fine fabric aside when he suddenly lifted her onto his lap, the better to make quick work of her stays. Laurel looked down at his calloused and stained hands, the hands of a workman on her lace trimmed French garment, and covered them with her own.

"Should we stop?" he asked gently.

Laurel answered him by shifting in his lap, and she felt the immediate and indisputable evidence of his need. But how would he know of hers if she no longer had the voice to answer him?

She slipped off his lap and stood shakily at the edge of the bed, her legs between his. After looking at him for one deep moment, she then turned her attention to her corset and loosened her stays with hands more accustomed to delicate tasks. When the garment fell away from her body, her sigh was an echo of his.

Wordlessly, he pulled her down beside him on their narrow bed, reaching for a frayed and folded sheet to protect what little remained of her modesty, since the air, even within the dark hermitage, was quite warm.

"It is not necessary," she said, and stayed his hand. "I would much rather there be no secrets between us."

He hesitated, and she guessed he would still hold on to his own secret. But she was too far gone for it to matter, or for her to care. Indeed, it was impossible for her to care about anything, but for the fact that his hand was inching up her thigh beneath the clean cotton shift, until it came to rest at the apex of her legs.

"Robbie, please," she pleaded.

"I will stop," he said, his voice hoarse..

She reached for his hand, and covered it tightly. "You will not," she gasped.

"I will not," he agreed, and with his other hand pulled the shift off her twisting body and threw it on the ground. But he did stop then, and Laurel watched him.

There was no mistaking the worshipful look on his face as his eyes traveled over her nakedness, pausing on her breasts, her belly, even on a birthmark that marred the smooth flesh of her hip. When he bent down to kiss it, she thought she would scream with pleasure. And when his lips traveled across her body, to her navel and below, she could no longer restrain herself.

His gentle fingers and teasing tongue explored every inch of her, until she thought she would die of passion. And when, suddenly and unexpectedly, her whole body shuddered in a release that was both pain and pleasure, she thought she had arrived in Heaven.

Robbie covered her panting body with his, warming her against the chills that now made her tremble.

"I did not know . . ." she began.

"Hush," he murmured, and pressed his body against her. His breeches were rough against her naked skin.

"But there is more, is there not?" she asked, and heard him laugh.

"Of course there is," she answered herself, increasingly aware of her newly found feminine powers. She dipped her hand between their prone bodies, until she was able to caress the most insistent part of him, even through the cloth. He raised his hips, and she struggled to relieve him of his garments and add them to the growing pile on the rough wooden floor.

Her hand ran up and down the naked length of him, wondering how on earth they would manage, and if she could possibly be mistaken about what she now wanted of him.

"Robbie?" she asked.

"Know that I would not hurt you for anything in the world," was all he said, and took her hand away to join her other on the pillow above her head. Then, his eyes never leaving her face, he poised himself above her and used his legs to spread hers on the mattress. Pausing just to catch his breath, he pressed against her to enter her, stopping at her cry of pain, and then filling her with sensation.

His body established a rhythm that she was powerless to resist, and she instinctively wrapped her legs around his waist. When he suddenly stopped, she thought she had done something horribly wrong, until he thrust again, gasping her name. A moment later, he collapsed over her, his heart racing like a stallion's after a race.

"Oh, my lord," Laurel sighed.

Robbie Darkwood turned to gaze questioningly into her eyes for a moment, before gathering her into the shelter of his damp body.

* * * *

Rob did not know how long they slept, but the man who thought he would have made a fine hermit awakened into a whole new world, with none of the old rules holding true. To be sure, loyal Prinny was stretched out on the floor beneath them, licking those parts of Rob's body that had slipped off the narrow mattress. One hand and foot were claimed by the dog. But everything else, including his heart, was now owned by the lady whose tangled hair was spread across his chest and shoulders. Pulling her against him, he heard her sigh and felt her uncurl her limbs so that she now was pressed against the length of him. All thoughts of Prinny vanished.

Her eyes were closed, their lashes fanned out on her cheeks, but he doubted she slept. One of her hands flicked away the tangled sheet and hovered about his hip, tantalizing him with the prospects of an examination either northerly or southerly.

She went southerly.

"We must not, my dear," he protested, though his body thought otherwise.

Apparently, Laurel Gardiner preferred to listen to his body, and perhaps to hear it better, started to work her lips down his contours, until her mouth met with her teasing, tempting hand. He could not tell, but preferred to think her eyes were open now, studying him, and she was learning what would please him most. When he thought he could contain himself no longer, he pulled her up to sit astride him, and, his eyes never leaving her flushed face, slowly entered her. If she had not been awake before, she most certainly was now, for he saw that what he did shocked her.

He cupped her hips, his thumbs arching toward her navel. She was smaller than he thought, and weighed hardly anything as she sat upon him. But it was enough, for he started a rhythm that she matched almost at once, her breasts rising and falling as she gasped for breath. So nearly timed were they, the explosion of their release came at nearly the same moment, for when he came to his senses, she had collapsed upon him.

Rob lay on his back, staring at the whitewashed ceiling, and knew that everything he had attempted to do for many months was now all for naught. He had sought to create a new person, born of the earth like Adam himself, and believed he might live a life untouched and free of obligations. But then an Eve was set down in his Eden, offering nothing more than herself as temptation, and he did not merely taste, but completely devoured every bit of forbidden fruit.

And yet, paradoxically, he found himself in Paradise.

What was to be done?

Laurel stirred, and sighed. Ever so gently, he pulled her hair away from her face. She pulled herself up onto his elbows, still balanced on his chest, and looked down into his face as if she had no idea how he came to be there.

Rob supposed he should be insulted, but, in truth, he scarcely understood it himself.

"Robbie Darkwood!" she cried.

"And none other, my love," he said, pulling the sheet up around her bare shoulders. "Nothing has changed in the past hour."

"You are quite wrong, I fear," she said, and then settled her head back onto his shoulder. "Indeed, everything has changed."

She was right, of course. However he now chose to extricate himself from the rubble of his past, he had to think about what he had done and accept the consequences.

"So it has," he said thoughtfully into her hair. "We shall be married, of course, and you shall have the protection of my name and my love."

Laurel shifted to look up at him again and trifled with his beard. "I am happy for your love, as I hope you are for mine. I do not know how this has happened, but I find I am quite powerless to resist it. Or you." She paused and kissed him full on the lips, tasting a bit like the soap with which he had bathed. "But what you propose is quite impossible. Marry a hermit? I fear I would sacrifice my own happiness in this matter, for to marry you would be the death of my father. However would he bear it?"

They lay for several moments in silence, while Rob thought about her words, and how her sense of practical obligations ran entirely counter to the abandon with which she had allowed him to make love to her. For the first time, he felt the protruding straws of their mattress scratching his sun-reddened back and the rock-hard lumpiness of the pillow.

But Lauren must have been thinking about her words as well, for she whispered, "But how would I ever bear parting from you or marrying another?"

Rob forgot about his discomforts and tried to claim some small parcel of hope for them both. "There are things about me you do not know," he said, even as he wondered what ought to be revealed, and when. "I am not what I seem."

"I should think not," she said, giggling, unmindful of anything compelling about his words. "For one, I would like to see what your chin looks like beneath this tangle. If it is as compelling as the rest of you, I shall be well satisfied."

"My dear, I am not trying to be clever."

"And I am not trying to be coy. I have already taken on a hermit, poor shrouded creature that he was, and discovered a splendid man. Can you yet have more surprises, another layer to be revealed?"

Rob grunted as he pulled the two of them up to lean against the wall behind them. The sheet slipped down to Laurel's waist and his, but she either did not notice or care. In fact, she seemed particularly intent on the hair that whorled around his nipple.

"I fear I do, and they may not make you happy," he managed to say through his distraction.

"Then do not say it. Let us stay as we are, safe in our hermitage," she said softly, and blew against his hardened nipple.

"It is not possible, no matter how romantic the prospect. We shall soon have to go back to being the hermit and Miss Laurel Gardiner. You have a house of guests to entertain, and a friend due to arrive soon. For if we continue as we are, there may be consequences of the love we share, if there is not already." If she did not already understand of what he spoke, he brought his hand down to the edge of the sheet and gently caressed her belly.

Laurel sighed. "For someone as sheltered from the world as you claim to be, you have a very honest view of our society, my dear hermit. I am not sure I ought to introduce you to my friend."

"It is as I wish, and have always wished."

"And yet I believe we cannot escape the acquaintance, as she is due to arrive shortly. You must promise me you will not reveal what has happened between us."

"That I love you, do you mean?"

"Of course not. Have we not already decided that it is impossible?"

"I believe you have decided that," he said calmly. "Is it rather that I have hopelessly compromised a very fine lady who should have had nothing to do with me after our first disagreeable meeting?"

Laurel found a scar that he had borne since he was a small child and kissed it. "I do not recall anything disagreeable about it, sir. Indeed, I could scarcely get you out of my mind since!" She abandoned the scar and lay down upon him, once again. "Oh, dear, Robbie, it is such a tangle. Quite as dreadful as your beard. I did not think such a thing could happen. But you will meet my dear friend, and you will find her quite acceptable, I am sure."

"I do not wish to find her acceptable. I do not wish to find anyone acceptable; I am a bloody hermit! Have you listened to anything I have said, Miss Laurel Gardiner? Or have you listened to your own heart?"

Laurel stiffened, and Rob hated himself for treating her rudely.

But did she truly imagine they could emerge into the sunshine without a backwards glance at what they had already shared?

"That does not make sense, sir hermit," she said, interrupting his thoughts.

"Then we are back where we started, I think," he growled, and rolled over so she was once again beneath him on the bed. And indeed they were where they had started, and their pleasure was in no way diminished for the repetition.

* * * *

Laurel walked as if in a dream, her lover clearing the branches on the path before them. She supposed she ought to feel shy after what they had done together, the extraordinary liberties she had allowed him to take and had taken herself, and yet nothing felt so right, so blessed, as his presence so close to her, his earthy scent lingering on her body. With his help, she managed to pull herself back into her garments, and in turn she assisted in covering up his splendidly muscled body beneath his tattered robes.

Now she was returning to her parents' house, a different woman than when she left it some time before. She stumbled, and Robbie's arm shot out from beneath the cloth to steady her.

"You are in pain, and I am sorry," he said. "If I had the slightest bit of resistance where you are concerned, I would not have imposed myself upon you again and again."

Laurel bit down on her lip. Surely he was being polite, preferring to ignore the fact she was a very quick study and had wanted everything he had offered. She did feel sore, but her hermit had offered her several compensations for any discomfort she might feel. She smiled, thinking of the delicious things they had done, unimagined in her experience only hours before.

"I will ask your father for your hand," he said once again. "There is simply no other way."

"If we have not made a child this day, then let there be an end to such protestations, Robbie. I do not feel ruined, nor might it ever matter, for I may not marry at all."

"You will not have me," he said, as if he could not imagine why it should be so.

"I have already had you, my love," she said, "as you have had me. We did not plan for it, and ought not burden ourselves with recriminations. Please, Robbie, do not take away from what we have shared."

He turned away and paused at the fork in the path. The sun was already low in the sky, and his body cast a long shadow on the path she wished for them to take. "I assume we are going to the smokehouse?"

"It is where I left a present for you. Truly, it was my only intention when I sought you out this day."

The hermit made a noise from deep in his throat. "It is I who should be bringing something for you, but I am quite unprepared. But I will accept your offering, if you will allow me to give you a token in return."

"It is not a token at all, dear hermit," she said, her thoughts racing ahead to other things of a more personal nature, with which she would like to indulge him.

"Very well," he said discouragingly, "but I hope it does not contain food, for Prinny will almost certainly have gotten into it. He has taken to the smokehouse, though I do not see anything appealing there but for your occasional presence."

Laurel knew she was fully devoid of all rational thought when the devotion of a mongrel could make her passions surge again with dizzying heat. But of course, she responded not to thoughts of the dog, but of his master. She attempted a smile and started to walk up the path, gently brushing against the large body that nearly blocked her way.

"He undoubtedly smells the beef that cured there long ago," she said, as she lifted her skirt to tread over the rocks.

Robbie Darkwood laughed, which proved a great relief, for it had the final effect of restoring some sense of normalcy to their conversation. "Or rather, he waits for your arrival."

They walked along for several moments in silence, until they crested the familiar ridge on the hillside. "And there he is."

Laurel looked up to see Prinny poised for their arrival, wagging his tail so fiercely she guessed that she might have been anticipated after all.

"You see I am correct," Robbie said

Indeed, he was. He was correct to offer her marriage, to voice his concerns and even regrets. He was correct to distrust her interest in introducing him to Penelope Croyden, as he undoubtedly would soon resist her efforts to make him dress like a gentleman. He was correct about many things, but he did not attempt to dominate or bully her in an effort to get his own way. She had never known a man like him.

"You are correct about your dog," Laurel said, trying to sound sensible. "I daresay one could write a long list of those things about which you are in error."

She felt him look down at her. "It would be longer than you could possibly know, my dear. But then, that is why I have chosen to live the life of a hermit, to correct them."

Laurel supposed her mind should be hard at work deciphering the meaning of his careless confession, but instead her heart soared to hear the equally careless endearment on his lips.

She looked up, and was right about the direction of his gaze. Under the shadow of his heavy hood, his light eyes surely recognized her flush as pleasure.

"Well, here we . . . " Laurel's words were lost as something crashed into her midsection, making her lose her balance. But the hermit's strong arms were around her in a moment, steadying her.

"Prinny! Behave yourself, boy!" Robbie Darkwood scolded, and then, softly, once again against Laurel's ear, "Did I not tell you where his affections lie?"

"So you did. I shall have to remember to bring him a gift the next time I am about, for he is sure to appreciate his more than you shall enjoy yours." She extricated herself from his hold, determined to behave herself. Things could not continue as they had begun. After all, had she not already resolved to redeem the happiness of her good friend? Had she not already decided that her hermit needed to be restored to society? And yet things seemed to be moving quite in the wrong direction, for if she continued to fall into his arms at every opportunity, the only society he would share would be hers alone.

The prospect was Elysian.

"Ah yes, your gift," he reminded her, as if he knew what she had been thinking and that it would lead them down the wrong path. "I confess, it does not sound very promising at all. You have not brought me food—more is the pity—and have just revealed that you do not think I will enjoy it. Was there ever a gift delivered with less hope of gratitude?"

Laurel looked over his hooded head to watch a hawk hovering above the lake and thought of what he had already revealed to her. He was a gentle man of intelligence and wit, with none of the deformities of which she had accused him at their first meeting, who hid himself away from the world because of wrongs he did not know how to make right. Somewhere there must be people who cared for him, who worried about him, who wanted him home, for all his faults. And yet he could not, would not, return, and instead tried to find hope in a life of deprivation and isolation. It was not a natural state for man. And certainly not for this man.

"I could offer you pity," she heard herself say. "But I am quite certain you would not be grateful for that either."

"Pity?" he laughed, though without the slightest trace of humor. "I have the sky above me, the lake before me, a companionable, but rude, puppy, and the warm earth at my feet." He turned to her and raised his eyebrow. "I only lack for . . . "

"Fresh clothing, sir," Laurel broke in quickly, not wishing to hear what she knew he would say.

Robbie Darkwood looked at her with such misgiving one might imagine she had proposed to make the garments herself, out of table linens and draperies.

"Clothing? You are quite mistaken, my love. I have all the garments I need. And I launder them regularly, no matter what you may think." He started to move away, like a guilty boy trying to evade an unpleasant task.

Laurel, having grown up in a household of such boys, lost her patience.

"In lake water, Hermit?" she asked, no longer in the voice of his lover. "If you continue as you are, the cats will take you for a trout, so strong will be the smell of fish on you."

He looked insulted, which she supposed was fair enough.

"If I correctly recall my purpose for living on your father's estate, Madam, it is to be left alone and not interfere with the company of others. Therefore, it should not matter to you or anyone else if I smell like a fishpond or a cabbage or a stable."

"Nor should it matter if you smell like lemon verbena or sandalwood or bay rum," she said. "And it matters very much to me, as you know too well."

He had already turned away from her, prepared, it seemed, to abandon her and her frivolous offering. But now he looked over his shoulder, where the cheap, dark cloth bunched up to make his broad back even more imposing, and where a jagged tear looked like a scar of war. "Have you just opened the door to admit my hope?"

"I do not know," Laurel confessed, a little desperately. "But I would like for you to meet my friends, including the dear lady who is soon to arrive."

A mask came down over his features.

"Of course," he said, and shrugged. "I will do it, for you wish me to do so, though I could think of several other things that would make us both happier. And they certainly have nothing to do with putting on clothing."

The hermit paused in his speech, though it was Laurel who needed the moment to catch her breath. Lord, what this man did to her!

"But I have already agreed to this, have I not?" he continued. "You caught me in a moment of weakness when I promised to meet your friend, but meet her I shall. I will dress up for her, and brush back my hair, and use your fine soap to wash the smell of fish from my body. I will leave my robe and Prinny locked in the hermitage. I will hold some discourse on the weather perhaps, or on the elegance of current fashion. There. Will that do?"

He paused but a moment before rushing on, and Laurel thought she heard the flickering of anger in his voice. "I will ask, however, for some discretion on your part. I do not intend to provide entertainment for other bored young ladies who do not succeed in finding a gentleman to cater to their whims or amuse them with witty conversation. I will agree to do this just once, and I will allow myself to be sufficiently impressed with your paragon of a friend. But let her be the last of them, for I have already made my choice. And if you will not have me, then I will have my solitude."

Laurel felt the sting of his rebuff, as he truly intended, and wondered at the unaccustomed authority in his voice. Whoever he was, whatever he had been, he was a man who expected others to listen to him and respect him. Perhaps even a hermit owned some measure of pride and did not desire to be burdened with the company of women who were rejected by other men, no matter how lofty their introductions. Laurel was suddenly mortified by her own behavior.

"I expect it will be the last of it," she said regretfully, and met his gaze again, "and I will not bother you again with my frivolous plans. In fact, it would be better if I do not bother you at all. I am sorry for having done so."

She saw the protest form wordlessly on his lips, and quickly cut off his opportunity for rebuttal by pushing past him to the entrance of the smokehouse. She felt him following her, felt the coolness of the shadow of his body against her back, and could not help wondering what he might have done in the close confines of the tiny shed if they did not enter as adversaries.

But he, perhaps wisely, did not enter. Instead, as her eyes adjusted to the darkness within, he waited for her in the narrow doorway, propping open the ineptly repaired door.

Groping for her bundle, she turned around, wondering if he would wish to try on George's garments, as she was a little anxious they would fit. But she saw him only as a dark shadow against the glare and decided they could best conduct their business in daylight. Apparently, he felt the same, for he moved as if he were the door itself, one shoulder at the hinge and the other arching open, and she walked through, trying hard not to touch him.

She did not, nor did he so much as graze against her hand as they opened the large bag together.

"Why, what is this, Miss Gardiner?" Robbie Darkwood asked as he held up a stiffly starched linen shirt. She was relieved to hear something of his old teasing tone. "This does not appear to be the usual fare for working men."

"I do not intend for you to wear it while you work. But I think it very fine if you were to join us at the ball we are to have in my friend's honor. It is already arranged, and all the neighborhood will be invited. And so you must attend as well."

"I do not think our arrangement extends to my appearing at a ball, no matter how varied the company. Indeed, I feel it is a very bad idea. Your father would certainly forbid it. And your brothers would undoubtedly toss me out with any impertinent servants, especially when they realize I am wearing . . ." His voice broke off as his fingers ran over the raised threads of embroidery at the neck of the shirt. "This is one of their shirts, I presume?"

"Neither Joe's nor Lewis's, so you need not fear," Laurel said, ignoring his other protestations. "These garments all belong to my brother George, and he remains in London, with Father's business."

"How very reassuring. Surely, Miss Gardiner, you will not have me wear another man's clothes?"

"I do not see why not. It is not as if George was murdered in them, or some other superstitious nonsense. He shall never miss them. We give our castoffs to the servants all the time, and they are grateful for them." She stopped speaking, wondering why a man who seemed to have nothing should mind receiving the bounty of another. It was the natural way of things, the most common form of charity. Unless, of course, one had never been the recipient of another's charity.

Laurel looked up at her hermit, wondering if he had ever been the object of someone's largesse.

"I am very happy, of course, that your beloved brother was not murdered in this shirt. Or at all, apparently. But that does not mean I will accept his clothing. I have superstitions of my own, you see. One of them is not to steal things belonging to another. I consider it very bad luck."

"My dear Mr. Darkwood, if you wish to tempt bad luck, I suggest you greet my good friend in that disgusting robe."

"At least it is mine."

"A point which does you little credit, sir."

"And yet, I do not assume another's identity with it."

"Have you not?" she said softly.

Awareness of her suspicions, of her growing understanding of him, of her intuitive knowledge, seemed to come to him in that instant, and he looked at her with something akin to shock. His defiance and boldness certainly vanished, though only for a moment, and was replaced with the somewhat confused expression of one discovered in a long perpetuated lie. Laurel felt an aching wave of compassion for him and for his desperate need to escape, mixed with a keen sense of guilt that she should be the one to expose him thus.

"No one will confuse you with my brother George," she went on, gently. "His hair is straight and of an indifferent brown, and his eyes as dark as mine. Oh yes; he almost never hides his fine features beneath a hood." Laurel did not pause to consider her words too closely, not really caring how she sounded But then, because he still had not answered her on the other, more disturbing point, she found herself pressing it again. "As you are no stranger to disguise, Robbie Darkwood, I do not understand why you are so reticent about this."

His unexpected weakness, briefly brought to the surface, vanished as suddenly as it appeared. She had not feared him when first they met, or when they fell upon each other among the statuary, or when he initiated her into the sweet arts of lovemaking. But yet, just now, there seemed something oddly threatening in his stance, something dangerous in his expression. Laurel guessed she would be called to account for her provocative remarks, and to reveal something of the picture she had already formed, during their many conversations, of disparate, dissected pieces.

"Whatever do you mean?" he asked, his silky voice holding a hint of warning.

The temptation to dive down with him into the depths of his mysterious past pulled at Laurel with all the accumulated weight of her unbidden feelings for him, but she resisted, not yet ready to take so precipitous a plunge. She looked unflinchingly into his light eyes and wondered if he saw in her an untutored girl who would play upon his emotions, or a woman worthy to descend with him, and yet survive. But she only saw the reflection of her own bright dress and nothing of the darkness within.

Laurel shifted her balance, and looked away. "I mean that you reveal yourself in so many unexpected ways. You would have me believe you some force of nature, at home in the wood and glades of Greenbriars, and yet I believe I myself know more about the flora and fauna growing around us. You say you know nothing of society, and still seem passably familiar with its workings. And you insist you are impoverished, but yet you have never met a gentleman who is willing to share the bounty of his discarded garments with you."

"Can it not be explained by the possibility I have never met a generous gentleman?"

"Or that you, yourself, are a gentleman?" she dared to ask.

She had him there; she saw it in the tight line of his jaw, and she believed she heard the click of more puzzle pieces coming together. She suddenly realized why he might ask her, a lady, to marry him, and expect that she would. But the picture remained far from complete.

"Would not a gentleman know the manner in which his garments were disposed?" he asked, as if stating the obvious.

Laurel would not be swayed by his perfect logic. "I doubt any gentleman pays much attention to the manner in which his clothes are discarded. Or laundered or repaired, for that matter," she said with the assurance gained from growing up in a household of brothers. "I wonder if a gentleman ever truly understands how a garment goes from lying in a soiled heap on the floor at the foot of his bed to a pressed and starched package in his armoire. What say you, Hermit? How do you suppose such a miracle is accomplished?"

She thought she saw him smile, and knew they no longer tread in dark waters, although the glimmer of amusement was quickly obscured by the seriousness of his response.

"My dear Miss Gardiner," he said, tantalizing her once again with his choice of words. "Of all men alive, I understand it is no miracle. I take great care to treat my poor clothing gently, for I know the burden of dealing with the consequences."

Now it was Laurel's turn to smile. "Then you truly are no gentleman, sir."

"I never said so, Miss Gardiner," he returned, and smiled again.

She seized hold of his good humor as if he threw a rope to save her. "All the more reason why you must accept this gift with gratitude. Imagine the hours it will save you, which could be better spent."

"I take it you mean with your friend?"

"Of course. I am sure you will find something acceptable here, something that suits both of you."

"And what if I do not?"

Laurel studied him with all the advantage of her growing understanding of him, caring not if he thought her impertinent. After all, she was also struggling to gain an understanding of what he might be thinking about her, and it made her bold. She could now envision him without the uneven growth of beard about his face, and the wild curls that framed his features. She thought a jacket would do much for him, even though she liked what she saw when he just wore a white shirt— or nothing at all. Leg-hugging pantaloons would have a decided appeal over the baggy trousers he wore. And if those garments were just a trifle too snug, all the better.

"I am certain something will suit, Hermit," she said, trying to sound cheerful. "Or I shall volunteer my own services to make alterations."

His answer was effectively drowned out by Prinny's barks, which may have been a very good thing indeed.

* * * *

Rob sucked in his breath and studied a portion of his torso at a time in the tiny reflecting glass that did service as the valet mirror in the hermitage. Damn George Gardiner after all. For not managing to keep his sister in London where she would have already been courted by a dozen eligible men. For not returning with her to Greenbriars and protecting her from poachers in his wood. And for being just a bit narrow in the chest and shoulders, so that his clothing might rip apart on a somewhat larger man.

Rob was now that man, somewhat improved upon by a regimen of hard labor and rustic living. And yet the borrowed finery proved to be an unexpected pleasure, for surely the last thing on Rob's mind when he abandoned the life he once knew was the fact that he would miss the fabrics and elegance of cut provided by the best tailors. When he packed only a few garments for a hitherto unchartered life, he had selected only the most practical sorts of clothing, and those items already showed signs of wear.

Undoubtedly, the impertinent and exquisite Miss Gardiner would chide him for not leaving such things for his servants, if ever she found out about it.

As he stood straight before the tarnished mirror, so that it reflected little more than the lower buttons on his jacket, he conceded that the lady knew a good deal more about his past than he thought he had ever revealed. Did he talk in his sleep perhaps? Did she overhear a rumor about him in town? But no, if she knew anything for certain, she would have tortured him with it at once. Or accepted his offer of marriage.

Instead, she thought to ease his way back into society by bringing him out like some prim miss in her first season. He was her damned cause, her reason to play the reformer. Well, fair enough. She was his cause as well.

He would not be satisfied until she agreed to marry him. For though he remained uncertain about a good many things, he knew he wanted nothing else but to share the rest of his life with Miss Laurel Gardiner, and could only curse the fact they had not met at another time, in another place.

But when, in the whole of his life before becoming a hermit, was it ever the right time, the right place? When had he ever had the freedom to choose his future and defy that which was always expected of him?

Never. He had chanced nothing until the calamitous day he uncovered certain painful, damaging truths and knew the only honorable course was to escape. To that point, nearly his twenty-seventh birthday, his life was as restrictive as the clothes he now wore.

Prinny barked, and Rob's thoughts changed abruptly to more practical matters, such as how to negotiate steps in such uncomfortable garments. Tentatively, carefully, he bent from the waist, thinking how familiar such movement was for him once, and how strange it now felt. He held out a hand to an imaginary partner—who closely resembled Miss Gardiner—and heard a slight tear of fabric at his shoulder. Perhaps he need not worry overmuch about George Gardiner accusing him of stealing his clothing, for it would be all but unrecognizable to the Londoner when utterly torn to shreds.

But yet the fine fabric held fast in the places that mattered most, and Rob thought they might do after all. He abandoned his imaginary partner with greater ease than he would ever abandon the flesh and blood Miss Gardiner, and thought of a more practical use for his new costume. Indeed, so many months had he been lost in his hermit's disguise, a pair of decent leggings and a well-tailored jacket made him feel as cunning as a man at a masquerade ball. With luck, he might remain as much a mystery dressed thusly as he could ever hope to be behind a mask.

And if he succeeded, he could also walk amongst the people of nearby Greenborough without arousing suspicion or particular inquiries into his life or identity. He might find companionship at the inn, and dispatch letters with the post. He could quietly retrieve the answers to those missives and determine how well his mother and young brother fared without him. He would not have left them in a muddle for all the world, but desperation had made him slightly mad and unforgivably thoughtless. Now, with the sobriety of time, he thought he might have handled the whole business somewhat better.

But perhaps it was not too late to repair the damage; surely it was not? He had spent months with little else to do but rethink the absurd and painful drama of his life and wonder how it might have all turned out differently—for better or, more likely, for worse. He thought of those he loved who had been hurt, and the home to which he somehow, precipitously, believed he might never again return.

And he thought, more and more in recent days, of how he might have hoped to be more than just a lowly hermit to someone whose opinion seemed to increasingly matter to him. Instead, Laurel brought him castoff clothing and leftover foodstuffs, as if he had never known such largesse, and let him know all his inadequacies as a farmer and a gentleman.

And yet, for all that, she allowed him to make love to her, to mark her for his own, to claim her as no one else ever had. Only once before had he ever behaved with such reckless abandon, so determined to overlook the consequences. And both times, his baser instincts triumphed over reason for the love of a woman.

Laurel Gardiner drove him to distraction; he simply could not explain it any other way. He was not so far gone that he did not appreciate the heated passion with which she returned his kisses on the night of the bonfire, nor the way she studied him when she thought he was unaware. She sought him out, often for no other apparent reason but his company, and more recently with the trumped up reason of civilizing him so that he would be presentable to her somewhat pathetic friend. But when she had found him a few days before, neither of them had given a bloody fig for her friend, nor for civilization, for that matter. For a brief respite, they had celebrated a perfect state of nature.

Mr. Gardiner had been right to caution him about his headstrong and beautiful daughter; Miss Laurel Gardiner made him see the futility of his escape from society, but also provided him with the very best of reasons why he ought to return and claim everything that was his.

Including her.

She was right from the start; he was not a very good hermit.

Nevertheless, if and when he ventured into Greenborough, where he might begin to carefully retrace his steps to his former life, he would have to be particularly alert she did not follow.

Chapter Nine

Miss Penelope Croyden stepped carefully from the dark interior of the coach into the late afternoon sunlight of the inn's courtyard and into her friend's waiting arms.

"Oh, Penny! I thought you would never arrive!" Laurel cried. "It is such a bore here without you!"

"Hush, Laurel! If my aunt heard you say such a thing, she would whisk us both back to London, to what she calls proper society." Penelope extricated herself from her friend's embrace and turned back to the coach, where Joseph Gardiner already assisted an elderly lady down the steps. "Aunt Jessup would have sent my sister Aurore to accompany me, but she appears to have some lively prospects in town. Our dear aunt therefore decided to sacrifice her own happiness to invest in that of my sister."

"I will not say I prefer the society of your aunt," said Laurel in low tones, "nor do I think the gentlemen here will enjoy it over that of another young lady, but I am only so glad to have you here that I would have invited Napoleon himself to ensure it."

"You joke, of course, but there are those who say my aunt shares certain character traits with that little despot. You will discover them soon enough, I am sure."

"What did you say? Of whom are you speaking?" demanded a voice behind them. Laurel glanced over the interfering menace of Aunt Jessup to Joseph, who just smiled and shrugged.

"Miss Jessup! How good of you to accompany my friend. If my mother but knew it, she would have come herself, instead of leaving the welcoming party as my brother and myself."

"I remember your kind mother from London and will see her soon enough. But your brother is no poor substitution, for Penelope recalls their acquaintance with fondness."

Laurel turned back to her friend, not expecting this revelation in the least, and saw Penelope blush like a provincial at her first ball in town.

"Yes, we all enjoyed ourselves very much during the season, for it may have been one of the grandest in anyone's memory," Joseph said graciously, and moved a little too quickly over to the coachman to show him where to put the travelers' bags.

"It is well Joseph chose to join us, then," said Laurel slowly. "We see him but rarely at Greenbriars."

"A pity. But now he will have further incentive to stay," pointed out Miss Jessup.

Penelope busied herself gathering her belongings and purposefully declined to join the conversation. But Laurel resolved to seek a confession later, if indeed it proved appropriate. Penelope and Joseph? It could not be possible, for she would have known something of it by now.

Could she have been so blind? If so—as unlikely as that was— she was no longer obliged to introduce her friend to the hermit, as she had promised. And she would not have to draw Robbie Darkwood out into their small society, which seemed a stupid plan, after all. He could remain her beloved hermit. And she could remain his . . . lover.

She could scarcely avoid the delicious truth.

"We have brought the cabriolet. There are many guests at Greenbriars just now, and since they all seemed so eager to come to greet you, we thought a small carriage would completely dissuade them. And you see, we have succeeded," Laurel said brightly, fully aware of the fact she was gabbling like one of the farm birds.

"It is very like the one I used at home, for I am not a great rider," Penelope sighed, and blinked back tears. "My old friend, the Earl of Westbridge, perfectly understood my fear of horses, for I was thrown when I was just a child. He encouraged my father to purchase a cabriolet for my own use, the better to go about the countryside and, indeed, the better to visit him at Waltham Hall. I did so, frequently." Penelope watched as Joseph strapped the boxes to the shelf in the back of the cabriolet and stood straighter. "But those days are gone. Westbridge is as far from my thoughts as he is from Waltham Hall."

Laurel supposed these ought to be encouraging words, though not to her possible career as a matchmaker. Indeed, what would have happened if she and Robbie Darkwood had not made love, had not shared passions and desires in the sanctuary of the hermitage, had not discovered truths about each other? The situation would have proved disastrous! Though, perhaps no worse than if things had gone as they had, and Joseph and Penelope did not now stand in the road looking like addlepated fools. To be fair, there was something charming about the situation. And there was no true reason her dear brother and her new friend should not find happiness with each other, but for the fact Laurel herself had nothing to do with bringing them together.

Laurel shook her head, becoming a little addlepated herself. "And yet the thought of Westbridge still brings tears to your eyes, my dear. Is that not evidence of the lingering ties of affection?"

Penelope Croyden sighed. "Perhaps it is. And yet I have scarcely spared a thought for him and my own sad situation for some weeks. Is it not strange? I spent nearly the whole of my life in his company, and expected to be even more intimate for all the rest of it. It was ever expected we would marry, and I never looked at another man. But now I wonder if he, older and more familiar with the ways of the world, felt the bondage as I now realize I would have."

Laurel thought bondage might not be entirely odious, if one were tied to a particular person. With dark, unruly hair and smoothly muscled arms, perhaps. She opened her mouth to speak when she caught Miss Jessup's impatient glances in their direction. Indeed, with Penelope's aunt at hand, and with Joseph nearly finished with the practical tasks of transporting ladies' belongings back to Greenbriars, here was neither the time nor the place for confession.

"Would that you chose a better hour for opening your heart, my dear," Laurel said, more impatiently than she intended. "But I will never believe anything good of your earl."

"You must," Penelope insisted, at the moment Joseph came up behind them and said, "Yes, it will certainly take the better part of an hour to arrive at Greenbriars."

Both ladies stared at him in confusion, until Laurel realized he had heard only the barest wisp of their conversation. Fortunately.

"Then let us be off, children," Miss Jessup announced. "I am hungry and impatient for tea, and I daresay the posting house's offerings could not measure up to my expectations."

Laurel expected the lady was correct, but spared a glance in the direction of the large, and slightly tilted, relic of another age. A large man stood in the ancient doorway, engrossed in conversation with the coachman who had delivered their guests. His face and most of his form remained in shadow, and yet he seemed at once familiar to her.

One of the servants from the estate, no doubt.

Joseph dutifully assisted the three ladies up into their seats, though Laurel suspected if she alone rode with her older brother, she could expect no such courtesy. But perhaps his purpose was more than show for the audience in the courtyard; he managed to urge Laurel to the seat beside Miss Jessup so he had Penelope to himself.

Penelope's aunt, grinning to reveal all her teeth as she watched them, clearly entertained hopes.

"Greenborough seems a pleasant enough town," Miss Jessup said, as Joseph directed the cabriolet through the congested streets. "You must have rooms here large enough for balls and gaming."

"Indeed we do," Laurel answered politely even as she strained to hear the conversation in the next seat. "But our favorite parties are those held in the large houses. The Duke of Wellsford resides in the neighborhood, when he is not in Italy buying paintings for his collection. And Lord Grandison is not very far off. And, of course, my parents are often obliged to host large gatherings, as they appear to have the most unmarried children."

"Your mother may be misguided in her efforts, Miss Gardiner," Miss Jessup said ungenerously. "I shall do whatever I can to assist her."

Laurel took a deep breath of the warm summer air, already regretting the circumstances that brought this lady, instead of the sweet Aurore, to their neighborhood.

"And yet I believe my mother's children do very much as we please in regard to affairs of the heart. Surely you cannot imagine we need supervision in telling us whom to love."

Of course, Miss Jessup imagined precisely that, and spent the better part of the hour—just as Joseph predicted—lecturing Laurel on that most particular, and personal, point.

* * * *

"You will see to it, yourself?" Rob said. "And deliver it to the young man in question? He is tall, and resembles me somewhat. You will know him by his gait, somewhat irregular due to an old injury, and the cane he often carries. It is . . . "

"Begging your pardon, sir," said the coachman, clearly amused. "Would it not be enough to know him by his name? And is it the very one written on this envelope?"

Rob smiled, understanding why the coachman would be wondering at such insistence to perform a very easy task. "It is indeed, my good man. Do see that he gets it. And here is something additional for your trouble."

The man looked down at the offering pressed into his palm, and his eyes widened. He put the slim envelope into his breast pocket and patted it reassuringly. "You can trust me, sir. But what if it is not possible to deliver, for all my efforts in finding the young man? Such things occasionally happen, you realize. Might I have your name as well, sir?

Rob hesitated, knowing this for the one question he should always have a care in answering correctly.

"Mr. Wood," he said, pulling yet another identity from his hat. "Mr. Robert Wood."

"Mr. Wood," the man nodded thoughtfully. "Of the Woods of Wichford?"

"I believe them no relation," Rob said firmly.

"Just as well, sir. They were a fine family until one of the sons turned up in London, involved in some nasty affair. A girl killed herself over him, and cursed him with her last breath."

Rob thought they might be related after all, for his own family story was no less sordid.

"The reputation of the whole family could rest on one soul, you see," the coachman continued. "Who knows how time will deal with them all?"

Who indeed knows? Rob reflected grimly. Will posterity judge him more harshly than his father? Or, even worse, will he be altogether forgotten, his portrait and name destined to some dark closet, closed to memory?

The thought gave him more pain than he might have anticipated, and he felt weighted by an overwhelming sadness. It seemed intensified, here in this sunny, busy place, but he could only account for it by the letter in the coachman's pocket, in which he sought reconciliation with his brother.

"Have a care!" the man suddenly shouted, and mercifully, it had nothing to do with himself. Rob followed his gaze to where another man carried a large box from the coach to a brightly painted cabriolet, supervised by three ladies. Poor gentleman.

One of the ladies turned towards another, and Rob recognized her as his beautiful tormenter. She wore some impractical blue thing on her head, which did nothing to protect her face from the sun, nor keep her curls contained beneath it. Her gown, which even he recognized as the popular military style, would have done more to stir the hearts of the French than an entire militia of his red-coated countrymen. Certainly, it was not the habit of officers to reveal anything of their breasts, nor allow an epaulette to be solely responsible for keeping their garments in place. But Miss Gardiner placed a good deal of trust in those insubstantial strips of fabric, and she seemed to care little if anyone took particular note of some the finer points of her anatomy.

"Sir?" the coachman asked, and Rob realized he cared all too much.

"Come, step into the doorway," he said, and fell into the shadow of the old timbers. "The sun is strong, and you have more to travel today."

"You are a thoughtful gentleman. 'Tis good you are not related to the Woods I know," the man said.

Rob looked up in confusion.

"The Woods?"

"The folks to whom you are not related, Mr. Wood."

"Ah yes," Rob nodded. "But then, one never knows when someone might turn out to be a part of one's own family."

* * * *

Laurel wasted little time in introducing Penelope Croyden to the many guests already at Greenbriars, who eagerly waited on their return. Sir John was somewhat acquainted with Penelope in London, and admitted to knowing the scoundrel who had disappointed her. The Winthrops mentioned a friend of their mutual acquaintance, and Miss Fellows expressed delight in having another lady in their company. Laurel wondered if such comment was intended as a slight insult to herself, for she had not proved a very attentive hostess, but there seemed nothing but perfect good humor in the welcome Miss Fellows offered Penelope.

Lewis's aloof response to the newcomer merited somewhat more curiosity, until Laurel saw the look he exchanged with Joseph and realized her brothers had something of an understanding. Not privy to their strategies, Laurel thought she ought to show the same deference as her younger brother to Joseph's interests. In the changing light of day, she realized how they would now enable several interests of her own, infinitely dear to her.

"Will you be with us for long, Miss Croyden?" Mr. Milton asked politely.

Penelope looked momentarily flustered. "Why, I cannot say. Certainly, it depends on the generosity of our hosts, for I will not overstay my welcome. And then, of course, there is my aunt. She was most kind to consent to come with me, and I hope she will also find much that is congenial at Greenbriars."

Miss Jessup, as if on cue, walked through the doorway with the one missing member of their party, and apparently thought the Duke of Montrose very congenial indeed. Laurel's mother, who found the Boy

Duke congenial for precisely the same reasons, followed behind them, looking somewhat unhappy.

"Why, here is Montrose, my dear Penelope," Miss Jessup chirped. "I knew his grandfather quite well, and of course was delighted to . . . "

"Your niece must be weary of her journey, Miss Jessup," Laurel's mother said firmly. "Perhaps Laurel would show her to her room, and we shall all rejoin for dinner."

Laurel recognized her own cue, and pulled her friend out of the circle of guests and back into her own private protection. Penelope seemed frankly relieved, though she hesitated on the stairway when Joseph came through the archway into the hall.

"Come along," Laurel said, and tugged on her friend's hand.

"I did not expect so many people here, though you did tell me to anticipate them," Penelope said as she was led into a large room that had once been Laurel's own.

"Poor dear. Is it so very hard to bear?" Laurel asked sympathetically. "I should have been more sensitive to your needs, and for your desire for privacy. And Sir John did not help matters much by speaking of the cursed Earl of Westbridge. I, myself, cannot even speak his name without utter contempt."

"Do not treat him so harshly, Laurel dear," Penelope said quietly, as she hopped up to sit on the large bed. "I think I have quite forgiven him, even though those who care for me do not. I am sure something dreadful happened, for why else would he not tell me he was leaving? And now I fear he is dead, perhaps set upon by thieves. I have already mourned him, for I loved him like a brother, and now I must go on with my life."

Laurel had been studiously arranging the flowers set out in a great vase on the bookcase, but she was distracted by Penelope's curious words.

"You have said those words before to me, and I did not consider them overmuch. But now I see something in your meaning and truly wonder at it. You were to marry Westbridge, yet you always speak of him as one beloved to you, like a brother. It is a very sweet thing but not . . . adequate." Laurel knew how lame her last word sounded but could not find something truer to what she felt. "I have brothers myself, and know I would not think of marrying any of them."

"Indeed not, "Penelope giggled, "but I would."

"Penny! Say it is not so!"

"But why not? I am quite over Rob, and I never desired to be a countess in any case. I shall mourn his loss always, but not for what might have been my life with him. I see it now as very much like what my whole life has always been. London has changed me, Laurel. I have seen new places, done so many things, met many people. Including other young men."

"Rob?" Laurel asked softly.

"The earl, of course, "Penelope said a little impatiently. "He only recently came into the title, as his father died last winter. He will always be Rob to me. When I hear the name Westbridge, I think only of his father. He treated me very kindly, to be sure, but it was certainly only by way of obligation to my parents. They were very close friends, and I think the old earl felt the loss almost as closely as my sisters and I. He became our guardian, of course."

"The old earl?" Laurel asked. "So now it is your Rob who is your guardian?"

"Rob," Penelope nodded sadly. "Unless he is dead, and then it is his younger brother, Harold. It would seem a little absurd, as Harry is of an age with my sister Miranda."

"I am surprised you never spoke of these things before, while we were in London."

Penelope's light eyes seemed to be looking at nothing at all, as she reached up to pull the pins out of her bonnet and release her thick black curls onto her shoulders. She shook her head and her hair managed to right itself into fashionable disarray.

"Perhaps I was not yet able to do so," she said. "It has been a very painful thing for me, and not helped by all the pitying glances to come my way. I could scarcely enter a room, but that my story would be the only topic of conversation."

"As it proved just now, downstairs. Curse Sir John!"

"Oh, not at all, Laurel. Do not be so hard on him, for he seems to be a man little blessed with conversational arts." She paused as Laurel laughed her agreement. "And I find it no longer matters so very much. Time, it seems, is a great healer."

"I thought I might do much to heal your wounds as well, my friend. I intended to offer you a salve, but now I realize it—he—would have inflicted additional pain, as he shares a name with your lost love."

"It is not so unusual a name, as it happens. It was the old earl's name, and a very popular one in our village."

"A happy coincidence. Your first guardian must have been so

popular a man, his neighbors sought to do him honor."

"You are generous, my friend. My Aunt Jessup has disarmed me of any such sweet beliefs. They are his by-blows, of course."

"Penny!"

Penelope's blue eyes met hers. "Do not be so shocked. Why should we not speak of what is true?"

Indeed, why should they not? Laurel once thought she knew much of what she needed to know about the relations between men and women, and had considered herself reasonably sophisticated. But it was not until recently that she began to understand something of seduction, of the hold a man could have on a woman, and how she might reciprocate in turn.

"I . . . I am only surprised he should be considered worthy to be your guardian."

"Perhaps he was not. But Rob is trustworthy."

Laurel said nothing, for how could she in the face of such unwavering loyalty? Penelope's name suited her uncommonly well, but even she would not wait twenty years for her Rob. Indeed, she seemed to have given him somewhat less than three months.

"If you believe it, then so shall I. But all the same, when he emerges to reclaim your hand after all this time, I should like to be the first in queue to give him a piece of my mind."

Penelope smiled as she started to unbutton her jacket.

"You are too late for that, my dear friend. My Aunt Jessup already reserved her place some months ago. And she owns a distinct advantage over you."

Laurel frowned. "Because she is your relation?"

"No, because she has been in the habit of thrashing men for many years. It is not by accident she never married."

"I share something of her skill, then, for how else does one survive with three brothers?" Laurel laughed. "And some day, when I am an elderly spinster, perhaps some sweet young things will say the same of me."

* * * *

After announcing how weary she was after her travels, Penelope retired to her bedroom shortly after tea. The others played at cards in the beachhouse by the lake while Miss Jessup, apparently not tired at all, imagined she entertained them all with tales of intrigue and fashion among the ton. Miss Winthrop was polite enough to ask several vague questions, of which she undoubtedly already knew the answers, but the rest studied their cards as if they were maps leading to a fortune. The older lady, either indifferent or unaware of their scarcely veiled attempts to exempt themselves from the conversation, rolled on relentlessly.

On the third attempt to do justice to the magnificence of Lady Armadale's newest ball gown, Miss Jessup paused long enough for Laurel to announce the Gardiner's intention of hosting a ball in several days' time. The card players, who, of course, knew of such plans, barely looked up from their hands. But Laurel, who hoped to ready them for the company of Robbie Darkwood, thought it an excellent time to introduce the subject.

"There will be a good many people from the neighborhood attending, Miss Jessup, and not all will be as finely dressed as Lady Armadale," she said gently.

"Of course not, Miss Gardiner! Lady Armadale is a paragon of style! She sets the standard for all who admire her, and has many followers. Last year she wore a plum and white striped gown to the Theatre Royal, and within weeks stripes were all the rage."

"And so it appeared as if one wandered amongst beach parasols when one went to Covent Garden during the season," said Miss Fellows, without looking up.

Mr. Holt laughed heartily, until one sharp look from Miss Jessup silenced him.

"One would not have been considered fashionable unless one owned a striped gown," she insisted. "But of course, now those dresses are relegated to the back of the closet, for one would not want to appear outdated."

"We are lucky to not have such restrictions here in Greenborough, Miss Jessup," Laurel said. "We wear what we like, and what our purses—or our father's purses—can manage for the year."

Miss Jessup, either not believing she could have arrived at a place beyond all hope, or imagining she brought fashion sense to the provincials, would not be denied satisfaction.

"But there surely is one lady among you here who is admired for her taste? One whose choices are copied by the others?"

"I believe you mean my sister, Miss Jessup," said Joseph. "I do not pay overmuch attention to such trifles, but I have heard Laurel Gardiner spoken of with a great deal of respect in these matters."

Laurel would have laughed if Miss Jessup looked merely surprised. But, indeed, the expression on the older woman's face was so stricken, Laurel only felt indignation.

"We do not judge people by their garments here, Miss Jessup," she said clearly. "We believe other qualities are worthy of the full measure."

"Perhaps that is why you did not do so very well in town, Miss Gardiner."

Laurel well knew such words were intended as an insult and that the others knew it, too. But she also knew the first words to come into her head would almost certainly guarantee the removal of Miss Jessup and Penelope from Greenbriars. So she gazed steadily into the dark blue waters of the lake, once again imagining the redemptive, cooling waters wash over her.

"I am happy as I am, Miss Jessup. I much prefer to invite friends to see me here in my own element than attempt to search for friends among the multitudes in London." She referred to Penelope, of course, but her brothers' companions around the gaming tables took this compliment to themselves. She knew, in that brief moment of cautious speech, she had gained allies. "And so, I hope you will not be repulsed by the array of guests we will entertain at our party this week. Some are very proper, indeed. But there will be others of more modest means, and with nary a clue as to what Lady Armadale wore last season, or this."

Miss Jessup looked rightfully indignant, but perhaps did not care to return so soon to town after her arduous trip. So she too might have looked to the lake and cooled her tongue.

"I suppose they are all respectable?" she asked.

Laurel wondered how respectable her hermit truly was, or if once he had been and no longer could claim it. But if George's clothing fit him, and he knew how to dance and made himself presentable to her friends, he would certainly give the illusion of it.

She stood, necessitating that the men do the same. Cards scattered on the table, for which she was genuinely sorry.

"My parents would not endure anything less than respectability, Miss Jessup. You have my assurance of it," Laurel said. "And now I believe I ought to see if my mother desires any help with the preparations."

"I will go with you, Miss Gardiner," Miss Jessup said quickly, and Laurel feared a renewal of their unpleasant conversation.

"But you must not, Miss Jessup. You are chaperone to this small party, are you not? I fear if you leave, it might get out that the afternoon's entertainment was not quite respectable."

The lady nodded sagely and cast a frown on the others, who had been quite accustomed to their own guidance for several weeks.

Ignoring the poisonous glances shot at her by her brothers and the others, Laurel gathered up her book and her embroidery basket and ran away with less than respectable speed.

* * * *

"I am glad you are refreshed, dear friend," Laurel remarked not an hour later. Penelope found her in the dining room with Mrs. Gardiner, considering which service of china to set out for the party, and joined in their planning. The Gardiners entertained often and seemingly without much effort, which perhaps was the consequence of not having been born to wealth, and knowing something of what a large gathering entailed. Undoubtedly, the many servants were grateful for this consideration, for they were rarely asked to perform the impossible, and were always well rewarded for their efforts.

Penelope seemed somewhat less familiar with such preparations, but drew up a chair so she might join them.

"I was not so very tired from the journey. I confess, my head ached from my dear aunt's incessant conversation," Penelope said wearily, and then looked quickly around her.

"Your aunt is down at the beachhouse, entertaining another captive audience,"Laurel's mother reassured her.

"Poor souls," said Penelope on a long sigh, and looked surprised when her companions laughed. "But then, I am grateful for the respite."

Their conversation returned to matters of plates and dinner napkins, when the sound of voices was heard from beneath the dining room windows.

"Oh dear," said Penelope, and then put a hand to her lips.

Mrs. Gardiner promptly stood. "I believe we are quite finished for the day. Would the two of you enjoy a walk around the grounds, perhaps? I believe you might set off through the door onto the veranda. You will find it very pretty. Very quiet."

Laurel sent her mother a grateful look and reached for her friend's hand. "Yes, indeed. Perhaps we can leave immediately."

It was not a question, nor did Penelope respond to it other than by clasping Laurel's hand and reaching for her bonnet. They managed their escape just as footsteps echoed on the polished floorboards of the front hallway.

"I suppose I ought to feel guilty," Penelope confessed.

"For avoiding your aunt? Forgive me, but I scarcely know the woman, and I already feel I have had my fill of her."

Penelope giggled. "She is not so very bad. And she has the care of my sisters and me, so I am very grateful."

"Then I should feel the same," Laurel said, somewhat chastened to be reminded her friend was an orphan.

"You need not. But we both might pity her, and take a lesson from her as well," Penelope said more seriously. "I understand she was quite cheerful and frivolous in her youth, and the beauty of her season."

"Many years ago," Laurel reminded her.

"Many, many years ago," Penelope echoed. "But she was very particular about her suitors, and eventually discouraged them all. Now she is quite alone, but for nieces and nephews, and a little bitter for her experience."

Laurel considered Miss Jessup's plight as she led her friend away from the house, pausing briefly when she decided to take a path parallel to the one with the Roman statuary.

"I am sorry for her, of course, for happiness seems to have eluded her," she said thoughtfully. "But I am not sure one's path to contentedness necessarily is laid with a marriage partner. Surely it depends on the man? And marriage to one who ill suits must be worse than not being married at all?"

"You are very sensible, Laurel."

"But this is not sense at all. Sense is guaranteeing a comfortable life in a fine home and a steady income. I am speaking of affection, of loyalty, of devotion, of love."

Penelope nodded, and looked out over the water as they began to approach the lake. "I, foolish girl once, thought I had it all."

"And so, perhaps you did. And so you will again," Laurel reassured her, though she based her certainty on nothing more than optimism and her brother Joseph's goodness.

They walked along in silence for several moments, taking great care not to trip on the rough stones along the way. Laurel's father had never intended his guests to use this path, for he had taken great pains and expense on the statuary way. Laurel again recognized her own stubborn preference for sensibility over sense in her desire to avoid the very place where her plan for Penelope's happiness was undermined by her own unbidden passions.

Penelope stumbled and grabbed Laurel's hand to steady herself. "I fear I may not have brought proper shoes to navigate my way around Greenbriars," she said.

Laurel felt guilty, both for endangering her friend, and for showing her father's estate in a less than positive light. A misstep, however small, would make her accountable to everyone about them, and especially her brother.

A familiar bark from above made her look up the steep embankment, but she saw nothing. Still, the arrival of the hermit might work very well under the present circumstances, for she would like to introduce her friends to each other away from the curious scrutiny of the others. What would Penelope think of the man Laurel had once intended for her, but now wanted only for herself? Would she think her a naïve romantic, one who thought happiness could be found on a lumpy mattress in a stone cottage? Or would she dare her to continue along a reckless path?

"How far will we walk today?' Penelope asked, her voice a little breathless. Indeed, the path was very reckless.

"Oh, we have not much more to go before we turn back. I thought perhaps we might continue along the right fork just yonder, for it is a pretty prospect. One never knows what one might see."

"I hear a dog not far off. Perhaps we shall see one of your father's tenants?"

"Perhaps," Laurel said, wondering if Robbie wore George's clothing or his own despicable robe.

"Oh!" Penelope cried, but her voice rose to a squeak as she pulled Laurel down on top of her. A little avalanche of pebbles, small but treacherous, tumbled down the embankment, and Laurel caught hold of a branch with her free hand, lest they follow.

"Oh, good heavens," Penelope murmured, shifting beneath her friend's weight. "This is hardly an inauspicious beginning to my visit to Greenbriars."

"Your aunt will not consider it at all respectable," agreed Laurel, as she pulled herself to her feet. She dusted herself off and examined a small rent in her muslin gown. Well, Miss Jessup will be happy to know my gown needs to be discarded, for it is all of six months old and surely no longer fashionable. She reached down to help Penelope to her feet, and thought her friend remarkably unhelpful in the effort.

In a moment, she understood why. Penelope fell back to the ground, falling heavily on the most padded part of her anatomy.

"Penny! What are you doing?" she cried.

Penelope bit down on her lip and struggled to a sitting position.

"I have done something foolish, I fear. My ankle feels as if it is broken or, at the very least, sprained." She edged up her gown, to reveal an ankle already swollen and showing signs of bruising.

Laurel dropped to her knees, feeling the full impact of the guilt she only imagined moments before.

"Oh, this is dreadful! I am so, so sorry!"

Penelope looked at her with something that might have been amusement, if such a thing were possible at this time. "It is not your fault, Laurel. How can it be?"

"I am responsible for your safety, as you are my guest."

"Then perhaps you might seek help? We can dispute fault for hours, by which time my ankle might look like a cabbage."

"Oh, of course," Laurel stood shakily, feeling even more foolish. How had she come so far as to forget herself? "I will find help. We are not so very far from the stables, and perhaps one of the grooms is about."

"Then go. I am quite settled here and will surely be here when you return."

As Laurel gathered up her skirts, intending to bypass the rugged pathway altogether and scale the slope of the embankment instead, she reflected on her friend's calm acceptance of her situation. Did such strength derive from her sad experience? Did pain make one stronger? As she caught hold of a bush and gained her foothold, she thought it could not have been worth the price Penelope had paid for blighted hopes.

Laurel concentrated on her task, wondering if, in her anxiety to reach the top, she sacrificed her own safety along the way. If she fell, not only would she likely land for a second time on her smaller, more delicate friend, but risked breaking her own ankle as well. Undoubtedly, it would serve her right, she thought grimly.

But by the time she crested the slope, she felt grateful for two things. First, the only damage she suffered was some additional indignities to her gown. And second, loyal Prinny was there to greet her, so his master could not be far away.

She stood upright, glanced behind to marvel at how far she had come, and considered that if the hermit came along, the day might come to a better end than she, at present, had reason to believe.

"Why, hello! Have you been mucking out the stables?" a cheerful voice called out.

Laurel looked up to see him approach and thought that even mucking out the stables might have a certain charm if she could but do it with him. He had tied back his hair with a ribbon she recognized as her own, and the fine contours of his face were fully revealed. The robe, always so odious to her, seemed curiously seductive, now that she knew everything that lay beneath.

She shook her head ruefully, wondering what she had ever hoped by her matchmaking scheme, for now she could not bear to imagine this man with anyone else. "Oh Robbie," she cried on a note of frustration, and instantly saw a look of hope and yearning on his face. "I have been walking with my friend, and we were so busy admiring the scenery, we did not study the path. I am afraid she fell and mayhaps broke her ankle."

"I am not a doctor," he said firmly, his own frustration clear, and pulled his wretched hood up over his head.

"But you are the only one who can help. Will you not come with me?" Laurel held out her hand, and after a moment's hesitation, he seized it and pulled her to his chest. When he kissed her, she tasted mint, as she had the night of the fire.

"Where would you like to go?" he asked in a husky voice, leaving her in little doubt of his intentions.

"I should like to go away with you," she said, fingering the fullness of his lower lip. "But I fear there are more pressing considerations."

She only meant Penelope, truly. But when he said, "Indeed there are," and demonstrated his need, she could think of little else but him.

"Robbie, she may have fainted dead away," Laurel said, after what seemed like ages had passed. "Please come with me."

His reluctance was apparent in every line of his body, even shrouded as it was under the dark robe. But something, which Laurel preferred to believe was his innate nobility, would not let him refuse her and her plea for help.

"Very well," he said abruptly, "lead on."

"I came up the embankment," Laurel said a little doubtfully.

"It is the fastest way. And if she fares as poorly as you say, we may have wasted enough time."

"Wasted?" Laurel asked softly.

He smiled mischievously at her and shrugged his body out of the robe. Laurel knew his intent was to make the descent easier, and she resisted the impulse to delay him yet again.

"She is on the path, near a bramble . . . " Laurel began, but stopped when he held up a hand.

"I do not believe there are many injured young ladies out upon the hillside. So I am certain I will find her with impunity," he said, and lowered himself over the crest.

Laurel wondered if she ought to follow, for Penelope might be fearful of a strange man in laborer's clothing. And Miss Jessup might be horrified to learn of her niece's unchaperoned introduction to the hermit, and she might remove Penelope altogether from Greenbriars.

So Laurel, doubting anything she might do to her gown would make any sort of a difference, followed Robbie Darkwood, catching a glimpse of his dark hair here and there among the shrubbery.

The descent proved a good deal harder than the way up, and Laurel needed to concentrate fully on her task. She heard footsteps crunching on the gravel, and what sounded like muffled curses, and knew he also found the way arduous.

Nevertheless, she was surprised when he suddenly appeared from behind a wild rose and scrambled up the path past her, without saying a word, and made his way back to the top.

Laurel, clutching a vine like a leaf in a storm, stared in amazement at his retreating back.

"Hermit! Why are you leaving me?" she cried, but he did not pause. Saying a few choice words under her breath—decidedly not respectable ones—she scrambled up behind him, readying for a confrontation over she-knew-not-what.

"Hermit!" she cried again, as she came to the top, and a large hand reached over the crest to grasp hers. His felt uncommonly cold, even though the day was warm, and he had just exerted himself. As he pulled her up, they were face to face, and she wasted no time in challenging him.

"What can you be thinking?" she asked, and then as a dreadful thought occurred to her, "Is it too late, then?"

"Too late?" he asked in a voice not like his own. "I say it is indeed too late."

"Penelope is dead?" Laurel gasped.

"Miss Croyden is sitting like a princess on a low stone, surrounded by roses and humming insects. She will live."

"Then explain your actions, sir. To run from a lady in need is despicable."

"It is not the worst charge that can be leveled against me, my dear Miss Gardiner. But I cannot help her."

"And why not?" Laurel asked, ready to push him over the edge herself, if need be.

"That is my business. And hers. Your interference is officious and will accomplish no good."

Laurel's hands dropped to her side, and she felt the bitter taste of a defeat she could not yet fathom.

"My . . . my friend is injured," she faltered. "I cannot move her myself."

The hermit seemed to consider the wisdom of this, and nodded. "I will borrow a horse from the stable, with your permission, and go for the doctor. You must go to the house and have your brothers arrange to have her brought there."

Laurel nodded, too numb to answer, but did not doubt his plan was a good one. She watched him run off, Prinny at his heels, and some minutes later heard the whinny of the horses who witnessed his approach. She had not yet moved when she felt the shuddering vibration of hooves beneath her feet, and she looked up to see him ride away. Even at a distance, she recognized him as an experienced horseman, comfortable both with speed and the rocky terrain.

Only then did Laurel fully understand how he came to have such skills.

And how he happened on Penelope Croyden's family name, when she knew she never mentioned it.

Chapter Ten

Dr. Arbuthnot, a useless ninny who treated head colds in much the same way he might dog bites or consumption, spent about five minutes examining Penelope's ankle, and a good deal longer in consultation with her aunt. Aunt Jessup, far from playing the role of solicitous relation, was anxious to grant the physician her time and serve him tea, and then question him on the possible cures to every ailment she had ever suffered in her life.

The role of sympathetic companion to the invalid, therefore, fell to Laurel, or would have if Joseph had not been so tiresomely pleased to acquire the pillows, blankets and ice without which Penelope would never recover. Once such necessities were in place, he pulled up a large wing chair and set himself up not three feet from the poor girl's head.

Laurel, who needed to look over her brother's shoulder when she spoke to her friend, decided Penelope seemed perfectly content with this arrangement and ungenerously wondered if the injured ankle was nothing more than a ruse to bring Joseph Gardiner to her side.

If so, Laurel could not really fault her friend's strategy. She might have done the same thing and found herself cared for and loved in the hermit's bed a good dealer sooner than it had happened.

She shook her head, clearing her thoughts. He was no hermit, she reminded herself. Such a thing would have been scandalous enough, but she had, instead, enjoyed an afternoon of passionate lovemaking with the Earl of Westbridge, her good friend's intended. She ought to be mortified, but instead the memory filled her with pleasure.

However, Penelope looked radiantly happy, even without her cursed earl. But then, her sweet friend entertained no notion about who her would-be rescuer would have been, for she seemed to have seen no one until Joseph came storming up the hillside like a deranged bull.

Now Joseph looked happy also, entertaining his adoring audience with an exaggerated story about a hunting trip to Scotland in which he played a conspicuously prominent part.

But the man Laurel loved, he whose dissatisfaction with life brought him to such desperate straits of solitude and despair, could not be in the least bit happy. Nor did he deserve to be. The small avalanche on the hillside had exposed a traitorous, ignoble coward in their midst, one who ought to be despised. But she could not despise him.

Indeed, she had never been more confused.

Circumstances and she, Laurel Gardiner, had revealed Robbie Darkwood to be something other than what he seemed—and what he wished—to be. Neither persona was honorable nor deserving of her love. For a man such as he, exile from society seemed only too generous a punishment. He deserved humiliation, censure, prison, removal from the House of Lords, to be stripped of his title, indenture as a servant in the colonies, and the contempt of all who ever knew him . . . at the very least. After all, he had jilted her friend. How could she expect anything better?

"Laurel?"

She looked up and realized her brother no longer leaned towards Penelope, but had turned towards her.

"I am sorry. Did you ask something of me?" she asked.

Penelope giggled, effectively dismissing any notion that she might be in lingering pain. "You murmured something and seemed very angry. I hope you are not mad at me for spoiling our little outing. I feel disappointed enough that I will not be able to dance at your ball."

"But you will come down, of course," Joseph said hurriedly. "I will carry you myself."

Penelope sighed and leaned forward to pat his hand affectionately. "You are too kind, Mr. Gardiner, but I will not ruin the pleasure of your evening."

Laurel could no longer see Joseph's face, but she fairly well imagined the idiotic look he undoubtedly wore.

"The pleasure of the evening relies entirely on your presence, Miss Croyden," Laurel heard him say.

"I will sit out several dances and give you company, Penelope," Laurel said clearly. "Joseph is a keen dancer and much in demand."

Neither seemed to hear her, which perhaps was just as well.

"I believe I shall take a stroll about the lake, if I am not needed just now," she ventured just as clearly. And then, when she received no response, "Perhaps I shall take a swim and dive for turtles."

That got Joseph's attention. He turned in his seat, entirely blocking her view of Penelope. "Do," he said tersely, and scowled.

Laurel did not need a second dismissal. She stood by pressing down on her brother's shoulders, forcing him to remain seated. Over his head, she saw Penelope's look of surprise, tempered by something that might have been delight. It seemed courtship trumped friendship in the games people played.

And Penelope ought to know, for she had once planned to marry the man who was her oldest friend. And yet that friend and lover were now all but forgotten.

To Penelope perhaps. And to Joseph, who surely hoped to forever take his place in her affections.

But not to Laurel. Knowing where the scoundrel lived, knowing what he had done and the punishment he now deserved, made it impossible for him to escape her thoughts. She nodded briefly at Penelope, flicked a fingernail at her brother's ear in a manner to give him just a tweak of pain, and went off to seek revenge—and answers—for the injury done to the woman whom, she guessed, might soon be her sister-in-law.

* * * *

Rob threw the last of his meager possessions into a wooden crate and knocked the flimsy container over, spilling those possessions onto the rug. He cursed himself soundly and deservedly and so wickedly that Prinny backed cautiously into the corner.

"It is fine, boy," Rob lied, for nothing was fine. If his whole complacent life had been turned on its head months ago, so did today's precipitous events turn it once again. And, in some ways, more cruelly.

Prinny wagged his loopy tail, and jumped into the crate.

"You are not going with me, boy," Rob said more gently, and as the truth of his words hit him, his pain became even more insufferable. Was it not bad enough he must be denied his life, and two women he had loved, but now his dog as well? The mongrel, his constant companion since his inauspicious arrival at Greenbriars, was not his to take on his journey, wherever it might lead. Prinny, like the hermitage, the furnishings, the farm animals and everything else on the estate, belonged to Mr. Gardiner, a man who took pride in his possessions and might well tally them daily. If Prinny went away with the defecting Robbie Darkwood, Mr. Gardiner had every right to have them stopped on the road and have his property returned to him.

Rob stood still in the center of his hermitage and realized how circumstances and fate left him so unhinged he hardly knew himself. Had he come so far to forget the sound judgement for which he was once respected? Did he not own a great estate himself, and know full well that he could never hope to count all the puppies and kittens that took shelter there and enjoyed the companionship of his tenants? What could Prinny matter to a man like Mr. Gardiner? Indeed, what could a hermit matter, when there would be another to readily apply for the position?

Man and dog could move on, pursued by ghosts and guilt, memories of the great lake and cool woods, and brief moments of happiness. Rob rubbed his aching forehead and wondered where it might all end. Once he had felt compelled to forsake his family and birthright, and abandon everything he ever knew or loved in the world. It proved a harsh punishment for something for which he could hardly be blamed.

But now the fault seemed entirely his, for he had allowed the illusion of his charade to blind him to certain reality. Why did he not become wary when Laurel Gardiner spoke of her poor distressed friend for whom happiness remained elusive? Why did he give in so easily to passion, when his sad history remained unsettled? And why, most absurdly of all, had he allowed himself to love again?

He did not need to venture out on a journey to know the answers to his questions. If he paid only indifferent attention to the matter of Laurel's friend, it could only be because his sense and senses were overly attentive to the matter of Laurel herself. Honor and duty once compelled him to jilt a very sweet lady. But honor and duty played little part in what he wished to do with the delectable Miss Gardiner.

And yet he would leave her too, while his will remained strong and he could still avoid her friend, whom he knew a good deal better than Laurel did herself.

It was a coward's escape, and he hated himself for it. But he had already borne the pain of the truth entirely alone and survived. If he shared the burden of that knowledge with those who remained confused by his actions, their pain would be as great and their survival less assured. Coward or not, he would do everything with his last ounce of strength to protect them.

Prinny looked up towards the door, providing the only warning of the invasion of the hermitage.

"I thought to find you here," Laurel said angrily and without preamble, as she marched into the room. Rob thought she might have kicked in the door.

"But not for long, Miss Gardiner," he said calmly and gestured with his hand. "As you see, I am preparing to depart."

"Are you?" she said nastily. "And with nothing more than a packing crate? Or will you borrow one of my father's horses? You seem to be a fairly proficient horseman, for a poor hermit."

Rob stood his ground, now knowing for certain she had guessed most of his secrets.

"Your father did not list 'ineptitude' among the qualities—or lack thereof—he desired in his hermit. I daresay many in my profession have particular talents."

Laurel stood silent for one blessed moment, drawing in deep breaths. Her breasts rose and fell in righteous indignation and, more likely, the exertion of her walk, and her hair fell down about her shoulders, curling madly. Her color, always high because of her inability to keep her bonnet on her head, was rosy and warm, and her large eyes glistened with what might have been tears.

He wondered at that.

"Did he list deception, betrayal and dishonor among the qualities?" she gasped in a tight little voice. "Did he desire someone who injured an innocent young lady, and damaged her for life?"

"I would not have hurt you for anything in the world. I love you," he said.

She stamped her foot like an impatient child. "I am not speaking of myself! And I already have evidence of the endurance of what you call 'love.' You have wronged Penelope Croyden most shamefully!"

"You know nothing about it, Miss Gardiner," Rob said, and crossed his hands over his chest, where they would not be so tempted to reach out and pull her against him.

"Oh, but I do, Mr. Darkwood! Or should I say, 'Westbridge?'" She waited just perceptibly, and he was certain she tested him. "My father got his money's worth when he hired an earl; he will rejoice to hear it."

"Why must he hear it, Miss Gardiner? You seem to be proficient at deceiving him in many things."

"That is an ungentlemanly thing to say, my lord. And it is not my morals under discussion just now, but yours."

She was right, of course. He must give her that.

"You know nothing of my morals or my motives, my dear. And they are none of your business."

"Oh, but they are," she argued, her color rising. "You have injured a very dear lady, one I call my friend. She has sought refuge in my father's house, hoping to escape her sad past and the knowing glances of all those in town who label her a woman scorned. I thought her safe here. I little imagined I would bring her in terrible proximity to the scoundrel who shamed her."

Rob felt an uncommon pain in his heart, knowing she spoke the truth, and more—that his burdens were already hers as well.

"And I am not 'your dear.'"

It was not the truth. No matter what happened, no matter where he found sanctuary, she would always be his dearest. He loved her, when he would have thought he was no longer capable of loving anyone. He desired her. He adored her. As he stood before her, resolutely determined to hold his ground against her bitter accusations, he recognized that his current pain and torment owed nothing to his abandonment of his family and friends. It was only and all about Laurel, and what the two of them already shared quite apart from wealth and title and the weight of guilt.

"Would that you were," he said gently, testing her as she did him a few moments before.

She gave a little cry, and he thought he had her then. He saw her body bend slightly to him, and her fists open and close like the wings of a butterfly.

"You are Penelope Croyden's, my lord. She is your oldest friend and your neighbor, and she has secured your promise of marriage. You must honor it or bring shame on your family and hers. I fear it may already be too late."

"Is she in a very bad way?" he asked, wondering how severe were Penelope's injuries, after all. She had looked comfortable enough a few hours ago when he saw her perched on the edge of the embankment, though she might not have been so happy if she had but looked up and saw him descending the hill towards her.

Laurel looked oddly disconcerted. "She . . . she is being consoled by my brother Joseph. I believe she will recover in time."

Rob thought her choice of words curious and leapt to the obvious conclusion. "Your brother Joseph? Are we speaking of a recovery of her ankle, or of her heart?"

"It is premature to speculate, but I have wondered, since yesterday, if her design in coming to Greenbriars might have more to do with my brother than with myself." Her hands dropped to her sides, and Rob realized the fierce winds that had propelled her sails to his door had already died down.

He cleared his throat. "I thought it had to do more with me."

"With you?" The gale, the fury, returned. "What has this to do with you?"

"Pardon me, but I thought it had everything to do with me. Is it not why you brought Miss Croyden here? To expose me and redeem her?"

"I . . . ." Laurel bit off her words, though surely not to spare his feelings. "I did not know you for her lover, my lord. I should have guessed the truth, but I did not. The Earl of Westbridge goes missing, presumed by some to be dead, and you suddenly appear at Greenbriars, an unlikely hermit."

She certainly did not spare his feelings.

"I thought myself fairly creditable," he said, quite beside the point.

"But you are not creditable, my lord. You are a liar and a cheat, and have scorned a worthy lady. You have abandoned your home and family, and you have deceived my father. I do not believe anything you can say to me, nor do I trust you."

"And yet you are here alone with me."

"Anger makes one reckless."

"As does love."

Again, she hesitated. "Is that why you jilted Penelope Croyden? Were you reckless in that?"

"I have a great regard for Miss Croyden, and a desire to never cause her pain or harm. But I have learned, since coming to Greenbriars and leading a contemplative life, that I never loved her as a husband ought to love his wife. My affections towards her might best be described as 'brotherly.'"

He saw something in his words shocked her, though he had yet to declare himself. He wondered if he ought to risk even more, if recklessness would give him voice.

"Brotherly?" she whispered, and it was his turn to be shocked. What did she guess?

"Perhaps I used the word ill. I am very fond of Penny, and feel great affection for her. I probably always will. But I do not love her as I love . . . "

Laurel studied him with an intensity that allowed him to believe that everything he valued or desired, everything dreamed and hoped for, would be his to win or lose in the moment.

He drew in a bracing breath and announced, "As I love you."

His words dropped between them into the stillness of the room, in the heated air of the summer sun and her passion, in the sweet smell of catmint that grew in tufts about the hermitage.

When she didn't respond, he reached one hand for her and asked,

"Will you believe me in this, even if you doubt my word on everything else?"

"I have no choice," she said solemnly, "and heaven help me, I will believe you." Ignoring the anchor of his outstretched hand, she came slowly into the haven of his arms.

Laurel was a tall woman, and one comfortably endowed in the places that mattered, but he embraced her as if she stood no more than a child against him, seeking shelter in the storm. Her lips reached to his collar bone, and he ducked his head, searching for her, remembering the mind-numbing kisses they had shared on the night he thought he would lose her to flames and carelessness, and again on the blessed day when she came to his bed. She met him as hungrily now as she did then, and he knew that this time her perceptions were not clouded by the romance of making love to a mysterious stranger, or to a man who seemed everything her other suitors were not. Her eyes were wide open, in more ways than one.

He explored her lips, her teeth, her tongue. The bitterness with which she had first confronted him was spent, and he found only sweetness there, and a hunger born of desperation, perhaps. His hands moved gently over her body, committing her divine form to memory, for he did not yet know how this affair would end. He wanted nothing more than to marry her and share all he had with her. But he had, for now, abdicated his position and his possessions, and could not claim her until he reclaimed himself. His life was a wretched business. But for now, she was here and, at least for this one blessed moment, she was his.

And, just as surely, she claimed him for her own. Her beautiful hands slipped under his loose shirt, and caressed the bare skin of his back, pressing him closer, closer. Her lips escaped him briefly, and she tasted his chin and cheek and rubbed her nose against his. He tried to seize the opportunity to capture her again, but her mouth entertained its own notions, and feathered kisses down the center of his face to find the shallow at the base of his throat. He shifted his hips uneasily, not sure if they dared risk everything for a second time.

"Oh, yes," she sighed, answering him.

"Laurel?" he said into her hair, moving his lips against its sweetness. "We must stop."

Now he had her attention. She ceased her erotic exploration of his body to glance up at him in surprise. Her lips were parted and reddened, and she sucked in deep breaths of air, which he not only saw but felt as her breasts pressed against him. His own breathing, which even hard work about his hermitage could not make erratic, was now as labored as Laurel's. And yet he had much to say to her, and quickly.

"We must stop this at once," he repeated, with a great deal of effort.

"But why? Why must we?" she asked plaintively, and brought her hands, now cool against his flushed skin, together at the base of his spine. "Because I was so very angry?"

"Because you no longer are and ought to be. I have done nothing to deserve your forgiveness, and I have behaved abominably."

"Yes, you have," she said, and her hands swept his waist to tug at his buttons. "But then, so have I."

It was impossible to argue with her or with himself. He lifted her against him and carried her to the edge of the ancient oak table to stand between her legs. Her eyes never left his face as he slowly, tantalizingly, pulled up her skirts until he exposed her to the light and cool air. She leaned back on her elbows, her lips parted, her quizzical eyebrows for once reflecting her confusion about the part she would play.

Barely able to contain himself, Rob settled the business to his satisfaction, and he believed, to hers. Reluctantly letting her go, he pulled at his buttons, hearing several of them scatter on the floor. Finally free, he leaned over her, his hands capturing hers against the table, and gently, slowly, he entered her. After her gasp of surprise, they began to move together, and he lifted her hips so she would be protected from the unyielding wooden boards.

"Oh, my lord," she cried, as she had once before. She had not understood the irony then, and he did not think she bothered to consider it now. And then he was beyond any reason as they reached heaven together on the aged, splintering boards of his dinner table.

Spent, he collapsed over her, his head against her breasts. How was it going to be possible to bid her farewell?

Finally, with Herculean effort, he straightened his arms and balanced himself above her. Her hands made a little butterfly gesture between them, and he bent down to capture them with his lips. Believing it to be a renewal of his lovemaking, she sighed happily and settled back against the table.

"Laurel, my dear, I must leave this place. I would like to spend many years risking my heart and soul for love of you, but it is premature to begin."

"I would think, my Hermit, we have already begun." She opened her eyes and looked at him as no woman ever had before. "Hermit? Robbie? You look to be in pain. Are you well?"

He sucked in his breath. "No, I am not well. Nor will you be, if we are discovered thus, and with no way to disguise what we have been doing."

"Do you think my brothers would beat me if they should find us? Or punish you with some unspeakable torture?"

Rob squirmed a little, already witness to what this divine lady read in the quiet of her chamber and how she knew of such things. Adding to his discomfort was the fact that he undoubtedly deserved whatever they might do to him.

"Physical punishment would be only too kind next to the censure of family and society," he said ruefully. "I know well what such things mean, and would not allow you to suffer so, not for all the world."

She reached out to him and caressed the line of his jaw. "'Tis a very noble sentiment, for a rough hermit," she said thoughtfully.

"But our problem is that my sentiments—and my actions, for that matter—will not be judged by the standard of the hermitage, but by those of the earldom."

"But why so? Can you not be simply judged by the standard of a man?" she asked and shrugged a little. Her gown slipped off her shoulder by the gesture, but she ignored it.

"'Tis a very noble sentiment," he echoed, trying hard to ignore the slipped gown as well, "for a wealthy lady of class and distinction. No wonder you would not wish for others to find your little library and see what you have been reading. You sound like a colonist."

"Do you really think so?" she asked, and blushed. "I think you have complimented me."

Rob combed impatient fingers through her hair, until it was spread out across the table. How was it possible to have intelligent conversation while she still lay half naked beneath him, and her lips were still raw from his kisses?

"Though you may think it an odd way of telling you so, I did intend to compliment you for these past fifteen minutes or more. If I somehow blundered in the delivery, allow me to tell you more bluntly how very much I adore you."

She blushed again, rather more fiercely, and lifted questioning eyes to his. He knew then his frustration entirely unjustified, for no matter what happened in the days and weeks ahead, no matter what trials he must rightly endure for the injuries he had brought upon others, Laurel would always know he loved her and that he endeavored, as far as he dared, to show her so.

"You did not blunder, Robbie Darkwood," she said softly. "I would have allowed you anything, and I think you know it. But then, you allowed me some liberties as well, and I am no where as sure as you in the matter. There are . . . some things one does not learn in books."

He stood, raising her up with him, holding her tightly against his chest.

"And yet you do not seem to need your books, my love," he said into her hair. "Your instincts belie your innocence."

"But I have not been an innocent for some time," she whispered.

Rob felt his skin grow cold and prickly, and cursed himself for his presumptiveness. What mysteries darkened her past? And was he as prepared to forgive her trespasses with the same ease with which she apparently did his?

"Indeed?" was all he could say.

"Of course not. I have imagined doing everything we have done, in all my dreams of the past few months. Since the afternoon I met you, I believe."

Rob let his breath out with palpable relief and hugged her closer.

"It is a most improper confession. You must not use it against me," she added.

"Oh, my love, I intend to use it against you at every opportunity. You may confess as often as you like."

She laughed, and was, once again, his innocent. "I must confess the experience did not exactly match my expectations."

Rob wondered if she played him with well-rehearsed intent, for it could not otherwise be possible to drive him from the heat of exultation to the despair of disappointment. And once again, he doubted himself because of her words. After all, though he had known his share of giving and generous women, during the last few years he had devoted himself entirely to a fairly chaste courtship of Penelope Croyden. And for all her sweet goodness, she somehow had never aroused him to misdeeds as did Laurel Gardiner.

"Did I disappoint you, my love?"

She lifted her face, and what he saw there told him he need not ever doubt himself with her. Her expression, part knowing and part wondering, proved for the greater part anticipatory. Rob could scarce contain himself for wanting her again and wishing to answer all the questions she did not ask aloud.

"Does the discovery of my identity not change anything?" he could not help himself asking, though the answer must be self-evident. After all, it was what had brought her to the hermitage, running into his arms. Indeed, it made no more sense than anything else in the months since his father's death.

"Oh, I suppose it does. Certainly, an earl is not nearly as romantic as a hermit. Westbridge must be sensitive to his place in the community and own much responsibility. I daresay he could never chop wood in his shirtsleeves or share a bed with a mongrel dog."

"I never!" he said, and then, catching her expression, "Well, perhaps on occasion, and even then, on very cold nights."

She snuggled deeper against his shoulder.

"Are you very disappointed?" he asked again.

"That Prinny shares your bed?" she asked.

"That I am not a hermit."

"My love," she began, and suddenly it scarcely mattered what else she said to him. "I believe you must own you were not a very good hermit."

He stood straight and made a small attempt to shrug her off.

They were back to that, then. "I beg your pardon, Miss Gardiner, but I considered myself an exemplary hermit."

"Oh, indeed. I think I made your inadequacies evident in the first days of our meeting. I need not repeat my criticism of your husbandry skills, nor your impractical manner of disguise. But let it suffice to mention that you could scarcely keep away from me."

"Vixen! You sought me out at every opportunity!"

"And you did very little to avoid me. What respectable hermit would do such a thing?"

"I see. And so you are disappointed."

"Indeed. However, I can hope you are a better earl than you are a hermit."

"I intend to be," Rob said roughly.

"Then you must return to your estate and right the wrongs your absence has caused," she said calmly.

He understood then why she would never disappoint him, why she would always be the one to make him see the way through the wilderness. Why she was the only woman he could ever marry. Her sanity gave him hope where he thought all was forsaken, and her love gave him the strength to endure whatever would yet come.

"To do so would set me before Miss Croyden, exposed to her

censure and contempt. If I manage to earn her forgiveness, the future may not unfold as you and I presently hope." He dared much beneath the simplicity of the statement, hoping she wished to marry him in spite of all that had happened. Surely she could not imagine that what passed between them just now could lead to anything else. Yet, he was not a free man, and the means by which he might have to extricate himself from an impossible liaison might give him liberty, but not the approbation of society. In short, the sociable, interfering, caring Miss Gardiner might find herself a countess, but a hermit in her own way: isolated from others, a recluse, an outcast.

"I trust you, Hermit. I have from the beginning, or I would not have followed you into this cottage on the day we met."

"One has naught to do with the other," he said slowly, entirely at odds with the beating of his heart.

"But of course it does." She smiled, and held up her clean, white palm for his inspection. "You see? I bear not the slightest scar of the injury you caused me."

Rob caught her hand and kissed the soft flesh of her palm. He flicked his tongue over her skin and thought he detected the slightest sliver of a healing scar.

"An injury of the flesh is easier to heal than one of the heart," he reminded her.

"And so mine would break if you would ever leave me," Laurel said. "But knowing it, feeling it, makes me Penelope's ally rather than her rival. I now fully understand what your defection must have cost her."

Rob released her and studied her face, not certain where she wished to go with this conversation.

"But it cost you, as well," she continued, her voice breaking. "One would have been a fool not to see it when you first came to Greenbriars, when you hid from me and everyone else. Something caused you to break away so precipitously, to become that island, entire of yourself."

"We recalled the poet's words at one of our first meetings," he said, on a note of irritation.

"And I wanted to be certain I remembered the words perfectly. It is why I asked for my copy of Donne's *Devotions* several weeks ago."

"And you received it. But I did not know you were using it as a reference while forming an opinion of my character."

"My opinion of your character was formed when first we met. I did not need to rely on John Donne or anyone else."

Rob turned away, not happy to be the subject of anyone's scrutiny, least of all the one woman whose opinion mattered more than anything else. He realized he now stood facing the bed and, thinking it not a very good idea, turned further towards the sitting area. Prinny looked up from where he sat on the large, old chair, expectant.

"And what did you discover on your own?"

"Many things," Laurel answered. "Your goodness, for one. Your inherent bravery, your willingness to help others. Your intelligence, something to which I had grown rather unaccustomed while idling my time with Lord Ballister in London."

"Ballister! Why did you never tell me? He was never one to be trusted . . . " Rob was jealous even imagining Laurel in the man's company.

"As I recall, he said something of the same thing about you." She looked around the room, far more at ease in it than he, and sat down at the table. "But then, so did everyone else in town. You are quite notorious, my lord."

He said something under his breath, not for her hearing. And then, "But you would tie yourself to such a one?"

"I would," was all she said, and he needed to hear nothing else. Particularly the words she carefully added. "But you have much accounting to do."

He caught himself quickly, for he was about to return to her side. She was right, of course. It would be wise for him to remember, if she ever had him for a husband, that she was often right. It was time for him to stop behaving like a love-sick puppy and heal the wounds he had inflicted on a good many other people who were also dear to him.

"I shall request an interview with Miss Croyden."

"Will that accomplish all?"

"Indeed, it will not, but there are things I cannot reveal until I have also spoken to my mother."

"It concerns her, as well?"

"Her son has gone missing from their home for all these months, and you think it does not concern her?" he said a little too loudly, and met Laurel's eyes. She knew more than she let on, he guessed. "It does," he said, more calmly, resignedly.

"Will you not tell me, Robbie?"

"Not now. Perhaps never."

Laurel stood up, knocking over the wooden chair behind her.

"Have I not shown you how you can trust me?" she cried.

"Then you must trust me. And believe this business to be more difficult than you or anyone else can imagine. It is not my story to share, unless I have Penny's and my mother's permission to do so."

"Robbie . . . "

"My name is Robin Waltham, Earl of Westbridge. Robbie Darkwood no longer exists," he said, more for his own benefit than for hers.

"Oh, he does. He does indeed, while you continue to hide your pain and the truth from those who love you," she said angrily.

He could think of a dozen retorts to her challenge, ranging from turning his back on her to blurting out the damned truth. But, absurdly, only one thing seemed to matter; there was only one thing he needed to know.

"Do you love me?"

Her dark eyes, glinting suspiciously in the dim light, never wavered as she stared at him. "Can you doubt it?"

He shook his head, knowing he did not. "Then you will trust me. And allow me to leave this place, your hermitage."

Her distress was all too apparent.

"Leave? But why so soon? And will you not speak to Penelope first?" She paused, and caught her breath. "And will you allow me to go with you?"

He put his hand up to stop her, but instead she seized it and once again came into his arms.

"I must go back to the place I should not have left, even in my darkest moments. I have done damage there, and it must be repaired, and quickly, if we are to have any chance at happiness. My defection seems to have been a mistake." He combed his fingers through her loose hair, this time spreading the dark curls on her shoulder and his. "You called me brave a moment ago, but I do not know how you think it. I behaved like a coward, and have no excuse, but my own despair and confusion. As I am, I am not worthy of you, dear Laurel, and would make a very bad bargain, indeed. So, you see, you have no choice but to let me go."

"Might I not come with you?" she repeated. "I will help you."

"No, my love. You have already helped me more than you can possibly know. But this is my battle, and mine alone."

She lifted her face to him then, and the kiss they shared was nothing like the flame that seared them when she first came to the hermitage.

It felt gentler, more temperate, and more enduring. It sealed his promise, and her acceptance of what he yet had to do.

"I am, perhaps, wrong about one thing," he said against her lips.

She leaned back and looked up into his eyes with that knowing expression she so often assumed. Perhaps she thought he might acquiesce into allowing her to accompany him to Waltham Hall, but he would disappoint her in that.

"My defection could not have entirely been a mistake, for I would never have otherwise met you," he said gently.

A smile teased at the corner of her lips but her expression did not otherwise waver. "And I am convinced that we would have met anywhere in the whole wide world. Remember that when you are far away fighting your battles. For we will always find each other again."

Chapter Eleven

"Laurel? Laurel, dear?" Penelope's gentle urging brought Laurel's attention away from the large window, through which she hoped to glimpse a sight of a man walking across the slope on the far side of the lake, accompanied by a very energetic dog. "Have you heard anything I have said to you?"

Laurel smiled, wondering how well she disguised her own nervousness. "You are too hard on me, my friend. I have listened ever intently to your words, since that blessed day we met in town. I took your disappointment for my own and tried to share your pain. I listened to every word, hoping to discover how I might help you through a most difficult time."

"I am sorry, my dear. I doubted neither your generosity nor your caring. I only wondered if you heard my description, just now, of the fabric we bought in town to make up as gowns for my younger sisters." Penelope smiled back, and Laurel knew her friend was fully aware of how silly that sounded next to her own protestations. And so she added, "And you did help me through a very difficult time. Do not ever doubt it."

Laurel picked up her embroidery and promptly stabbed her finger on the needle hidden beneath its folds.

"Ah, but I do doubt it, my friend. How can I not, when I have ample evidence of the greater redemptive effect of my brother on your wounded spirits? I think one of you might have thought to mention to me something of the true state of affairs." Laurel knew she sounded petulant, but she felt reasonably justified in it.

"But there was nothing to tell," Penelope assured her. "Until this very day, or the last."

"I do not believe you, truly I do not," Laurel insisted. She did not particularly wish to be difficult, especially to a friend whose accident would preclude her participation in a good many events the Gardiners planned, but Penelope's answers mattered very much to her and to her hopes for her own happiness. "You must have reached some sort of understanding before you arrived at Greenbriars."

"Indeed, we did not. And, in truth, neither do we have what you would call an understanding now."

"And yet the relations between you seem very . . . comfortable," Laurel remarked.

"They are," was all Penelope said.

Laurel would not let the matter drop. "Do you not consider it rather sudden?"

Penelope looked at her in surprise and with a knowing air that made Laurel feel far younger than her own twenty-three years. "I am not an expert at such matters," she admitted, "for I enjoyed an understanding with a gentleman for all my life and felt very satisfied with the arrangement. I now appreciate the understanding had nothing to do with me or with him, but, rather, was the greatest wish of our families. Rob was a very good man, and I am sure I would have been happy with him."

"But?"

"But what I felt the day I met Joseph seemed an emotion unprecedented in my experience. Even now, I am not sure I can put those feelings into words."

"Will you try?" Laurel asked for somewhat selfish reasons. She felt something of those emotions herself and knew not how to explain them.

"Perhaps I can, but not to you." Penelope made no attempt to excuse what might well be perceived as rudeness, but then, Laurel's inquisition might have been the greater lapse in delicacy.

"And what of your Rob? Will he not be devastated to learn of the transference of your affections?"

"As I was devastated when he left me with no explanation, apologies, or promises?"

This seemed a more resolute, determined Penelope than the jilted girl Laurel had known in London. But then, what had she, herself, said to the hermit? How anger made one reckless?

"Perhaps there existed a good reason for his behavior," Laurel said, knowing her opinion on the matter was turned quite in the opposite of its former direction. "What if he returns and delivers you a very good excuse?"

Penelope twisted in her chair, and one of the pillows slipped from behind her. Laurel started to stand so she might retrieve it for her, but Penelope waved her back.

"I believe the only good excuse he may deliver is if he does not return at all. If he is dead, then I shall mourn him. Otherwise, I will not hear of any excuse."

This seemed a very different Penelope indeed. Perhaps Rob was equally right when he said love made one reckless as well.

"Your heart is healed," Laurel said, "But I fear it may have hardened somewhat."

Penelope sighed. "Do not scars inure us to further injury?"

Laurel looked down at her palm, where a slender line of whitened skin caught the light.

"And certainly," Penelope continued, "I could not offer my heart to another if it still bled for Rob. It would neither be fair nor generous of me."

"And does the other . . . Joseph . . . know of this?"

Penelope blushed very prettily. "I believe I have given him a fairly good idea of the way matters stand."

"He must feel the same; I am sure he does. Looking at you thus, I am sure he cannot help it. And knowing him as I do, he is ever serious and unbearably honorable."

"To his sister, perhaps."

"Penny!"

"You will not make me confess it, for it is between Joseph and myself. I hope you will understand someday."

Laurel opened her mouth to let her friend know she was not so innocent as Penelope presumed, but then thought better of it. One wrong word would reveal too much, and Laurel did not even imagine how she would someday let her know Robin Waltham had transferred his affections to herself.

"There is a great deal I have yet to understand," Laurel said quietly. "But you will let me know the truth of one matter?"

Penelope looked up expectantly.

"Did you come to Greenbriars to visit my brother or me?" Laurel asked, hoping Penelope could forgive the inquisition.

"Could I not come to visit both of you? I already depended on your friendship, and could do no more than hope for it from Joseph."

"He does not disappoint you."

Penelope shook her head, loosening several of her dark curls. Her blue eyes twinkled happily. "I doubt Joseph ever could."

"You doubt I ever could do what, Miss Croyden?" asked a familiar voice, sweeping into the parlour without preamble. "Carry you into the drawing room, where my mother would have you play for us? I am sure I can manage it very well."

Penelope laughed. "So you have given me sufficient proof," she said, as her light gaze brushed across his wide shoulders.

Laurel, not unreasonably, was warmly reminded of the way Robbie Darkwood's eyes were wont to look upon herself in recent days, and wished she could be as free to announce her expectations as Penelope. But then, what were her expectations? What if Robin Waltham did not satisfactorily fulfill his obligations and remained bound to Penelope? Would any happiness come of such bitter resolutions?

Joseph bent from the waist and retrieved Penelope's little embroidered pillow, and she did not protest when he put it gently behind her back, supporting her balance by taking both her hands in his. They made a pretty picture: she with her dramatic coloring marked by the darkest and lightest tints, and he with his somewhat burnished hair and deepest brown eyes. Curiously, the contrasts between them were somewhat akin to those shared by Robbie and herself. But in this great moment of doubt, she wondered if anyone would ever notice—or care.

She sighed heavily.

"Did you not say you were diving for turtles, Laurel?" Joseph said pointedly, clearly wishing to be left alone with Penelope. Whatever divine manners he displayed for his beloved were not in evidence in front of his younger sister.

"Turtles?" Laurel asked, as if she addressed a madman. "Of what can you be thinking? I would no sooner dive for turtles than I would marry Lord Ballister."

Penelope laughed, but Joseph did not look away. "A heavy indictment against that gentleman."

"Perhaps he is not so much a gentleman as you suppose, Joey," Laurel said sweetly. "In fact, next to marrying him, diving into muddy water might be heaven itself."

"Why do you not determine the truth of it, dear sister? I am sure Miss Croyden can spare your company."

Laurel looked over Joseph's shoulder and saw Penelope's expression, a mix of contriteness and hope.

"I am sure she can. But I have other matters to which to attend, so the turtles are saved for another day. Perhaps Montrose would like to play with them in the summer house. I think he enjoys that sort of thing."

"He is occupied just now with Miss Jessup. I believe she is making a case for her niece." He stopped and turned to Penelope, clearly thinking he owed her some sort of explanation. "He is a duke, of course."

Penelope whispered something to him, which Laurel could not hear. But it seemed to have the effect of reassuring Joseph of whatever doubts still lingered.

"I shall see to my business, then," Laurel said quickly. "Though I have a feeling all urgency is gone."

* * * *

It certainly appeared to be gone. Laurel went first to the smokehouse, thinking herself very much accustomed to finding it isolated and not likely to feel the loss of her hermit there, even though they frequently shared it. The door he had once struggled to align with the stubborn, rusty hinges stood tightly in the jamb, protecting the empty space within from the great empty space without. How could it be otherwise, even in the light of so much natural beauty? Without his presence, the nearness of his society, all the world seemed an empty place, and she did not yet understand how she could be happy within it.

Laurel released the latch and opened the door, blinking into the darkness. It appeared she was wrong, for the small room was not entirely empty. On the rough table, once used for slabs of meat, and more recently for the exchange of books and other things between the hermit and herself, lay a small volume. Three steps proved sufficient to bring her to it, but only one moment to realize it not a part of her own collection.

She remembered her first visit to her hermitage after her return from London, during which she noticed strange books on the uneven shelves in the room. Robbie Darkwood, who abandoned nearly everything of his old life, had nevertheless brought books with him and might have acquired others since coming to Greenbriars. Laurel did not yet know how many of his possessions had returned with him to Waltham Hall, but she guessed he did not leave behind this token by chance.

And yet, it could not have been his, for it was not a gentleman's book. As she walked to the door, into the light, she turned the fragile pages and recognized the sonnets of Mr. Shakespeare on them, accompanied by illustrations far more flowery and giddy than the poet's words. The collection was not complete, for the volume was far too slim to contain them all, but most of the more notable sonnets were there, and several marked by notations in the margins. Laurel ran her fingers over the fading script, admiring the neat, feminine hand that had once delighted in the meanings of the metaphors and allusions.

For reasons she could not explain, other than it seemed to replicate the confusing pattern of her present life, Laurel turned the pages from back to front, so the flyleaf came at the conclusion of her perusal. There, in the same delicate hand, was written:

"Miss Amanda Wood, 1785"
and beneath it, in darker ink:
"Amanda, Countess of Westbridge, 1791"

Tears, unexpected and sweet, welled up in Laurel's eyes, and she fumbled for her lace before their salt could stain these precious pages. Surely this book belonged to Rob's mother and was the reminder of her he took from their home to comfort himself for the duration of his bleak existence as a hermit. Laurel at once did not imagine him so sentimental, nor yet able to part with something so obviously dear to him. And what did he mean to leave it where she was sure to find it?

It did not require a great mind to quiz it out, and spurts of laughter punctuated her sobs. The warmth of his presence seemed to suddenly surround her, and the landscape no longer appeared the void she had imagined only moments before. The book sealed his promise, and the great desire he undoubtedly had to be reunited with his book spoke of the certainty they would meet again.

Feeling as if an uncompromising weight had just lifted from her breast, Laurel made her way quickly along the familiar path along the lake, wondering if her brothers' friends, who boated amiably on the still water, even noticed her. She doubted it. But if Miss Winthrop's bright green eyes were suspicious, or if Sir John's boredom was aroused by the sight, they might think her nothing more than her father's hermit, making his way to the cottage built into the stone wall.

The sheep and goats were gone, their pen opened to give them their freedom. But whether Rob had just allowed them to take their chances on the estate, or if he had consigned them to the care of another tenant, she did not know. Certainly, they would be safe enough from harm. But she did not imagine her father would be very pleased if the goat showed up on the veranda and sampled the exotic flowers the gardeners displayed there every morning. However, it would certainly be diverting.

Laurel knocked on the door, an act patently absurd when she considered the last time she made an entrance here. Then, she might have found her hermit in any state of undress, or engaged in some activity she should not witness. Perhaps she had. For she did not know if he had intended to inform her of his imminent and hasty departure. Yet, for all her doubts, she could not harbor any regrets for what took place in this room only hours before, nor did she imagine Rob did either.

The hermitage, once her sanctuary and her secret joy, was now returned to her care. But the triumph she might have once felt was replaced by a keener sense of loss and loneliness. For now it seemed the real pleasure she found here was not in her solitude, but in the time she had spent with a stranger who withheld so much from her, and yet had somehow revealed the things that really mattered. The place, and the memories it held, were forever changed.

And Laurel could not yet know if those changes were destined to make her happy. Matters might soon become very complicated, and even unpleasant.

Robbie Darkwood might never be restored to her, for a dozen obstacles might keep them apart. He remained bound to another, and his family obligations seemed even more ancient than the home he had abandoned. Far from Greenbriars, from the intimacies and freedoms they enjoyed, he might find himself most comfortable in his more formal role, that to which he had been born and educated. Or the deceptions capable of keeping his true identity hidden from her for all this time might yet deceive her again, and he could prove no better than a common seducer.

Or what if, upon learning of the resignation of his hermit, her father set out to find a suitable replacement? Another man might settle in her beloved sanctuary and exclude her entirely from the spot. Bereft of intellect or sensibility, he might be absolutely indifferent to a lady who attempted to blackmail him and oust him from the premises. He could be very old and very ugly. He might use her precious books for kindling, and smash all the possessions she had brought here over the years. Or, far worse, he might be entirely indifferent to her.

And certainly, it was impossible she could fall in love with every hermit hired to live in her father's hermitage.

She sighed, and the sound echoed off the empty walls.

Truly, it was impossible she could ever be in love with anyone other than Robbie Darkwood. Robin Waltham. Westbridge.

She did not know what to call him, but it did not seem to matter overmuch. She only knew that when he called her, she would come.

* * * *

Rob stood in the shadows of a stand of ancient oaks and gazed up at the great house he had once thought never to see again. But his exile imposed so precipitously and vengefully upon himself was of his own doing, and he bore no ill will towards the assemblage of towers and halls built somewhat arbitrarily by the earls of Westbridge over the reigns of several monarchs. His own father did little to improve the place; indeed, it might be said the old man aimed to pull the whole place down in a shower of scandal and grief. But he, Robin, had really just come into the property, and he had a sudden optimistic vision of what his future here might bring.

Prinny whined, clearly impatient to move on. And why not? They had travelled much in the past few days and felt somewhat the worse for it all. Over one night, they had settled comfortably in a hay field, pressed close to each other for warmth and comfort. But the next, when a misty rain fell upon the countryside, Rob had felt the necessity of investing in a night's stay at an inn, and he had explained to his four-legged companion that he would do very well in the stable. Prinny did not seem as convinced of the business, and in the morning, when they were reunited, he stayed even closer to Rob's side than usually his habit. They did not separate for the next night, or the next, and here they were arrived at their destination before seeking haven for another night became a necessity. Of course, for all Rob was master of this estate, he knew his mother would not take kindly to Prinny finding rest in the upstairs bedchambers.

They walked together up the drive, Rob noting which rooms were lit and which were dark, and Prinny noting every rabbit who poked a curious nose out of the hedgerows.

At the door, elderly Mr. Avery nearly fainted away when he saw Rob's anxious and weary face, and the two hugged each other in a fortifying embrace.

"Do they know to expect you, my lord?" Avery whispered, patting Rob's chest and shoulders, as if he could not believe him real. "I cannot believe it, for I heard your dear mother sobbing not two hours past, and I know all she worries about is your safe return."

Rob felt his own heart pain him for the damage he had unthinkingly done to others, and wondered how long it would take to make things whole again.

"Is she here now, in the parlour?" he asked anxiously.

"My lady rarely goes out, for she is still in mourning," Avery pointed out, and then amended his statement. "For your father, you understand.

She never believed you dead, nor doubted you would return."

"If you heard her crying, then she may well have doubted me. But I did send a brief letter not very long ago."

"Of course," Avery said, and Rob reflected that the servants knew more about the comings and goings of a household than did any of the family. "But it only just arrived. It appeared to have been misdirected."

"Damn the man!" Rob said. "I hired someone in the village to deliver it here, not expecting to be home so soon thereafter. I directed it to Harold."

"Your brother is here, of course. And . . . " Avery's voice tapered off.

"Yes, Avery?" Rob asked, somewhat distracted by the removal of his bulky pack from his back.

"Forgive me, my lord. But your young lady? Miss Croyden? She is gone from home as well."

"I saw her only recently, Avery. She had a minor mishap and is recovering at the home of a mutual friend. It is nothing, and I have every hope of her future happiness."

"Here at Waltham House, my lord?"

Rob would curse Avery's impertinence to ask it if he did not believe the old man entirely devoted to him. "I cannot say. Time will yet reveal the answers to your questions."

"Very well, my lord." Avery bowed, once again the proper servant. "Would you care to bathe before you are reunited with your family?"

Rob looked down at his ragged and filthy clothing and flicked off a hayseed.

"That bad, am I?" he asked cheerfully. "But no, I can not prolong this any longer. And perhaps if I appear before them thus, they will have more sympathy for me and forgive me."

Avery stifled a laugh, and then his face sobered. "You would have had to commit a much greater crime to lose their forgiveness, but I doubt any such thing would have been in your nature, my lord."

Rob looked long and hard at the old man, wondering if he knew more than anyone about the reasons Rob had left his home and everyone he loved. But he could see nothing there but an attempt to be clever, and a natural consideration of Rob's emotional state.

"I am ever full of surprises, old friend," he said, and patted Avery on the back. "And now, let me pull one out for my mother and brother, and hope for the best."

Leaving Avery standing in the hallway, possibly wondering what to do about a muddy mongrel who made himself quite comfortable near the fire, Rob walked past him to where bright lights shone in the dining hall.

He slipped quietly through the door and paused for a moment to observe the homey scene. His mother sat in her accustomed seat, trifling with the stem of her wineglass. Her pale hair, though laced with gray, looked golden in the candlelight, and Rob wondered why neither he nor Harry were blessed with her fairness. With their dark hair and light eyes, they were both the very image of their father.

Harry sat near her, talking rather more animatedly, and looking older than when Rob saw him last. He had had an unexpected burden to bear, and the additional uncertainty of knowing if he could claim the title in the absence of his brother. It would age even the most lighthearted soul.

But Harry had not claimed the title. Rob did not have to look further than the empty seat at the head of the table to know his own return was expected and desired. He himself had only sat in that seat for a few months before vacating it, but he imagined it still warm and comforting.

He came forward, not sure what to say.

"Lindford, my son would like some more of the roast, I believe," said Lady Westbridge, and looked up to meet his eyes. The goblet dropped and shattered, but not even the servants seemed to notice. "Oh, Rob. Oh, Rob," was all his mother managed to say.

Harry was a little more energetic. Rob thought he would dash right over the dining table in his rush to reach his brother's side, but instead he opted for the long way around, foregoing the use of his cane, and merely knocked over three chairs. Their arms were around each other in less than a minute, and their mother joined them only moments later.

"We received your letter, old boy," Harry said. "We only imagined you would follow, but we did not think it so soon."

"Should I stay away, then?" Rob made a feeble attempt at humor.

The look in his family's eyes told him exactly how feeble it proved.

"Why did you go?" Lady Westbridge wailed, letting go the control that must have ruled her usually dignified behavior for all these months. "We did not know what we did to send you away."

Rob stiffened, wondering why he had not considered this. Surely his family would only have thought him solely to blame, though even there they would be mistaken.

"It was never you. You must know that, Mother. My reasons are good ones, though they seemed better at the time." He wondered how long he could put off the inevitable. Surely until after he managed a long, hot bath. "We must talk, and soon. But for now . . ." He paused and looked over his mother's pale hair to the large platters of food remaining on the sideboard. "Might I take my place at the table?"

* * * *

Laurel watched the Duke of Montrose leave the parlour, sulky after being bested at a game of whist. Sir John, Miss Fellows and Mr. Holt looked somewhat apologetic for having been triumphant. The duke was a boy-man everyone sought to please, as they would a younger brother or ward.

Laurel smiled knowingly at her mother, who finally understood that her daughter did not expect to be the duchess, and deflected her attention with a nod to the other side of the room. There, Penelope Croyden stood taking several tentative steps on her weak ankle, assisted by a very solicitous Joseph. Lewis approached the couple, and then apparently thought better of it and walked out of the room instead. Miss Winthrop was about somewhere, so Laurel did not doubt he would be entertained as well.

"She might have had an earl, but I believe she prefers your brother," Mrs. Gardiner said softly. Miss Jessup sat snoring in a nearby chair, and no one had any wish to arouse her.

Laurel considered how her mother would respond if she told her the earl might be had by someone a good deal closer than Miss Croyden, but she did not dare share any of her fondest hopes or the subject of her nightly dreams. Nothing was yet decided, nothing resolved. Robin Waltham left her with a slim volume of poetry, the memory of his caresses, and some vague vows protesting his love for her. Surely he once had offered no more or no less to Penelope.

"I cannot say I blame her, Mother. Once burned, she will not touch the hot stove again. And our Joseph is ever trustworthy, reliable, and will never leave her."

Mrs. Gardiner smiled indulgently. "I suspect you do not see Joseph as other young ladies might, for he will always be your brother. He is very handsome, cuts quite a figure, and is truly very passionate."

"Joseph?" Laurel scoffed.

"Do you not see it?" Mrs. Gardiner laughed, and Miss Jessup stirred in her chair. "I am sure your friend does."

Laurel watched as Joseph led Penelope gently across the rug, allowing her to lean heavily on his arm. She stumbled once and quickly reassured him, and then said something to make him fiercely blush. It seemed there was a part of Joseph his younger sister had never seen before, and she suspected it proved a new experience for Penelope as well. Had she not confessed how her love for Rob seemed sisterly? Did Rob not reassure Laurel his love of the lady next door felt brotherly? If they were both truthful with each other, and, indeed, with her, she understood something of what was lacking in the love they shared.

And how they each could so quickly find happiness with another. Or believed they could.

Laurel had heard nothing of the hermit, of Robbie Darkwood, or of Westbridge since his leaving. Mr. Gardiner seemed blissfully unaware of his employee's retirement, and no one seemed to notice the lack of the silent figure who decorously slipped in and out of the woods and remained silently at the side of the road while the carriages passed. Most of the household happily anticipated the ball to be held the next evening, and no one suspected that Laurel had once hoped to surprise them with the addition of the hermit into their midst. It was as if he had never existed, which was perhaps the very point.

She sighed, perhaps too loudly, but only her mother heard her. Her concerned mother leaned over and gently reassured Laurel with a caress on her shoulder, obviously thinking she pined for a love of her own.

Her dear mother did not know the half of it.

The gentle peace of the large room was interrupted by loud footsteps and a conversation heard just beyond the door. Lewis came in, holding an envelope, and delivered it just short of his mother, who clearly expected to receive it.

"It is for Miss Jessup," he said clearly. And then, in a whisper, "Should we wake the old b . . . "

"Leave it with me, Lewis," Mrs. Gardiner said firmly. "One does not startle an elderly lady, no matter the hardiness of her constitution."

Even so, after coaxing Miss Jessup awake and gently arousing the lady to receive her message, Miss Jessup seemed very startled indeed.

"Good heavens!" she shouted after reading it. "Penelope! Come here at once! There is great news from home!"

Her aunt seemed unaware that Penelope still relied on a crutch and on Joseph to get about, and urged her to make haste. In truth, Penelope did not appear all that excited, and Joseph, perhaps sensing the worst, even less so.

"What is it, Aunt?" Penelope asked. By this time, she enjoyed the audience of everyone in the room.

"It is Westbridge! He is returned!   He asks to speak with us as soon as it may be arranged. We must leave at once!"

Penelope wavered where she stood, and she might have fallen, if Joseph had not caught her by the waist.

"Come, girl! We must pack our trunks immediately and leave this very night."

Penelope looked long and hard at the man at her side before turning back to her aunt.

"We will not," she said firmly.

Miss Jessup scarcely heard her, so great was her anxiety. But when no one else in the room moved, she caught herself and looked up into her ward's face. "I am sure I did not hear you correctly, my dear."

"And I am sure you did, dear Aunt. I have no intention of quitting Greenbriars so soon, certainly not when our host and hostess are hosting a ball. I intend to dance," she announced, and caught hold of Joseph's arm again. "I have not heard from Westbridge in all these months, nor has he seemed to care what has become of me. Surely you cannot imagine I would feel compelled to do his bidding now."

"He is your betrothed," Aunt Jessup reminded her, but stared at Joseph until he slipped his arm from Penelope's grasp. "And he is an earl."

"The first is a relationship he chose to ignore, so I do not think it valid any longer. And the second is a title only recently acquired and bears little connection to the boy I once knew. In any case, neither name bears any connection to me. Not any longer."

After this bold and spirited speech, Laurel thought her friend deserved a full round of applause, but her mother's glance froze her on the spot as she said, "Miss Croyden, there will be other balls. You must obey your aunt."

"Thank you for your good advice, Mrs. Gardiner," Penelope said without the slightest trace of irony. "But with your indulgence, I will stay until after the ball. I do not choose to wait until the next celebration. And Robin Waltham, for all he is an earl, can wait until his horses fly. I will return in due course."

"You seem a determined young woman," said Mrs. Gardiner, and Laurel knew her mother meant it as the sincerest compliment.

Penelope smiled up at Joseph. "I believe I am," she said.

Chapter Twelve

Laurel turned her head one way and then the other, her eyes following her startling reflection in the large mirror of her dressing table. One of the new maids had just finished braiding and pinning up her hair, and the girl seemed blessed with rare talent for such things. Dark tresses were neatly swept away from her brow, revealing the sparkle of diamond earrings. Laurel could not say why her parents decided to bestow such a rare and beautiful gift on her without benefit of an occasion, but she guessed her mother might have imagined her unattached daughter needed some reassurance in the face of her friend Penelope's undisguised happiness. And Mr. Gardiner, who firmly believed money could buy a good deal of happiness, must have readily corresponded with his jeweler in town.

In any case, Mary Ann, the new girl, seemed determined to show off her mistress and the diamonds to their best advantage. She had started braiding Laurel's hair while it was still damp from a bath, and she had marveled at its thickness and curl until Laurel felt quite superior to all the royal duchesses, and perhaps to one or two princesses. Lavish compliments did as much as the diamonds to restore her confidence, if not her complete happiness.

The gown was one of her own choosing, and it felt mildly disconcerting now to remember how she once had wondered if the hermit would like it on her. She now appreciated how very much she had deceived herself, imagining she might have presented Robbie Darkwood to her bereaved friend, when she knew from the very start how much she wanted him for herself. If she had succeeded in bringing them together, and somehow had contrived to have both at the ball this evening, why would it have mattered if Robbie thought she looked like a princess or a drainpipe?

Because it did matter. If she had been the slightest bit truthful to herself, she would have acknowledged how she felt about the mysterious stranger, even after their first tumultuous meeting. If she owned the smallest bit of discretion, she would have remained far, far away from him, never even thinking about meeting him on the path, or demanding he provide a delivery service for her. If she was the truest friend to

Penelope, it would have not mattered in the least if the hermit preferred Miss Laurel Gardiner in green or blue.

But she rather thought he would have preferred the green. And so she sat now, admiring the way the brilliant diamonds set off little flashes of reflected green silk, and how the ribbons Mary Ann wove through her hair were precisely the right color. Her corset, new and very stiff, nearly took her breath away, but the effect seemed worth it. Her breasts were raised to the limit of respectable decency, and her curves required no powder to make them look flawless. Bending slightly forward, she felt even more satisfied with herself. Her brothers would be less satisfied, but she did not dress to suit Joseph and Lewis.

Indeed, for whom did she dress tonight?

A slight tap at the door diverted her attention from the alluring lady in the mirror who just happened to resemble herself.

"Enter!" she called out. "Mary Ann, I am of a mind to . . . Penelope!"

Laurel turned in her seat, startled to see her friend walk in without the slightest difficulty. If a trace of a limp remained, most of the guests would attribute it to the newness of Penelope's dance slippers, or to a clumsy partner. And if the girl begged off from dancing midway through the evening, she would have sufficient company to join her and no one would think anything amiss.

"Mary Ann is with Miss Winthrop, who seems to have lost her own maid. The dear girl stopped by my own chamber, but I assured her I could manage quite well."

"Indeed, you have," Laurel assured her, and moved over on the bench so her friend could join her. "You are managing even better than I hoped."

Penelope blushed gracefully and looked down into her lap.

"Indeed, your ankle, feared broken only days ago, seems miraculously recovered," Laurel noted a little tartly.

"It remains somewhat painful," Penelope said as she stretched out her leg and pulled up the hem of her gown. "But the swelling is nearly down. Dr. Arbuthnot is a remarkable healer."

"Dr. Arbuthnot would not know a dog bite from the pox, and yet we all foolishly call upon him to make pronouncements upon our health." Laurel looked back at her reflection and nibbled on her lower lip until the color was bright and the delicate flesh slightly swollen. "Nay, I might say there is a more remarkable healer among us."

"You might, but you will not?" Penelope laughed.

"I hesitate, because I wonder if great skills at healing are needed if the injury is not so very bad as reported."

Penelope sat silently for a few moments, and Laurel felt her tremble beside her.

"I might say you accuse me of a great injustice," Penelope said at last.

"You might, but you will not?"

"Of course not. I cannot say it, because you are absolutely correct," Penelope said, and burst into laughter.

"Oh, you are a wicked girl indeed to play my brother falsely!" Laurel shook her head, smiling.

Penelope sobered at once. "But I am neither wicked nor did I ever play him false. It is just he is so very shy and could barely speak to me when we met in town."

"He thought you betrothed to another, you may recall."

"I am not likely to forget it, my dear friend. But the fact did little to stifle the attentions of other young men who somehow thought despair enhanced my attraction."

"Indeed, it might have done just that. But to deliberately injure yourself? You might have suffered a good deal more than you intended."

Penelope nodded. "It was not entirely deliberate. I did stumble, and fall, and could only be grateful I did not bring you down with me! But you cannot fault me for clumsiness, for I was quite distracted. I could only think of your brother, who yet greeted me with his usual reticence, of my aunt, who felt the immediate allure of a duke in our presence, and, of course, your own purposeful mission."

"My mission?" Laurel squeaked, wishing to forget the brilliant scheme which had become her excuse for courting the hermit. "I intended nothing but . . ."

Penelope silenced her with a glance in the mirror. "You intended me to meet a charming swain on the estate, as I recall. You told me you thought him far more worthy than any of the gentlemen we knew in town, and infinitely preferable to my Westbridge. I am sure he would have been perfectly congenial, and I did not want to ruin your little experiment. But surely you can see that I did not want to complicate my already uncertain life. To dance with your swain would have made you happy, and possibly him, as well. But to spend my time, and dances, with Joseph would make me happy. And after my recent sad experience, is it so wrong for me to wish myself happy?"

"No, of course not, Penelope," Laurel said gently, thinking of the elusiveness of her own happiness. "And so you fell and made us believe your injury somewhat more serious than it seemed, and so earned the solicitous attention of my otherwise shy brother."

"You will not ever tell him?"

"No, it is for you to tell him. Someday, perhaps, when you are marveling at the wonder of your meeting and how you fell in love. It is really quite romantic."

"I believe it is. I can only wish the same for you someday. But you are so practical, and difficult to deceive, I daresay there will be not the smallest bit of artifice or play acting in your own courtship. The man you love will have to be straightforward and honest, to measure up to your own strict standards."

Laurel caught her breath and coughed.

Penelope slapped her on the back, anxious and concerned. "Are you well?"

"Goodness, yes. It is only this corset. I do not know why I wear it but to torture myself."

Penelope sat back on the bench, tipping it slightly. "You wear it because you look absolutely splendid in it, my dear. And if there is a man here with half an ounce of sense in his head, he will demand every dance upon your card. Now I am so happy, I would wish all my friends the same absolute joy."

"Do not raise your expectations so high," Laurel said dampeningly. "I have spent the last few weeks in the company of my brothers' friends and have not detected the smallest interest on their part. Nor on mine."

"Not even from the little duke?"

Laurel laughed.

Penelope smiled. "And yet, when you greeted me on my arrival, I thought you looked wondrously well, with the suspicious glow of one who is in love."

"You are a romantic, Penelope. I had only been in the sunshine overlong and was probably feeling the effects of the summer heat."

"With your swain, perhaps?"

"He is not mine. He is yours still," Laurel said, with more gravity than Penelope might have thought the situation merited.

She looked surprised, but did not dismiss the pronouncement. "Do you require me to release him to your care?"

"Yes, I suppose I do," said Laurel, nodding thoughtfully.

"Will I see him soon? This very evening?"

"I am certain you will meet shortly, but I do not expect him tonight."

"It is just as well," Penelope said, slipping off the seat and standing sturdily on her feet. "I wish to spend all my time with Joseph. When I leave with my aunt to confront the Earl of Westbridge, I would not have any doubts lingering in your brother's mind."

"Then I consider him a very lucky man," Laurel said, and truly meant it.

* * * *

"Miss Laurel?" One of the servants stopped her on the stairway as she descended unescorted to the ballroom. "Your father wishes to see you in his library."

"Now, James? Is he not with our guests below?"

"I believe he already made a brief appearance and is now hiding. He may not care for the entertainment."

Laurel laughed. "I daresay he does not. But does he wish for me to hide from the music and guests as well?"

"As to that, I cannot say," James answered solemnly

Laurel caught herself quickly. "No, you are quite right. I will see him at once."

She moved quickly down the stairs, wistfully yearning to be among the guests and their laughter. She did not really think her father would keep her from all that, and yet it seemed odd he would demand an audience at such a moment. Perhaps he only wished to hear how much she appreciated his little gift to cheer her spirits.

As she knocked gently on the door, she heard the musicians start the first set and realized Mr. Holt would be looking for her in the crush. She had, however, the best excuse.

Her father opened the door himself and closed it quickly behind her.

"Father! Is all well?" she asked.

"Why would it not be? There are a hundred people in my home, spilling drinks on my priceless rugs, appraising the tableware. I have had guests here for weeks, and none of them seem in the least bit inclined to leave, nor offer a proposal of marriage to my only daughter."

"Oh, indeed," Laurel said humorously, not at all sure where her father's tirade would end. "But then, I never would have accepted Miss Fellows or Miss Winthrop."

"I am not amused, Missy. I did, however, have hopes for Montrose."

"One hopes he will grow to be a man, but we need not expect anything more at this time."

Her father grunted, and Laurel knew she had won that brief skirmish.

"Your brother informed me just this night that he intends to marry Miss Croyden."

"But that is good news, surely?"

"That your brother is courting a woman betrothed to an earl? It does not sound very good to me. What scandal will ensue! Will others find his courtship presumptuous? Will the Gardiner business lose clients as a result?"

"Father, you need not worry. I have spoken to Penelope and she has quite forgotten—if not forgiven—her earl. Her heart belongs to our Joseph, of that you can be certain. Do not think any scandal will fall upon us."

Her father looked anything but convinced, and yet he did not pursue the argument. Laurel suspected there remained another issue, and since she was the one summoned to his audience, she could only believe it had to do with herself.

"Thank you for the earrings, Father," she said, hoping for the best.

"More than you deserve, my girl," he said, confirming her suspicions. He cast his hands about on the huge desk, visibly frustrated until they rested on one sheet of creamy paper. Across the expanse of the oak, Laurel saw a small crest imprinted at the top of the page. Her father fumbled for his spectacles and then peered at the words, written in a bold hand.

"But worse luck is mine today. It seems I have lost one of my trusted employees," he said.

"Surely there are many who seek work? Lewis and Joseph could find you a man in the village."

"Ah, but the man I lost had very specific, not to mention peculiar, qualifications for the job. One might call him uniquely suited."

"How so?" Laurel asked innocently, knowing what was to come.

"Why, because the man is a hermit. Dedicated to the noble life of isolation, contemplation, completely independent from society. Where will I find another?"

Laurel knew her instincts were right to already regret the loss of her hermitage. "It does not seem so very hard. I daresay there are a good many malcontents to be had, who would never admit of their pleasure at being paid for doing what comes naturally. You paid him well, I assume?"

Her father narrowed his eyes. "He seemed content. I take it that was your impression as well?"

"Certainly, he could complain of nothing to . . ." Too late, Laurel felt the trap. "Are we speaking of the hooded man who kept company with the dog?"

"Do I employ any other hermits about the place?"

"I could not say, Father. But one would think a community of hermits would quite defeat the purpose," she pointed out, remembering doing the same to Robbie Darkwood.

"Almost certainly. I do know my man wished very much to be alone and communicate with no one. The dog seemed as much company as he desired."

"Then he must have been quite content, sir."

"Apparently not. Though I left him alone to his own devices, and cautioned your brothers to do the same, my hermit did not find the place to his liking. Indeed, he claims to have found a place where he might settle his differences with society." Mr. Gardiner's finger tapped a tattoo on the letter. "The implication is Greenbriars did not provide sufficient exile to do the very thing."

Laurel heard the music and the thrum of voices from the ballroom. "But Greenbriars is not a place where one escapes the rest of the world," she insisted.

"I suspect my hermit might have escaped the rest of the world, but not the attention of one small person."

Laurel straightened her back, although reminding her father of her height could not be the most important point of their discussion. "Does he indict that person in his letter to you?"

"He does not have to, for I have no doubt of her identity. And he does not write the letter. It comes from the Earl of Westbridge, who apparently dashed it off in the same burst of energy as his message to his all-but-forgotten beloved. The coincidence is very odd."

"Perhaps the hermit informed the earl Miss Croyden visited here and has, therefore, been rewarded with a position at Waltham Hall."

"Perhaps that is it," her father nodded. "It is very useful to claim a connection to an earl; do you not agree?"

"Very useful. And yet, Miss Croyden would spurn it for love of my brother."

"Love does strange things to us all. But I do not wish my daughter to seek it in the arms of a hermit."

"Father!"

"Do not dispute me, Missy. I am ever aware of what goes on about me."

"Then I am surprised you are upset over the departure of one so unworthy."

"Unworthy? Nay, I never said my man was unworthy. Indeed, he seems to have more sense than my own daughter and departed before any real damage might be done."

"Would you prefer my leaving to his?"

"I would have you with your mother and me always, if I thought it would make you happy. But it would not. Nor, do I think, would you be happy living in the hermitage."

"I have no intention of doing so. And, I must add, no damage has been done to my reputation," she said warily.

"And to you?" he asked, as she knew he must.

"I cannot dismiss the charges so easily, Father. I am certain I love him."

Her father sank back into his seat, but he appeared quite calm and very thoughtful.

"It is worse than I imagined, then."

"And yet it may be a good deal better than you think. You must trust me on this, sir. I am ever your daughter and know what I am about."

"I do trust you, or I would not have looked the other way when I knew you bothered the poor boy."

"I did not bother him," Laurel insisted, and then, at the look on her father's face, "Perhaps on occasion."

"I also trust you will do what is right. Or, at the very least, allow him to do what is right."

"I shall, and so shall he. But the time is not yet at hand."

Her father looked up from his seat, a questioning look on his face.

"But I believe it will be soon, Father. I pray it shall be so."

"I will add my prayers to yours then, and hope the matter may be settled one way or another before your dear mother learns our secret," he said, and dropped Rob's letter into a drawer of the desk. "And I suppose we must join the dancers, or she will demand to know what we are doing here."

"Will you escort me?" Laurel asked, and offered her father her elbow.

"I will, for I would not have it said my daughter wanted for partners." He came around the desk, straightening his jacket, and smiled at her. One finger came up and tapped the diamond dangling from her ear. "These are for you, not part of the dowry to offer the man who one day would be your husband."

"Thank you, sir. But you need not worry. I will not sell them to buy food or drink."

"I am sure you will never need to," she thought she heard him say, but his words were lost in the gaiety of the music that enveloped them when they opened the door to the hall.

* * * *

Although Laurel had already witnessed ample evidence that her poor fragile friend was already healed of all her injuries, she did credit her for some discretion during the hours of the ball. Penelope danced very prettily several times with Joseph, igniting sparks of rumour and speculation throughout the circles of guests whose business it was to gossip as much as to step to the music. And, surely to satisfy her aunt, Penelope danced twice with Montrose and once with Mr. Winthrop. But, for the rest, Penelope sat enthroned at one end of the great room, holding court with those who had heard about her accident but who, more likely, wanted to meet the young lady who was rumoured to already claim one of the children of the wealthy Gardiner family, even while still betrothed to another.

Joseph proved solicitous and attentive, bringing her a pillow with which to prop up her ankle, and serving her so many drinks of lemonade the poor girl would surely have to excuse herself frequently and for some duration by the end of the evening. But then, Laurel reflected with just a touch of envy, Penelope somehow seemed to manage the business of her life very well, even while giving the impression to others of her wounded helplessness. It was a talent Laurel herself had never nurtured, though with three brothers, it might have come in very useful.

Laurel reflected on these things as she took her turn with the Duke of Montrose, a partner with whom she could comfortably converse even while her thoughts were on other matters. Though still a boy, he proved a very creditable dance partner, perhaps because the lessons from his dance master could not be very far away in his recollection. In time, he might make a woman a very excellent husband, but that time was not yet.

"I believe I must travel from Greenbriars later this week," he said, as they came together briefly during the quadrille.

Laurel watched Penelope's face turn gratefully to Joseph as he brought her some delight from the buffet tables, and knew she should never judge her friend ungenerously again. Penelope loved Joseph; she revealed that love in every line of her expression. Nothing else mattered.

"Will you be sorry to see me go, Miss Gardiner?" Montrose asked.

Laurel, confused and a bit impatient, turned to look at him. "Of course I shall, your grace. But all dances must come to an end. You must, of course, go on to another lady."

He looked at her as if she was mad, and for the first time since they had met weeks ago, Laurel caught a glimpse of the man he would become. He would be intelligent and inquisitive, though blunt in his approach. His wit was of an unremarkable sort, but, in time, he might be made to laugh. But never at anything aimed at himself or to those he cherished. He simply would not see anything funny in it.

He caught her hand so they might change positions on the floor, and his grip felt surprisingly firm.

"I am not speaking of the termination of our dance, Miss Gardiner. Laurel, if I may be so bold."

"Of course, your grace." Laurel paused only fractionally, trying to think of his name. But she could not.

"I am speaking of my departure from Greenbriars, Laurel, a fact I have mentioned thrice since we started dancing."

"I . . ." Laurel stuttered, and glanced to where Penelope still sat, drinking her lemonade. "I am sorry. I must have been caught up in the music. But when will you depart? Is it imminent?"

"For my part, I have scarcely heard the music. I have only thought of you, and of how much I shall miss you when I depart at the end of the week."

The dance steps, allowing Laurel to turn her back on her partner for a few moments, granted her a few moments of reflection. "I shall miss you as well," she said companionably, when she turned back towards him.

"Will you indeed?" he asked, and the look on his face made her instantly understand how poorly she had chosen her words. "I prayed you would say such a thing."

"You must not read too much into my words, your grace. I merely meant that it has been lovely having guests at Greenbriars, particularly those as lofty as yourself."

He stood a little taller. "I am a duke, of course."

"Of course. How could I not know it?"

He glanced at her, and she knew her instincts were correct: he would not be laughed at.

"But I enjoy a good many things. Particularly nature and wildlife."

"I noted as much. Did you not spend a good deal of time at the lakefront?"

"There is much to be discovered there, even in an artificial lake. But I am certain you already know this, for you are an avid explorer as well."

"I am . . . I am not certain I heard you correctly, your grace," Laurel said, though she knew she had heard him perfectly. Of what could he be thinking?

He went on, either unwilling or thinking it unnecessary to repeat himself. "I have observed you frequently taking walks about the estate, favoring the lake path at the north side. And, just yesterday, your brother mentioned you had been diving in the water for turtles. It is most unladylike, but an excellent method for studying the creatures."

Laurel murmured something also unladylike beneath her breath, ruing the day she had tried to provoke her besotted brother with her ridiculous words.

She opened her mouth to protest, to explain, even though she had not a thought of what she would say. But, for better or worse, the music stopped just then, leaving her mid-step and not quite prepared for her final courtesy.

Montrose, however, seemed perfectly prepared. For, not only did he bow deeply, but he grabbed her hand as he did so.

"The dance is over, your grace," Laurel said, increasingly uncomfortable.

"It may be, but my speech is not," he answered, and pulled her from the floor. Laurel was aware of several interested glances her way, and knew she was well and truly caught. To protest, or to slip away, would have raised far too many carefully plucked eyebrows.

"We were speaking of turtles, I believe?" she asked blithely as they circled one of the columns of the room and fell into its shadow. They remained in plain view of most of the guests, so there proved nothing improper about their tête-à-tête. But neither would anyone dare to interrupt them thus.

"We were," Montrose said, "but I am not so interested in them as I am in you."

Laurel knew her discomfort fully justified, then. For Montrose spoke like a man with a purpose, and she began to understand what that purpose might be. But where had he learned such things? Who would have guessed the petulant child at the card table, the boy who threw shiny pebbles into the water while she exchanged passionate kisses with a hermit among the statuary, would rise to the occasion as one confident and well rehearsed?

And how would she refuse him without causing him to run off in a childish snit?

"I am younger than you, I know," he said thoughtfully.

"Thank you for reminding me of it, your grace," Laurel said.

He looked at her, defensive perhaps against the blatant sarcasm in her tone. "It is simply a fact, Miss Gardiner."

"Indeed, but more to the point is why such a fact matters in any discussion we might have."

"Miss Gardiner, I have come to appreciate your talents in the past weeks. I see you are also kind and loyal to friends and family. Your beauty is a matter of record; I heard of it long before I met your brother Lewis. I know you are not titled, but as I myself have no family, I have no one to whom I must answer or explain a single thing." He paused and drew himself up to his full height which was not, alas, as elevated as Laurel's. "Surely you know why I have drawn you out of the crowd."

"To bid farewell? You say you are leaving soon?"

He blinked once, and then again.

"I hope we may never need to bid each other farewell in the future, Miss Gardiner. Laurel. I am asking for your hand in marriage."

Laurel sank back against the column, wondering why she had failed to foresee this until moments ago. A man prepared to offer his fortune and his estimable name to a woman must have observed her most particularly, though she never was aware of it. And she must have offered some encouragement, though she had remained equally unaware of that.

"I have surprised you," he said, more astute than she would have guessed him. "I have done it poorly, I suppose. I have been rehearsing all week, and thought I would be quite persuasive."

Laurel straightened, realizing he had just granted her an unexpected opportunity for a graceful reprieve. "You have not done it poorly, your grace. You spoke like a true gentleman, very sincerely, and with determined elocution. You nearly took my breath away. But . . ."

His pleasure at her words came immediately between them. "Did I indeed? I asked your brother for advice and found an excellent volume of speeches in your father's library. For I knew someone like yourself, who heard proposals from gentlemen before . . . Oh, forgive me, Miss Gardiner. I know nothing of it, of course."

"Of course," Laurel readily forgave him, if indeed such was needed.

But she really was thinking that here was her third proposal in months. Possibly. She did not yet know what to think of those final words with her hermit in his cottage.

"There is but one thing lacking," he said and took her hand in his.

Laurel noticed two old biddies watching them and hoped he would not dare to kiss her, for resistance would be awkward, if not downright impossible.

"You are quite right," she sighed.

Montrose said nothing for several moments as he stood holding her hand. She had the impression he waited on her word, and she knew what it ought to be. "I have played my part, Laurel. Now it is your turn to play yours. I only await your assent. It is the only thing lacking."

She pulled her hand out of his, and ran a finger affectionately down his arm. "No, your grace. There is another thing, far more difficult to realize than a lady's acceptance of your proposal. It is love, of course. In all your study for this great moment, did you not once read how very much a suit is strengthened by protestations of love?"

He pulled away from her. "I love you, then. Is there another reason why I would propose marriage?"

"Oh, your grace, you are very right in noting I am older than yourself, for at the moment I feel many, many years older. Of course there are many reasons for marriage; I have heard several of them. But love is what will make me marry, if and when I do." Laurel felt an ache in her heart, thinking of what she had lost, and what she yet hoped to regain. "And you do not love me, your grace."

He started to protest, and she placed her seductive finger upon his lips. She heard a lady to her right giggle.

"And though I am very fond of you, and am truly humbled by the honor you bestow by this offer, I am not in love with you," she added.

She took her finger away and waited for what would come. She thought she could read him fairly well, for she believed she saw the precise moment when he acquiesced.

He sighed. "I am sorry to hear it, for I thought we could get on fairly well."

"So we might have, but more like brother and sister, I suspect. And I have quite enough of that, you understand."

He smiled unexpectedly and boyishly. "And yet your brothers love you very much."

Laurel thought of George and Joseph and Lewis, and of the sentiments both Penelope and Robin Waltham betrayed about their feelings for each other.

"They do, but it is not the same." Laurel heard the opening chords for the waltz and saw young Miss Branwick, the niece of the Duke of Armadale, looking anxiously their way. She would be able to leave Montrose in good company. "There are many things I do not yet understand, your grace, but I know it is not the same."

Chapter Thirteen

Greenbriars seemed a very solitary place, even though its finely plastered walls still reverberated with the gaiety of the ball and the cheerful farewells of so many guests only recently departed. And while Laurel professed a great satisfaction in having the house and its property restored to the use of the family, she regretted the loss of so many diversions, and the general tumult that had managed to keep her from inspecting her own private affairs too closely, for she could not readily make sense of it all. Nor did her lover yet call for her to join him so she might understand what stood between them. And what she might do to help.

Instead, she wandered along the familiar paths and sat among the statuary that had witnessed far too much, and she pained her fingers working all the needlework she suddenly decided she needed to accomplish. Her mother, who plucked errant stitches from the cloth as soon as Laurel left the room, asked only once about Montrose and seemed not in the least bit disappointed for Laurel having rejected his suit.

Lewis left with their guests, happy to remain in the society of Miss Winthrop, but claiming obligations to their brother George as his excuse to return to London. Joseph stayed, undoubtedly finding London to have little allure, especially since the object of his affections journeyed in quite the opposite direction with her aunt. Laurel could not know, of course, what passed between Penelope and Joseph, but the expression on their faces as they parted each other could leave little doubt that they anticipated a reunion in the very near future. Miss Jessup, urging her niece every step of the way, seemed convinced Penelope would soon be restored to her one true love and said as much. Penelope did not argue with her, but Laurel noticed she refrained from actually mentioning the man's name. Joseph did not seem to doubt his identity. And, to be honest, neither did anyone else.

Truly, it must be an enviable feeling to be so certain of one's destiny, and to know one's deepest desires would soon be realized. Joseph seemed to have nothing on his mind but to fish with their father in the early evenings and to ride out with his sister in the afternoons. Laurel heard him whistling cheerfully in the hallways and occasionally laughing at nothing at all.

"You seem very happy today," she said one morning as they rode to town.

"You say it as if it is an accusation," he answered, handing her the reins of the cabriolet so he could shrug off his jacket "Do I not have the right to be happy?"

Laurel looked up at him, seeing the boy who had treated her with brotherly teasing all her life, and the man who hoped to marry her friend.

"You have every right, Joseph. More than most, I should think. For you are good, and kind, and patient, and all good things are due you."

"It is quite a statement, coming from my censorious sister."

"I have never been so! Indeed, I am often your greatest champion. And have I not thrust any number of women in your direction?" She paused, thinking she did as much for the woman he most desired, though she then had no idea of his interest or hers. Instead, she said, "You seemed to find more joy with them than I did with Montrose."

Joseph laughed. "Montrose was Lewis's idea. I thought him a little young for you."

"You make me feel an elderly spinster."

"And so you shall be, if you keep turning down eligible men."

"I have not turned down more than two in the past several months. I refused Ballister for he preferred Father's wealth to me. And I refused Montrose for . . . "

"He preferred turtles."

"You set him off on that; do not deny it."

"I will not. But I will say he seemed most impressed with your credentials. And Father would have liked for his daughter to be a duchess. Why, I would have liked it very much myself."

"I daresay you'll have to settle."

Joseph turned to her then, his eyes narrowing against the sun. "Is there someone else, then? And I not know it? I thought you said there were only two eligible men."

Laurel paused somewhat guiltily. She could not be sure Robbie Darkwood would prove eligible. Certainly, the Earl of Westbridge did not.

"I said there were two eligible men I refused."

Joseph gave a long, low whistle. "Then there is another for whom you continue to hope?"

"There is."

"And he has given you reason to hope?"

"He has."

Laurel did not think she wished to say more on the subject, and was grateful when Joseph stopped his questioning. And yet, as the tower of the town's modest church came into view and she slackened the pace of the cabriolet, she spoke again. "I suppose Penelope also gives you reason to hope?"

Joseph looked surprised. "Indeed, she does."

"Even though she remains betrothed to another man? And does she ever speak of . . . that one?"

Joseph nodded, and Laurel thought it might be his only answer. But then he spoke, and his words were unintentionally reassuring. "She grieved much at his defection, for she trusted him for all her life. But I think in these months, while she awaited word from him and it did not come, her despair turned to something else. I prefer to believe it allowed her to be open to new possibilities. After all, she scarcely knew other men, so long were she and Westbridge intended for each other."

"You do not think she will return to him?"

"As she already has?" Joseph asked, and then laughed. "No, not in the way you mean. I have every assurance she is now mine."

"Then I congratulate you on your excellent luck and wish you all joy."

"As I wish the same for you. I hope your ineligible gentleman has the courage to offer for you and, if he is worthy of you, that you accept him."

"I grow more confident of it with every passing moment," Laurel said, and pretended she did not see Joseph studying her profile.

* * * *

Laurel fancied a new travelling bonnet, for one never knew when one might be invited to visit friends or family sufficiently distant to warrant a carriage journey. She already owned a complete and highly fashionable wardrobe, but as she last made use of her crisp brown crepe Kutusoff hat when she arrived from London, it came accompanied by unpleasant memories. If she happened to be called away from Greenbriars any time soon, she wished to travel unencumbered with any such reminders.

Joseph sighed, more for dramatic effect than actual weariness. "I will accompany you as far as the posting house, no further," he said.

"If you cannot, at this advanced stage in your life, make so simple a decision as what you wish to pin onto your feeble head, I surely am unable to help you."

"You have already referred twice to my advanced age, dear brother, and I can only point out that you are older than I. You will probably say it does not matter so much for a man, but I, for one, am surprised Miss Croyden would have you. You are, after all, beginning to sprout gray hairs."

Laurel knew her barb hit home, as Joseph turned and frowned at his reflection in a tavern window.

"But you need not fear," she said relentingly. "She might have made herself happy with Montrose, but, like myself, decided puppies require a good deal of care. So she cast her sights on one already weaned."

"You are full of compliments today . . ."

"No more than yourself."

". . . but I believe her Earl of Westbridge even more advanced in his dotage than I."

"Is he indeed?" Laurel wondered, realizing she knew very little about the man she loved above all others. He liked animals and managed to make his own dinners. But she did not know what creatures he bred at Waltham Hall or how he preferred his tea.

"He is a year my senior. Old enough to know his own mind and act in accordance with his conscience," Joseph announced.

"You sound very hard on the poor fellow. And you cannot have it both ways just to please yourself. If Westbridge were not such a scoundrel, Penelope would not be yours for the taking. He hurt her, to be sure, but we do not know his reasons. And, unlike other maidens who wear their disappointment like a mourning veil to the end of their days, Penelope seems to have made a full recovery."

Joseph added a little hop to his step and smiled a little too broadly. Though he said nothing, the proof of Laurel's words carried through every line of his lean body. Here was love, she thought, a pure unadulterated joy announcing itself without any words. Pretty sonnets and lacy tokens of affection were nothing compared to this.

They walked past the posting house. Laurel said nothing, for she was happy to remain in Joseph's company, though he might be indifferent to hers. She did not require her brother's escort, either for propriety or for his opinion on her purchase, but gossips were less likely to accost her if she remained with him. It was not so much she disdained society, but rather that she did not wish to share what was so preciously her own. Perhaps she was a bit of a hermit herself.

"Mr. Gardiner!" a voice called out just behind them. Joseph turned on his heels, pulling Laurel with him. A white-shirted clerk, his sleeves stained with ink and grime, waved a small envelope in the air. "Something arrived for you, sir!"

"Penny," Joseph breathed out slowly, and moved towards the man. Laurel felt her own heart skip erratically, knowing whatever the letter contained would resolve her own future as well as her brother's.

"Begging your pardon, sir," the man apologized, placing the missive in Joseph's open palm. "But you will save me the trouble of a ride out to Greenbriars. This came within the hour, addressed to yourself."

Joseph's easy dismissal of the informal delivery of his letter was clear by the generous amount of coins he dropped into the man's hand.

"Is there anything arrived for me, Mr. Cankin?" Laurel could not help asking. "Miss Laurel Gardiner?"

The man chuckled. "There is no one about who does not know you, Miss. But I am sorry to disappoint you, for I have nothing for you today."

"My sister has lost her prime correspondent to me," Joseph said a little smugly, running a finger over the delicate script on the envelope. Laurel thought she detected the faintest scent of lavender wafting through the still, warm air.

"There is, however, another letter addressed to Greenbriars, though I will not ask you to deliver it. It is for the tall fellow, the one who walks into town with the mongrel."

"One of our guests, I suppose," Joseph said, still distracted. "But they have just left our home, so I suppose the letter must be redirected."

Laurel, however, did not recall Sir John or Mr. Winthrop ever befriending a mongrel, nor could Montrose ever be imagined to be tall. The letter, however, would undoubtedly need to be redirected.

"To whom is it addressed?" she asked innocently.

"To Mr. Robert Wood. Do you know the fellow, then?" Mr. Cankin asked earnestly. "He seemed oddly reticent about revealing much about himself."

Laurel could not conceal her grin. Robert Wood, indeed. Would there be no end to the man's permutations on his own given name?

"I do know him, Mr. Cankin. You can hardly imagine there could be a man upon the estate unknown to us?"

"If you know him, Miss Gardiner, perhaps you would not be adverse to seeing he gets this. He seemed most anxious about his letters when he first came to introduce himself to me."

Laurel reached out for the envelope, noting the prominent crest in the sealing wax. "I will see he gets this," she said, and glanced at her cheerful brother. "Indeed, I intend to deliver it myself."

* * * *

Laurel's new hat, purchased in town on the afternoon the two letters arrived, proved very elegant, but it was a trifle too expansive to fit within the confines of the Gardiner coach during the journey she made with her brother some days after. As they passed the gatehouse of the lovely estate on which the Croyden sisters remained with their aunt after the deaths of their parents, Laurel reached for the hat and placed it on her crushed curls. In doing so, the feathers tickled Joseph's nose, and he awakened from his fitful sleep.

He brushed one hand across his face, though the feathers were already aloft on Laurel's head. "'Tis not amusing, Laurel. I would never have flattered you in that damned hat if I knew . . . "

"No, it is certainly not amusing, dear brother," Laurel interrupted. "If your beloved opened the coach door and heard you snoring so, there would be nothing funny about the consequences."

Joseph snorted and sat up in his cramped seat. "Are we arrived?"

"Indeed, we are. You could not be very anxious about visiting Penelope if you managed to sleep for the whole journey."

"You misunderstand me, Sister," he said and grinned. "It is only that I shall require all the reserves of my strength for this encounter."

Laurel did not answer, but merely raised her eyebrows. She could not take him to task on it, but what would his trials be next to her own? For his part, he knew he already owned Penelope's heart. But the Earl of Westbridge was neither Robbie Darkwood nor her own lover, and Laurel could not be so confident of success.

And yet she accompanied her brother, who appeared so anxious to respond to Penelope's missive, he would have left directly from the post house days ago. When they had returned to Greenbriars and he announced his intention to fly to Penelope's side, Laurel asked permission to travel with him. Joseph did not seem particularly pleased, but did not flatly refuse her. Their parents seemed to think it a reasonable plan, and offered no opposition. And so Laurel justified the purchase of a new traveling hat and had her maid pack her favorite dresses for their journey.

The Croyden's home was modest by the standards of Greenbriars,

but very lovely nonetheless. Situated on a rising prospect, it was graced
by a small wood on the east. Past it, rising starkly against the cloudless
sky, stood the towers of a larger, distant home. Laurel did not have to
guess who lived there, but she did wonder if any of its inhabitants
happened to be gazing out onto the vast fields below and might observe
the approach of the Gardiner coach. And if so, how long would it take
for him to leave that place and arrive at the Croyden's door? And did
he even expect her?

If Westbridge did not, clearly Penelope compensated for the loss.
As the carriage swayed into the last broad curve of the drive, the
figures of four women came into sight. Penelope, the tallest, waved a
white cloth in greeting, even as a stouter figure, easily identified as
Miss Jessup, tried to pull her niece's arm down. Undoubtedly, she still
harbored warm hopes for Montrose and would not want her niece to
deliver too impressive a show. Her insistence on propriety might well
have worked on the other two women, however, for they stood unmoving
and close to each other. As the carriage neared, Laurel recognized
them as younger counterparts of her good friend.

Penelope shrugged off her aunt's restraints once the carriage came
to a halt, and she ran to the door. Miss Jessup, wearing her niece's
cloth like a sign of surrender, followed at a more respectable pace
while holding back her two other charges with her outstretched arms.

Laurel stepped out first, and her friend launched herself into her
embrace. For all this show of enthusiasm, however, Laurel realized
Penelope's eyes were looking over her shoulder, watching the next
visitor emerge. To hug a friend while one would prefer to caress a
lover is indeed a poor substitute, but Laurel could voice no indignation.
What else could Joseph and Penelope do before a curious audience?
Particularly when nothing was yet settled between them and the
expectant world?

"Mr. Joseph Gardiner," Penelope said clearly, across Laurel's
shoulder. "Welcome to our home."

"Miss Croyden," Joseph paused, emphasizing each syllable as if
acting on the stage. "I came as soon as you summoned me to do so."

The simplicity, the complete artlessness, of the words belied the
heat of their meaning. Their intensity made Laurel breathless just on
hearing it, and it made her own heart ache for that which she did not
yet possess.

"I came as well," she said in a small voice.

"Of course," Penelope said, and released her. "I am so glad you did. Though not, perhaps, as much as is another."

Laurel wished to know more, but the opportunity to do so was not yet present.

"Allow me to introduce my sisters to you. Miss Aurore Croyden, and Miss Miranda Croyden. Of course you already know my Aunt Jessup. Sisters, here are my friends from Greenbriars. Miss Gardiner, and her brother, Mr. Joseph Gardiner."

Miranda, the younger of the two, giggled, and Aurore stamped on her foot. Looking from one lovely face to the other, and then to Penelope, Laurel realized they were not as similar as she first thought. While they were of the same general build, Penelope's coloring appeared more vivid and startling. Her hair was curlier and thicker, and it gleamed darkly in the sun.

"Shall we to the house?" Miss Jessup asked dutifully. "You must be weary after your long journey."

"One of us must be weary, to be sure," Joseph said cheerfully. "The other managed several hours of uninterrupted rest."

The Croyden girls laughed along with him, and Laurel could only wonder at it; he was not that witty. But it could not matter in this blessed company, for Joseph, surrounded as he was by women, played the scene to his best advantage.

They walked into the house together, following the coachman with his burden of boxes. Laurel turned to Miss Jessup, her remaining companion. "We have missed you at Greenbriars, Miss Jessup," she said. It was entirely true, though not necessarily in the way Miss Jessup might imagine. "But I hope your homecoming proved a happy one."

"Happy is not the word I would use, Miss Gardiner. Indeed, it seemed anything but." She pulled her arm through Laurel's; it was an unexpected familiarity and yet a comforting one. "But I believe it will all work out for the best. My niece reassures me of the fact on a daily basis."

"I am glad, not only for her, but for the sake of others. How often our happiness is a consequence of a chain of events, over which we have little or no control."

"Oh, my dear, you are wise beyond your years," murmured the older woman. "And yet, you do not know the half of it."

Knowing, in her aged wisdom, that the half pertained directly to herself, Laurel nevertheless resisted temptation and went silently into the house with her escort.

* * * *

There remained much business to attend to this day. Rob knew it not only because he had already resumed his place as master of Waltham Hall, but also because his younger brother and estate manager reminded him of the fact at breakfast. His mother and brother now understood the circumstances of his leaving, as painful as the explanations proved, and both admitted they did not know what they would have done in his situation. Yet, while they granted him acceptance, he did not think they entirely felt forgiveness. And so, even as he burdened himself with the responsibilities he had temporarily abandoned, he still needed to atone.

Harry seemed impatient to finish with the business of fencing near the stables. He produced a plan drawn up several weeks before, showing the enlarged area over the current one, and seemed uncommonly pleased with his effort. Rob stood at the window overlooking the valley, watching as a small dot of black on the road gradually grew larger until it materialized into a coach and four. He heard what his brother had to say, but did not necessarily listen to it.

"Rob? Are you with me?"

"I am. You believe Maples is the man to construct this enclosure? Did he perform well on the new tenants' cottages?"

"You saw them yourself. They are adequate, though not inspired."

"I am not sure one looks to a farmer's cottage for inspiration. If it is sturdy and well lit, and is graced with a drawing chimney, it should prove more than adequate. I know of what I speak."

"I am sure you do." Harry laughed. "Sometimes I suspect you would prefer to live in that little stone cottage than in the Hall. Certainly, I know Prince would."

Rob turned away from the window and glanced down at poor Prinny, who endured a name change in order to gain respectability in the house of an earl. The dog would have liked nothing more than to roam the fields and harass the wild things, but since coming to Waltham Hall, he scarcely left Rob's side. And since Rob could no longer spend his own days in the woods and streams, with the heat of the sun on his head and the cool clear water running down his body, Prinny made his own prison. But then, so did he.

Rob slid a finger, the nail of which was neatly buffed and no longer broken, between his neck and cravat. He wondered what his valet had done with his old white muslin shirt.

"I have not spent enough time with Prinny, poor boy. He was my constant companion at Greenbriars, infinitely patient and always cheerful. I am sure I do not know many people of whom I can say the same."

"I prefer to believe you might say the same of me, Brother," said Harry, for once quite serious.

Rob nodded, and returned to the window. The carriage was not entirely out of view, though a thin line of dust rose up from beyond the trees, revealing its location as it moved. "You have been more generous than I deserve."

"It is the very least I can do. Aside from all that led to your abrupt departure, it has taken you time to be restored to your position here. When one has a dog for one's only companion, allowances must be made."

"I am sure I never said Prinny was my sole companion."

In the window's reflection, Rob caught Harry's moment of doubt, and then the growing realization of his meaning.

"Who arrives at the Croyden house this day?" was all Harry asked, fully aware he did not change the subject.

The line of dust vanished, and it seemed nothing in the landscape had changed from an hour before. And yet Rob knew everything had changed, and if his prayers were answered, nothing would ever again be the same.

"A brother and sister whom Penny befriended in London. They are two of the Greenbriar scions and invited her to visit them there. The brother, Joseph, has managed to supplant me in the lady's affections, a fact for which I am eternally grateful."

"And the sister?" was all Harry asked of him.

"Yes, it is she," Rob affirmed, as if that answered everything.

* * * *

Laurel spent more time than necessary freshening up after her arrival. For all that, she did not think her hair required more than a few pins, and her cheeks were quite pink after the excitement of the welcome. One of the maids helped her remove her traveling dress and select a lighter day dress from the many she had packed for her journey. She changed out of her sturdy boots and into delicate slippers, and she eschewed a cap so her curls could spring back to life.

But all this did not take more than half an hour. She nevertheless preferred to stay in her bright little chamber to allow her brother a few moments of privacy with his beloved before she came in on them in the drawing room.

If she waited much longer, however, she would die of hunger, for she had not eaten since breakfast.

She opened the door to the stillness of the late afternoon. The work of the upstairs maids was done, and no one seemed to stir in the adjacent rooms. But from below, the steady hum of conversation could be detected, like a weary insect caught between two windowpanes. Laurel walked slowly down the stairs, savoring her last moments of solitude, and followed the sound to the large arched opening to the right of the great staircase.

"Ah, Miss Gardiner! You have rested, I assume. And do you like your accommodation?" Miss Jessup asked.

"It is very lovely, Miss Jessup. You have done much to assure my comfort, and I am appreciative."

"It is our very best guest room," Aurore chirped, and handed Laurel a tray of tiny pastries. Their cook was French, Laurel guessed, and knew her father would be quite envious.

"I hope my brother fares as well? He is, after all, the one your sister invited."

Miranda giggled. "Oh, I believe he fares very well," she said and gestured with her shoulder to where Joseph and Penelope stood against a marble mantelpiece. "As to his room, it is on the floor above ours. It would hardly do for him to be so near."

Indeed, it would not. But Laurel knew what this young girl could not: it did not matter what artifice was arranged to distance a man and woman in love, they would come together just the same, and just as passionately.

"You sighed, Miss Gardiner. Are you very weary?" Aurore asked.

"Perhaps I am. As you may have guessed, it was my brother who slept nearly all the way to your home."

"He certainly looks revived," Miranda pointed out.

He did. Whatever Joseph discussed with Penelope did not seem to be constrained to his words, but somehow involved his whole body. He leaned forward, waved one hand and poised his legs like a runner entering a sprint.

"As does your sister. I hope whatever caused her difficulties last spring has been fully resolved?"

No one spoke, and Laurel instantly regretted her insensitivity in speaking of it so soon. The sisters could not yet know it was somehow her business as well as theirs, and the subject was likely to have brought them much pain.

"I do not know if the matter will ever be happily resolved, Miss Gardiner. The roots run so deeply, they may never be fully extricated. But Penelope is prepared to be very happy, and we have decided to forgive our neighbor, for the fault cannot be said to be entirely his. The past is with us, but can be buried."

"You do not find my brother's suit officious or sudden?" she asked in a low voice.

"Be assured, we do not. It is welcomed. More so by Penelope than by us." Aurore laughed, attracting the attention of everyone else in the room. "And more by us than by Aunt Jessup," she finished in a whisper.

Laurel laughed as well. "Your aunt still harbors hope for an earl or a duke? Poor lady. You must not disappoint her, then."

"Oh, I suspect earls are highly over . . . " Aurore's voice dropped off and she gazed over Laurel's shoulder.

The voices in the room went silent and everyone gazed in Laurel's direction, though not at her.

She froze, knowing who stood behind her, for she sensed his height and warmth as keenly as if she lay against his chest. A vague soapy scent reminded her of a heated afternoon in the hermitage, though the sensation was unadulterated with the accompanying scents of sunburned flesh and labor-dampened flesh. But she knew him, as she would know him anywhere. As she knew him in the woods, or in the garden, or in her uneasy dreams all these weeks past.

of effort. But if she remained thus, facing the room while he saw only her back, she would look a fool. Or worse: a fool in love.

"Westbridge," she murmured, as she finally turned to him.

"Miss Gardiner," he said, and politely took her hand. There was nothing in it, she told herself, but her flesh caught fire and the heat spread quickly through her body. "You called me by another name once."

She studied him as if there were no one in the room watching them. But this moment was theirs, and it might be all she had.

He seemed taller, and certainly more imposing in form. But perhaps it was due to the finery of his garments and their gracious fit, which managed to reveal as much of his body as the open shirt and the trousers he once wore. The beard she had once abhorred was completely gone now, and the line of tanned skin against the lighter flesh of his cheeks remained the only hint of what once was. His hair had been tended by a valet, who surely had expended much effort in keeping the unruly curls under control, and probably trimmed them each week. Laurel glanced down, past his short jacket, and looked quickly away. Her imagination was already too much aroused.

"But you were someone else, once. You are no longer that person," she said at last, but not for the first time.

"I am as ever. But it is true I would not wish to be content with remaining so, for there is so much more I desire."

"Oh," was all Laurel could manage to say, for he confused her mightily. She knew everyone else in the room watched her, awaiting her response, but she could say nothing else.

"You must desire a pastry, my lord," Miss Jessup said impatiently.

"And to convey my greetings to you all. Mr. Gardiner? We have met before, but under entirely different circumstances. I offer a welcome to you . . . and my congratulations, I suspect."

He dropped Laurel's hand, and a satisfied murmur went up in the room. Everyone seemed pleased with the manner of this reunion. Everyone but Laurel, who wondered how many arrows Cupid was willing to fling before one hit true and held fast.

Chapter Fourteen

Laurel walked quietly through the small wilderness at the home of her hostesses, quite alone and unprotected. She did not particularly wish to examine from whom she ought to be protected, but her feelings of vulnerability were coupled with an inescapable sadness. All joy should be hers, she reminded herself at least hourly, for her brother and good friend were all but betrothed. And the man for whom she would have had to defy all her family to marry when he was a lowly hermit, now proved to be an esteemed member of the peerage. But she owned no confidence that their circumstances were very much improved.

She sighed and sat upon a fallen tree trunk, wondering how an adventure begun with such happiness of promise should now be fraught with misgiving and confusion. She and her hermit could never again be what they were; in that they were in perfect accord. But Laurel did not really know who Robbie Darkwood was, or if she would even like his noble successor. Or if that lofty gentleman would still have her.

She prayed he would, and had not scrupled to travel all the great distance to him on the gamble that the promises said and unsaid back at Greenbriars were still cherished. But when she saw him yesterday afternoon, arrived in all state in the Croyden's drawing room, her confidence began to falter. He was no longer her hermit, whose ease of body and spirit seduced her and made her love him. In his country finery and neatly cut hair, he looked like any proper gentleman of her acquaintance and a good deal more regal than most.

Laurel stood, uncomfortable upon her seat, and resumed her restless exercise. She did not do Westbridge justice to imagine his appearance no longer warranted her favor, she reminded herself severely. In truth, he remained the handsomest man she knew and one likely to turn heads in any society. But fewer heads of eligible ladies were likely to turn when he was but a hermit, and now that he was released of his long standing promise to Penelope Croyden, he was free to marry wherever and whomever he chose.

All this was patently possible for days, but Laurel had never doubted him or herself, until she accepted his cool and polite welcome the day before and realized she had no more standing than any of the other guests when he invited the whole company to dinner at Waltham Hall for the evening next. This evening.

And though he remained with them for some time, and all this day held the possibility of a reconciliation, he had made no effort to speak to Laurel in private or offer her any assurances.

She had made a mistake in coming here. Joseph and Penelope did not need her, for they somehow managed to settle their own affairs without the slightest bit of her interference. Miss Jessup did not need her, for the latest gossip could be had with considerably less bother through the post. And Robin Waltham, the Earl of Westbridge, did not seem to need her either, for he somehow managed to resume his estimable place in society without any of her help.

She had made a fair muddle of everything, she admitted. How very presumptuous she had been to imagine she could repair Penelope's affairs when she had failed miserably at all of her own. As she lifted her skirts to avoid the muddy tracks at a little garden gate, she wondered what the Duke of Montrose was doing, and if he might yet be available.

No, she did not want Montrose; she never had. She only wanted Rob.

The wilderness, with its fallen trees and mossy ledges, gradually gave way to an open field. In the distance, a glistening ribbon of water ran through a valley and the modest cottages of farmers were nestled along its banks. Newly sheared sheep raised their heads to gaze at her as she passed and, finding her lacking, returned to their business of keeping the field grass at a manageable height. A dog, barking some distance away, undoubtedly kept their many wooly cousins out of harm's way.

Just ahead, where the field yielded to a different sort of cultivation and a riot of red roses claimed a rusted iron trellis, the remains of an old tenant's cottage boldly withstood the ravages of weather. The chimney had collapsed on itself, and birds built nests beneath the rotting thatched roof. The door, standing at an odd angle, seemed secured by nothing more than a length of twine, and rough boards covered the windows. The remedy so lacked proper workmanship, they may have been done by an inexperienced hermit.

Laurel smiled, and the slight pull at the edges of her lips painfully reminded her she had scarcely done so since greeting the Croydens the day before. Ignoring all the intruding thoughts that were so worrisome, she found a rickety bench and sat herself down warily upon it. She needed nothing else, she told herself, for here was heaven itself.

Several sheep kept her company while she sat and rested there, and so might they all have remained if their eager sheepdog did not find them. Instead, enthusiastic barking grew louder, and the poor creatures, not knowing quite what to do, ran off in a dozen different directions.

Not a very efficient sheepdog, Laurel thought, and then when the barking animal came into view, she thought he did not look the part very well, either. In fact, he looked like something else entirely.

"Prinny!" she cried, as he leapt onto the bench beside her and put large muddy paws into her lap. Laurel did not care, for so unexpected and delightful was his company. She let him nuzzle his wet nose against her breast and press his large head against her cheek before she realized he might not be unaccompanied. As she pushed him away, her knitted shawl slipped down off one shoulder and loosened curls fell down her back.

"He is well trained, you see, to discourage trespassers," said a deep voice, sounding very severe. Westbridge stood near the trellis, a somber form in a black jacket and dark trousers against the brilliant red of the roses. He clapped his hands once, and then again, but Prinny would not be deterred from trying to nose his way into Laurel's bodice.

"Oh, very well trained, indeed," she gasped, when speech was finally possible. "I suppose if I gave him a side of mutton he would lead me straight to the Westbridge jewels."

"It would not be so very bad if he did," she thought she heard him say, though Prinny lapped at her ear.

Westbridge clapped again and, for some reason, the dog remembered his manners. Or else he was finally satisfied in having utterly destroyed her new gown and what remained of her fragile composure. As Prinny leapt from the bench, Laurel tugged on her bodice and shook her hair back behind her shoulders.

"And I am not trespassing," Laurel said, defensively. "Penelope told me to explore where I may and gave me the run of the place."

Westbridge did not move but to run gentle fingers between Prinny's twitching ears. It was several moments before he answered, several moments during which he seemed to frown upon the wretched state of Laurel's appearance.

"I am sure she allowed you every liberty on her family's estate, but this land and cottage and garden are mine."

Laurel's heart turned in her breast, as his words called to mind the glorious misunderstanding that was theirs upon their very first meeting.

"I did not walk very far, my lord," she said quietly.

"No, I do not suppose you did. But the Croyden's property is very modest, and mine is . . . quite large. And so, you see, you are trespassing."

Laurel, achingly restless and somehow unable to leave her bench, wondered why he insisted upon it, and what it all might mean. And then, watching his fingers nervously caressing his dog, she realized that he was as unsure as she, and did not know what to say to her or how she might receive his words.

"You look like Eve in the Garden of Eden," he said at last.

Whatever she expected, it was not this. She looked at him, surprised. "I imagined it myself once, when we met before. But we were other people then, and that was another place," she reminded him.

"I think . . . " he began, and his fingers left Prinny's smooth head. "I think wherever you are, I am in Eden."

If he had difficulty speaking the words to her, Laurel remained at a complete loss to answer anything at all. Instead, she sat in his garden and watched him as he moved away from the trellis, releasing a shower of red rose petals onto his dark shoulder. He ignored them as he walked to her, his clear eyes never leaving her face, and pulled her up into his arms and kissed her.

The Earl of Westbridge certainly knew his business better than did his mongrel dog, but yet he followed a path similar to Laurel's earlier seducer as his lips worshipped her ear and neck, and moved towards the curves of her breast. Laurel, for her part, gently explored his back and arms, and thought his proper starched garments offered even more resistance to her lovemaking than his disgusting hermit's robe. But she never doubted she would gain access to him and his strong body, as she had before.

"That is enough," he choked, and held her at arm's length. His cravat appeared in complete disarray, and the mud Prinny had left upon her bodice now streaked across Rob's crisp white shirt. "We may be on my lands, but we are not alone here."

"I see," Laurel said, and did. They risked a good deal while nothing was yet settled between them. "And is this also part of your plan to deter trespassers?"

Rob grinned, and she recognized the man she had met months before. He reached for her hand and pressed it against his chest, over his rapidly beating heart.

"You trespassed months ago, though you may not have known it then. I scarcely knew it myself."

She came back into the circle of his arms, little caring who might witness their intimacies. His lips pressed down upon the top of her head and she nestled into the crook of his shoulder.

"Knew what, Robbie Darkwood?" she dared to ask, believing she already knew the answer.

"That I loved you, of course. I willed myself to ignore the thunderbolt that nearly left me a simpleton on the day I first met you at the hermitage, for I knew no good could come of it. And yet I could neither escape you nor the truth of my own unhappy life and, more to the point, neither did I desire to do so for very long. On the night I thought I lost you, I realized there was yet hope for me to regain what I abdicated. And to have more than I ever dreamed possible."

"Of course you shall," Laurel said reassuringly, and caressed his cheek with her fingers. Though the beard and mustache were gone, his skin retained the roughness of their shadows. "But do you not know how much I love you as well?"

"No. Not yet. There is too much to explain, and none of it happy. I will not hear any vows from you until you know the truth."

"Rob, there is nothing you can tell me that will make me believe otherwise. And if you continue to do that with your tongue, I will be so distracted I will not hear a thing you tell me in any case."

"Perhaps it shall be my best defense," he said against her neck, and continued to do it.

* * * *

Though he knew her dress already ruined by mud and by Prinny and, indeed, by himself, Rob thought it wise—and divinely pleasurable— to carry Laurel over the patches of earth made fetid by the recent rains. She did not resist when he lifted her into his arms, and it seemed to him she already knew her place there, where her body fit perfectly against his. They said nothing for some time, even when the impressive towers of Waltham House came into view and he lowered her to her feet to lead her in the opposite direction. For his part, he still needed time to summon the words he needed to say. And for her part . . . he simply knew not.

He glanced down at her, at the vision of the sun illuminating her dark hair, and at her rosy flesh, which shrugged off protection. Surely, if it shrugged off any more, he would go quite mad and only prolong his agonies, suffered while he waited to claim her as his own.

For she would be his; she must be his. A lady who would readily accept a malcontented hermit would allow him, the man who loved her, grace and forgiveness. And if she refused him, he would necessarily become a hermit again and seduce her with his paltry forestry skills and raggedy clothes. Of course, he considered as he tightened his cravat, she seemed to prefer him in those clothes.

Or not entirely in them.

"Here is the boundary with the Croyden estate," he said suddenly, and not entirely irrelevantly. "You can see how very close it is to mine, for Waltham House is just scarcely out of view."

Laurel's eyes narrowed against the bright sky, and he knew she just feigned interest in his observation.

"It is at the heart of the problem, you see," he continued. "It is where the troubles began."

Laurel turned to face him and caught his sleeve. "You will not have me believe you went off into exile for some paltry boundary dispute," she said angrily.

Surprised at the strength of her conviction, he realized she was as tense as he and with all the more reason: she yet remained in the dark.

"No, my love. The lines have been well drawn for centuries, though there has always been intercourse between the families and across the lands." He cleared his throat, regretting his choice of words. "We have always been the closest of friends."

"You need not explain more, Rob. Both you and Penelope precisely explained the close ties that bound you both since childhood, and how you knew each other as you would a brother or sister." She walked along beside him, frowning slightly and, if he recognized her manner as well as he hoped, mulling over her words. "It surely would allow no surprises between you, no room for . . . oh!"

He saw the precise moment when she understood what it was all about, what tortured him and what would be the burden he would necessarily carry on his shoulders all his life. He saw it in the stiffening of her back, the flush spreading across her skin, in the look of horror and repulsion on her hitherto innocent face.

He caught her by her elbow and propelled her along the path, not allowing her to stop. For, he sensed if they stopped now, he might never regain the momentum to continue.

"Robert and Amanda Waltham, my parents, were best friends to Maryanne and Jasper Croyden, Penelope's parents. When the Croydens died, just weeks apart by the fever, my parents were in a wretched state, but my father, damn him, was inconsolable. I was not much more than a boy at the time, but thought it might have to do with the fact he stood guardian to three young girls. I knew there were few financial concerns, and could not imagine what else would allow him to grieve as he did. And, but for chance, I might never have known until much damage was already done."

Rob paused, watching Laurel for her response, waiting to hear what words she had to restore sense into his senseless world. She said nothing, but looked directly ahead as they continued together on the rough path.

"As you know, my father died not many months ago, and of no apparent ailment. He prepared me well through the years for the responsibilities of the earldom, and often told me nothing would please him more but for my son and Penny's to be the means by which the neighboring estates would be united. The Croyden's home is left in trust to the eldest grandson of Jasper Croyden. I know this, of course, because I am now the trustee for the property, and guardian to the girls. It would have been a convenient circumstance were I to be related to them all, as well."

Laurel stumbled on the path, and Rob caught her with greater strength than he intended. Still she said nothing, and paused only to tighten the lace on her shoe.

"But that is not all I know now, for it remained my privilege and responsibility to examine all the papers pertaining to the estates after my father's death. And there, on one rainy day after I had just completed studying a report on drainage in the cow pasture, I found something that sent my complacency crashing down about me. There were specifics, neatly spelled out, about an inheritance due to Miss Penelope Croyden, were she not to marry Robin Waltham, his son. It was hers, not because she was my father's ward, but because she was his daughter."

Rob nearly choked on the last word, for it remained a very bitter pill. But there was no escaping it, as there had been no escaping it on that dismal day when he read it for the first time.

"My father freely admitted to the affair he had with Amanda Croyden, of which Penelope was the result. My own mother, now painfully humiliated, learned the truth only days ago when it became my unpleasant duty to explain the reasons for my defection. As for Jasper Croyden, or anyone else, I cannot say." Rob knew there remained much to be said, as much for his own benefit as for Laurel's, but there could be no point to it if she would not have him after these revelations. "And I . . . I reacted foolishly, perhaps, but in the only way to make sense at the time. I could not marry Penny, nor could I present the truth without doing harm to the women I then loved best in the world. My mother would have to learn the truth, how her husband and best friend betrayed her trust. And Penny would learn of her illegitimacy, and how the man she always assumed she would marry was the one man ineligible to do so. I ran away then, hoping I would be forgotten, leaving all I loved for the sake of those I loved. I am cursed, and the taint of it remains upon me."

Rob stopped as they crested a hill, unable to go on. On one side of them lay the great expanse of Waltham House and all the surrounding lands. He wondered how anything so beautiful could have borne such deceit and despair.

"I fail to see how you are cursed, or why you imagine yourself at fault for anything imposed on you by a man wicked enough to urge a marriage between two children of his own body," Laurel said in a voice quiet but steady.

Rob looked down at her, and thought her color restored and her expression one of calm equanimity. Family loyalty would have him defend his father, but what did she say that he hadn't said to himself a hundred times already? His father may have erred twenty years before, but he nevertheless sought to compound that error by defiling the next generation. He would have married his oldest son to his oldest daughter, destroyed the incriminating legacy, and no one would have known any better. Or worse.

"Because I am my father's son," he said, realizing for the first time how shallow those words sounded.

"But you are your own man," Laurel said, and finally turned to face him. He saw in her eyes the very things that gave him pause when first they met outside the hermitage all those months ago—her determination, and wit, and sharp intelligence. Now, he thought he also saw compassion and sympathy. Her next words oddly echoed his own sudden understanding. "You were not your father's son when I met you first, when you sought to live by your wits and strength as the most humble of men. I accused you then of escaping your past, but is it not possible you found yourself at the hermitage, fully revealed?"

"Is it not possible I found my future?"

She continued to look unwaveringly up at him, and he recognized with all certainty that her love had not diminished. "Indeed, it is very possible. But first you must know yourself."

"And those around me. I discover I have a sister, one I shall soon give away in marriage. I discover my mother is stronger than I thought, though I doubt she will remain as true to my father's memory. Nor should she. I learn my younger brother is reasonably competent to run an estate and wiser than his years."

"And you learn you, yourself, are a fair cook and a serviceable laundry maid. You can tend goats and sheep and . . . She paused and laughed as Prinny ran an impertinent snout up her stockinged leg. "Teach unruly mongrels to do that which you do not dare."

Rob took her again into his arms, wondering how he ever could have imagined she would be repulsed by his family's dreadful history, or how he could lose a love so patiently gained.

"You will find, my lady, I will dare a great deal."

Her hands went to either side of his face and she stared intently into his eyes. He would have wanted to know what she saw there, and if it could ever equal the measure of what she first saw months ago at the hermitage at Greenbriars.

"I am not your lady, Robbie Darkwood. I am plain Miss Laurel Gardiner."

"But I intend to change that as soon as your father will allow it"

"Will I not have anything to say on the matter?"

"I believe you already have," he said, and kissed her.

* * * *

With the notable exception of the bride's mother, all the many guests gathered into the little church near Greenbriars agreed that the thunderous skies and torrential rains were a good portent for the happiness of the marriage of Robin Waltham, the Earl of Westbridge, and Miss Laurel Gardiner, spinster. The Gardiner servants hurriedly erected a tent of sorts between the carriageway and the church entrance, but the ceremony was so well attended, the guests spilled onto the unprotected lawns and road. And the reception, so carefully planned for the splendid gardens in which the celebrants might mingle with the more reserved presence of Italian statuary, was now to be held in the Gardiner ballroom. Mr. Gardiner, caught in the dilemma of allowing his greatest art treasures to be damaged by the carelessness of any of his guests, while nevertheless wishing for them to be seen and envied, was convinced by his eldest son that the most prestigious acquisition was the one Laurel had somehow managed to gain. And by his wife that there was no treasure as valuable as his only daughter's happiness.

"'Tis a dreadful pity the weather did not look kindly on this day's events," Mrs. Gardiner whispered during a lull in the proceedings. "Laurel will always regret her choice of date."

"If so, I daresay it will be the only thing she will ever regret about her wedding day," Mrs. Joseph Gardiner answered, and smiled at her mother-in-law. "Does Laurel look as if she cares for anything but Rob?"

The elder Mrs. Gardiner nodded thoughtfully. "Indeed, she does not. Nor does it appear she regrets a single thing, as becomes a bride." She studied Penelope for a moment, not daring to give voice to any of her own lingering doubts.

"Nor do I, dear Mother. I can not imagine a happier conclusion to the tangle that was our lives only months ago." Penelope glanced up at her new husband. "I do love your son."

"The happiest conclusion," Mrs. Gardiner agreed, and caught her breath as Westbridge sealed his marriage to her daughter with a kiss that would leave none of the assembly in doubt of his affections.

"But there remains the business of the leaking roof," Mrs. Gardiner continued, turning towards her husband, who stood on her other side.

"A leaking roof? At Greenbriars? How can such a thing be possible?" Mr. Gardiner said, in rising alarm.

"Hush, or you will disrupt the ceremony," Mrs. Gardiner said between her teeth. "I do not mean in the house, but in the hermitage."

"Why should it matter . . . oh, no. Say it is not so," Mr. Gardiner groaned, but his wife saw the tickle of a smile at the corner of his mouth. "We have given them a wedding journey to Italy as our gift. And did Laurel not promise to bring me home some statuary?"

"It is only for one night, my dear. I offered to outfit the place as elegantly as possible, but your daughter and new son-in-law would not hear of it. They wish to start their marriage in the very place they first met."

"A bit of romantic nonsense, to be sure. And highly impractical in this climate."

"And yet observe what joy has come of it. Who might have imagined this ending from such poor beginnings?"

Mr. and Mrs. Gardiner sat in contented silence when Lord and Lady Westbridge started up the narrow church aisle to lead their wedding guests into the rain outside. The young couple paused briefly at the Gardiner's pew to accept her parents' blessings and to bid them hurried words of gratitude. The earl looked directly into his father-in-law's eyes and offered his hand, much as he had many months before. The older man clasped his hand for a moment, and released him to continue up the aisle with his new wife.

"I imagined this ending," said Mr. Gardiner as he helped Mrs. Gardiner to her feet. "I never doubt that any plan of mine will meet my happiest expectations."

As, indeed, it had.

LaVergne, TN USA
08 February 2010

172450LV00001B/116/P